REST IN PEACE
BOOK TWO: CHANGES

Evelyn Sciarratta

First edition Dec. 2012

Front cover illustration by Michael J. Pohrer.

Printed in the United States of America

This novel is my legacy to my children and all those that follow them.

Anthony, our firstborn, taught us the meaning of being a parent, and loving him for it.

Cynthia was definitely her daddy's girl.

Denise had but a brief hour in our lives, and waits for us to join her.

Nick and Nico, our twin sons, made their dad's chest expand a bit further.

And Zachary, the last of the pack, quickly claimed his place in his dad's heart.

CHAPTER ONE

What will she do with her papa's truck? She couldn't leave it stranded on the road next to the rock pile, possibly all day. Someone will see it and will know to whom it belonged. They will report it. The sheriff will be called in to investigate…the same sheriff that always had to investigate. He will find her hidden in the NO TRESPASSING area. He will take her back to Sunni. She will never again see her lover. She pulled over to the side of the road. Woods and fields were the only noticeable things in her line of vision. She did not turn off the engine.

The Doc is extremely thoughtful when it comes to Sloan. He is always checking her gas gauge, adding gas if needed from the containers he stores in his garage. He knows this is a hazard and yet he couldn't break himself of the habit. He felt that if he were to be called out of town on an emergency, and his car showed the gas gauge to be low, he could count on his supply.

Sloan placed her elbows inside the opening in the steering wheel, her face supported with fisted hands pressed into her cheeks, thinking, always thinking. Within minutes, she again gunned her engine, heading towards town. She knew her plan would work; of course she would need some support from another source. She pulled into a parking space in the town's shopping center. She turned off the ignition praying that what she had in mind would work, for if it did not, she would have to restart her papa's truck, losing more and more confidence with each try. She parked near the gas station.

She would work her way down one side of the street and then the other, until she found what she was searching for. She took her time, she had to; her mission was to listen to the conversations the tourists engaged in. Today was Friday. This could be a bad day; the tourists may stay through the weekend. She noticed on her drive into town the cabins were almost full. The cabin where she'd had her first sexual experience appeared to be empty. The door was open, but secured with a screen door. The owner, it appeared, was airing out the place. "Cheap" it's called, no air-conditioner running when it's unoccupied. She followed as close as she dared without being conspicuous.

The minutes were ticking away; her watch read 10:40 a.m. She thought she would never find what she was looking for. *Doesn't anyone talk when they walk?* she wondered. Her plan wasn't going to work. What will she do now? Will Clay leave, assuming she had changed her mind? What if he had already been here and gone? Will she have to return to a life with Sunni, one she now knows will be a lifeless existence? She had to do something, but what? She was beginning to get sick at her stomach when it finally happened.

"Sweetie-pie, I really think we should leave now if you want to visit with your brother Horace and his wife Francine. We need to return home by Sunday; our neighbors cannot care for our dogs past that day."

Those were the words of a couple in their eighties. His posture told of a severe case of osteoporosis. Upon his head sat a Kansas City Royals baseball cap. He was wearing those stupid half glasses, but he did have a charming smile; he was grinning from ear to ear, at what Sloan had no idea. His choice of clothing was a light blue polo shirt, which was way too big, and green walking shorts that revealed no apparent ass. He was wearing red, white and blue striped tennis shoes with no socks. There was no way his wife had lent a hand in his selection. Age can really do a number on some folks; sadly he was one of them.

His companion was perhaps the cutest and tiniest woman Sloan had ever seen. She was endearing with her quite curly, pearl white hair partly covered with a red flowered hat. She too was wearing glasses, but hers were stylish and full-framed. When she smiled at the Kansas City Royals fan, her whole face joined in. She was adorable in a sleeveless, belted multi-colored flowered dress. She was carrying a large red tote bag; low-heeled shoes were a color match.

"Sweetie-pie, are you listening to me?" They were definitely a Mr. and Mrs.

"Yes, I am listening and I agree, but first I would like to pick up some sweets for them…okay?"

"Whatever you say, sweetie-pie."

If Sloan lives long enough to be with the same man, she will never allow him to call her such a pitiful name. She tapped the gentleman on his shoulder.

"Excuse me, sir, but I'm in a little bit of trouble. If you can help me, it will be greatly appreciated."

Both the assumed Mr. and the Mrs. turned towards her.

"What seems to be the problem, little lady?"

She knew it was just an expression for she was way taller than either of them.

"I can't get my papa's truck started. I came to town looking for a job, but no one was hiring. I need to return home so my papa can come back and pick up his truck; there's never been a time that he couldn't get it started, plus, he needs it for his job. He loads hay for a farmer. It's quite a distance to walk. I have a little money I can give you for your gas." She tugged on her purse for emphasis.

The gentleman was the first to speak, hushing his sweetie-pie, who was about to take the initiative. That was another thing Sloan could never abide: being put in her place. She had lived her life being told what to do and what not to do, but never again.

"It will be our pleasure to help you. But we need to know your name, and then we won't be considered strangers." She gave them a fictitious name of Brook.

"We were just about to leave; it's a good thing you happened by when you did. Our car is parked near the post office—it's a little green Ford Mustang. Just follow us. We were going to get some sweets, but we can do that after we take you home. And little lady, please do not insult us with your offer of money. There are several things God expects of us; one of them is to take care of those that are unable. You, my dear sweet child, more than qualify."

She did not think he would accept money, and it was a good thing he didn't: she had none.

She kept thanking them over and over. She stared at what she was to climb into.

She could not believe how small their car was.

"Do you think I will fit into the back seat of your car? It really looks small."

"Sure you will. Come on; I'll hold the seat down, just climb on in."

Sloan struggled, but he was right, she did get in, just barely. Her knees joined her chest. She was tall, but this was ridiculous. 'Why would anyone buy a car this small?'

Not until Sweetie-Pie turned in her seat to face Sloan did she realize she had her seat pushed all the way back.

"Oh my, you poor child, you're all cramped. I forgot to bring my seat forward. I do this all the time with our friends. I guess I'll never learn."

Sweetie-Pie leaned forward to release the seat, forcing it forward. Sloan's legs found relief.

"How's that? Better, I hope?"

"Oh yes, much better, thank you. I've never been in a car with such a small space. How does anyone fit comfortably?"

Sweetie-Pie giggled along with her husband.

"They do if they're old and short like we are, and I remember to pull the front seat forward."

As they pulled out Sloan told them the direction to take. She turned around to look out the back window of the Mr. and Mrs.' car, taking her final look at her papa's truck. Tears started to cloud her eyes; she quickly brushed them aside. She did not want to create any suspicions should the driver notice.

The Mr. made a right turn at the start of the cabins as Sloan instructed. The cabins were filled almost to capacity. Cabin 1—her cabin, as she would like to call it—and Cabin 3 were minus cars.

Sloan had to ask. "Do you plan to visit with us again?"

The Mrs. this time found her voice.

"Probably not. We really only stopped to get something to eat. We stayed longer than we intended, but I just had to see some of the cute shops."

Sloan could not believe how slowly they drove; at this rate they would never make it home on Sunday. *But where is their home?*

Her inquisitive side took over.

"Just where is it that you live?"

"Kansas City, Kansas," was the Mr.'s reply.

They'll never be home by this Sunday; possibly next Sunday, maybe, was Sloan's opinion.

As Sloan's newly found friends were approaching the end of the cabins, she told the Mr. to turn left and to follow the road; she would tell him when to stop. After several minutes, it wasn't hard to notice the mountain of rocks at the side of the road, though it did appear that someone had removed a few. She was confident that Clay would have no problem finding her. She would not take a chance of discovery to rebuild what had been taken down. She would stay hidden behind a wall of overgrown bushes and listen for the cars that passed.

Before thinking, she yelled at the Mr. to stop.

"Oh, I'm so sorry; I didn't mean to shout out like that. I was afraid you were going to pass the area where I'm to get out."

Mr. and Mrs. looked around, and as far as the eye could see there was nothing but woods, not a house in sight.

The look on the Mr.'s face told of his disbelief in her story.

"Child, are you playing games with us? I see no house."

"Oh, it's there, trust me, you just can't see it from this vantage point. I can get home much quicker if I cut through the forest by foot; it's a huge time saver. You've helped me considerably and I can't thank you enough." But before she waved them off, she thought it proper to ask their names.

"Our friends call me Clem, but I prefer Clemens, and they call my wife Flo instead of Flora. We think they do it to get us riled, but we just turn a deaf ear, which is easy to do at our age. Well, enough said. I think you better be on your way; your papa might become concerned. It's been a real pleasure to have met you, Brook. May God keep you and your family in His graces."

Sloan graciously thanked them again and told them to drive safely. She gave a hearty wave and headed towards the woods across from the pile of rocks. Mr. and Mrs. Harper made a slow U-turn in the road and headed slowly back into town. She waited until she was out of their line of view. She looked up and down the road to make sure no cars or trucks were approaching and then ran fast, diving into the tangled mess of vines and underbrush.

It was worse than she imagined. She knew it grew fast but this was absurd.

She failed to protect her face and arms from what felt like an attack. The tangled mess would surely leave its mark. She pulled and tugged, knowing she had to get them out of her way or she would surely be seen.

She heard something in the distance coming towards her. She shoved through, not thinking of the consequences, and fell face forward into what looked like a jungle. She looked to the heavens to thank God, while breathing a sigh of relief as a truck sped by; had the driver looked to the right as he headed into town, he would have seen her lying among the weeds.

The limbs and brush banded together, interweaving with the material of Sloan's dress and preventing her from standing. Tugging was proving to be an impossible task. She could not take the time to carefully remove what was tearing at her dress, not when she was still visible. Never again would she wear her favorite dress. Now able to stand, she shoved the brush back into place enough that no one would notice the freshly disturbed opening.

She looked at her watch, a gift from Sunni; it was 11:12 a.m. Sunni was and would always be a special friend. Sloan doubted she would ever feel for another the bonding they shared. She began feeling remorse for betraying Sunni, but quickly rid herself of those thoughts. Sunni would survive without her, but Sloan would die without Clay.

Hearing what sounded like another truck, she took a peek. This time it was a car; it too was heading into town. Her stomach was telling her it lacked sustenance. She had not entertained the thought of eating before she took off, plus the heat was taking its toll; although water was not a problem, standing for any length of time without support would wreak havoc with her endurance. She had to sit; her back and legs were about to give out. She looked around for a rock large enough to sit upon and close to the opening should Clay's car appear.

Sloan refused to count the hours of waiting. No matter the sound, when she heard a commotion she flew to the concealed hedge, but time and again it was a disappointment. She clung to the mass of vines, refusing to move until her eyes meet Clay's. She would be hanging for quite a while.

She was beginning to feel the pangs of betrayal. She was also sweating horribly; she needed to feel the spring water rush over her, to cleanse her body, as well as her mind. She ran to the "hole," tossing her handbag while kicking off her shoes.

Sloan waded in for several feet before she was able to swim. She had forgotten the pleasure and excitement her family was denied when Timmy died. The tears found their way back, remembering the joy she and her siblings shared when Mama announced it was break time, a signal for everyone to gather their swimming gear. She would keep those memories secured in her mind and heart.

She swam until she was exhausted, then collapsed into a seated position at the edge of the water. She stared at her tattered dress, no longer caring, while trying to smooth out the knotted and twig-entwined mess within her hair. The spring water refreshed her as she drank from it; where it was fed from she had no idea nor did she care. Sloan began to cry. She would have to return, she would never leave Mason's Mill.

Leaning forward, her hands covering her face, Sloan sobbed for what she now knew was never going to be. Then arms reached out and lifted her away from the water's edge. She no longer feared her attacker; she welcomed death. She turned, the tears would be non-ending, and she could not speak. She wrapped her arms tightly around the heartbeat of her life.

Clay was astounded at such strength.

"Babe, what's wrong? Did something happen?"

She continued to cling to him, as though he would leave again for some unknown reason.

"Come on, babe, talk to me. I can't stand not knowing why you are crying. Is it because of me? Is it because I was late in getting here? If that is the reason, I have an explanation. There was a four-car pile-up on the highway. I was stranded for hours."

"I thought you didn't want me anymore. I thought you weren't going to come for me. The hours continued to add — it was an eternity. I just wanted to die."

"Oh babe, I'm so sorry. I couldn't live without you, don't you know that? I have never felt as alive as when I am with you. You have my heart, babe, you always will."

Their lips locked. The splendor of that kiss once again drove them to heights they had experienced before. They couldn't get enough of each other. He had her trembling, she could feel her strength begin to leave her body and he was aroused to the point of hurting. He needed her now, but she quickly came to her senses and she broke the spell.

"Clay, we need to get away. I've been gone way too long. Soon they will come looking for me. We need to leave immediately."

She was tugging on his arm, pulling him towards the opening. He pulled back.

"Hold on, babe. A few more minutes will not make a difference. I need to know if your parents were agreeable to this. You did tell them about us, didn't you?"

Should she tell him the truth? No, it was too unbearable to relive that experience. She could not do it. What's another lie?

"Clay, I got into a huge argument with my papa. He refused to let me go with you. I had to leave without their permission. That is the reason we need to hurry—they are probably out looking for me now. If they find me, they will force me back. Trust me, Clay; we need to get out of here now. Where did you park your car?"

"It's up the road about the distance of a block."

"Oh my God, someone has probably seen it by now; that road is heavily traveled. If I get caught with you, all hell will break loose. You need to turn the car around and if you see someone approaching from behind slow down and let them pass. I'll stay here. When it's clear, beep your horn and open the door. I'll lay low on the floorboard until we leave town. Please tell me you have a four-door—two are an abomination."

"Yes, it's a four-door, but babe, you need to slow down; this isn't a race against time. You're acting as if someone is chasing you with a gun. I've been on the road for hours; I'm exhausted. Besides, I reserved the same cabin as before. We can relax and enjoy each other without making a mad dash for the highway I just got off of. Come on, babe, I've been so hungry for the feel of your body against mine I could hardly drive. I promise to make you feel really good."

"Clay, please don't do this to me. Just the thought of your lips on me is making me crazy with desire, but I've been gone since early this morning and I'm sure a search is on. You don't know my papa; I'm all he's got. He'll never let me go, he'll see you dead first. Trust me; we need to get out now."

Clay had never had a woman deny him; Sloan was a first. They made their way to the now exposed opening. Sloan listened for the sound of traffic. When she heard none, she gave him a shove.

"Run fast before a car comes. Remember what I said about the car door. Go now."

Clay, as you recall, was not much for running. But he tried the best he could. Sure enough, by the time he got to his car, he was breathing heavily. He did not have time to think about his breathing; Sloan told him he had to hurry.

The road was clear; he sounded the horn while stretching over the front seat to give the back door a shove. Sloan was on the floorboard before he took another breath.

As he began to drive, she shouted.

"My God, Clay, give it the gas. You're driving like an old man. This is insane. You are my only means of escape and you are barely moving."

"Well, it could be because there is a truck in front of us."

"Oh my God, someone saw us."

"No, I don't think so." He could hear her start to cry. "Babe, you're safe, I'm sure of that. Please stop crying."

He drove by the cabin they were to stay in. *So much for good times.* Making a left turn into the shopping center, he noticed the young man he'd collided with when he first encountered Sloan. That same man was now coming out of the doctor's office. He slowed his car; the guy was about to climb into a Dodge truck parked in front. Clay thought it would be a good thing if he apologized again.

"Babe, do you mind if I stop? I see your friend, and I would like to make amends."

"You must be out of your mind. If he sees me, he'll probably kick your ass, and when he's done with you, he'll take me away. What do I have to do, jump out and prove what he's capable of doing? You have to understand, nobody must see me. After a while, I'll be considered a runaway. So please, run with me."

Clay pressed his foot to the accelerator, but not before Marc noticed his car, but would he remember the make and model? Maybe or maybe not. Once Clay entered the highway Sloan was up and over the front seat. She looked down at her dress; felt her hair; the presentation she had planned was ruined. She started crying again. He pulled to the shoulder of the road and gathered her close to his chest.

"Hush, babe, there will be no more tears. You will never have to worry or have fear from this day forward."

"Oh Clay, I'm crying because I look like a grimy bag lady, and I so wanted to look pretty for you. I am from a poor family and I never had many pretty clothes. This dress was given to me by a dear friend, and now it's not even wearable. And the one thing I'm most proud of is my hair, and now I can't even own up to that."

She couldn't keep her crying in check.

"Wasted tears for something that is fixable with a shower and a comb. I think what we need to do is find a place to spend the night, then you can shower and I'll scour the area for some personal items to carry you over until we get to New York."

"Oh God, Clay, I don't know. If they find me, they'll take me away from you."

"Look at me; do you honestly believe I will allow that to happen?" His lips were moving but his eyes were what spoke the truth.

She reluctantly agreed to stop.

He had driven for one hour when he noticed a sign for lodging. He pulled off the highway onto the designated ramp. Facing the highway was a Ramada Inn. Sloan refused to go inside, embarrassed with her appearance.

Clay parked the car in the front of the entrance while she sank low into the seat. If anyone were to notice they would assume he or she were cheating on his or her spouse, or both. He returned shortly with the key and proceeded to the assigned room located on the main level.

When the door opened to the suite, she gasped.

"Oh my God, I just stepped into one of my magazines. I always dreamed of the 'someday' without ever actually believing it, but here I am living in my dream."

Sloan moved about the room touching everything in her path. This was such a small thing to appreciate. He could not wait to see her reaction when he presented her with the world.

Clay's body as well as his mind was exhausted; he surrendered to a small divan. She finished running her hand over all that pleased her, and then knelt before him. He took her face into his hands, tasting the sweetness of her kiss.

She yielded, searching out the depth of his mouth. She willed herself away.

"I need to take a shower."

He threw his hands up in the air with a sign and a smile commenting, "I think before you do anything, I should rid your hair of the weeds…agree?"

She nodded.

This was a magnificent moment. For the first time in two weeks, Sloan was calm and relaxed. She cupped her hands into her lap. A waste basket was within his reach. She was in awe of him, his forehead furrowed, his eyes serious. He was giving his best effect to remove the debris, his hands ever so gentle.

Before he disposed of the last of the twigs, Clay had something to say.

"I think we need to slow down and think about what we are doing. My conscience is wearing heavily. I just can't run off with you without knowing why your father is against me. I think we should go back and straighten out the mess we created. Once I explain my intentions, I don't think they will object to us being together. I want them to think kindly of me, not as a kidnapper of their daughter. Babe, we are acting as fugitives, running not from the law, but from your family. What we don't need is to start our lives on something that can be easily resolved."

"Clay, can't you please just let it be. You need to trust me; I know what I am doing. I will tell you this much, it has nothing to do with you; he will never allow me to be with any man. Do you now understand?"

She figured a lie was no big deal when there was no one to question it.

Was Clay reading more into it than what she actually meant? *Surely her father wasn't abusing her.* He did not push the issue; the subject was now taboo.

"You do know once we do this, there is no turning back? I will not be able to right the wrong You may never again see them or this town. Is this really what you want?"

"Yes, Clay, that is what I want."

"Then so be it, but there is one thing you need to know. You must never leave me to return home. I will never allow anyone to take you from me, do you understand?"

She was quick to respond. "Clay, when I surrendered my body, my heart went with it. No one can separate two hearts that beat as one, don't you know that? That day on the platform sealed our fate, a connection that can never be severed. Wherever our journey takes us, our love will endure."

He took her face into his hands. "Kiss me, my darling, and let me feel that love."

She reached for him, placing her mouth onto his. He devoured her lips, his tongue working its way into her mouth. She felt her heart beating out of control; she needed him much more than he needed her. She couldn't get enough of him as she worked her way up from the floor, her lips never leaving his as she began to remove her dress and panties; her purse for the first time left its place of honor.

She released her lips, licking at his mouth before making a statement.

"I'm going to take a shower. Would you like to share the water with me? We'll have no need for it to be hot; once our bodies come together there's going to be enough steam to humidify this entire suite."

She gave him a provocative smile that caused his groin to ache. He did not think he could last as long as he did the last time. His need was agonizing. His clothes were added to hers.

She slowly made her way to the bathroom, pointing her moving index finger at him in a come-hither sign.

She felt the heat of his body blend onto hers. The warm water coated their bodies. He held her breasts in his hands, licking and rolling his tongue over her erect nipples before he bathed her body with the fragrant bar of soap the motel provided. Soon the suds were covering her from front to back. He began caressing her body. The soap was no longer necessary; his left hand found its container. His right hand began to make designs meant to please; she began to moan. He continued with his strokes. He knew what pleased her, and only when she begged would he finish what he'd started. He licked at her lips, while she continued to groan with pleasure. He lifted her high, bracing her against the shower wall. She wrapped her legs around him, holding onto his head for support. She began to scream in ecstasy. He stopped, she pleaded with him to continue, he did not give in. He removed her legs from around his body. She was now standing, though weak in body strength. He began to wash away the suds, never missing any of the vital spots that brought her extreme pleasure.

She screamed out, arching her back as she began her climb into the wonder of lovemaking. "Don't stop, please don't stop. Oh my God, yes, yes."

She slid down to the floor of the stall but did not stay there long; he took her into his arms and made his way towards the king-sized bed. Clay had techniques that he had used many times with women he had cared about at one time or another, causing them to scream out wanting more of the same. He would now use some of them on Sloan; she too would plead for a repeat performance.

They lay entwined for better than an hour. She was weak from the raptures that rippled throughout her body. No words could describe the fireworks once they got started.

They were about to embark on a journey that neither one of them should take. They would not leave their hotel that night.

Clay was the first to awaken. He glanced over at a sight never to be witnessed by anyone but him. He was beginning to get aroused. He knew this had to stop; if he continued at this pace, he wouldn't last out the year. But, by God, she was truly beautiful, with her long hair fanned out upon the sheet. Her nude body was like nothing he had ever seen. The texture of her skin was smooth and soft. He groaned with wanting her as he leaned over, gently pressing his lips to hers. Her eyes fluttered open as she returned the kiss; again she appeared ready to make love. He gently pushed her aside, reminding her he needed to shop, and his plane was waiting to take them to his home in Manhattan.

Sloan fell back into her prior position, somewhat disappointed. "I'll take a shower and be ready when you return."

Clay's visit with his grandmother Lydia two weeks prior had been overwhelming. She remained in the same condition, which was good, considering the circumstances. When he relayed the news, she was ecstatic. While looking for and finding his mother, he found Lydia's baby girl living in the same town—who would have thought?—and add to that an extraordinary find, the woman to claim his heart. But in her wildest dreams Lydia never expected her baby girl to have twelve babies of her own. She confided in him how the guilt of her lies lifted, that God must have forgiven her, for it was only by His power that Ali and Jena were found safe and secure.

Clay did wonder why it was taking Ali so long to call him with her flight plans. Surely she had made them by now. He still had another week in which to hear from her; there was no need to panic.

He was beside himself with guilt over not seeing his mother. He had planned to pay her a repeat visit before he picked up Sloan. But because he was caught up in the traffic due to the accident, he was afraid Sloan would return home, possibly thinking he had changed his mind. He couldn't take that chance. There would have been no problem if she had given him her phone number or address.

Clay closed the door to the suite and went immediately to the registration desk to request the use of a telephone. He dared not use the suite's phone; he was not ready to answer questions, questions to which he did not yet know all the answers.

He wanted desperately to hear the sound of his mother's voice; he was already missing her. He reached into his wallet, where a scrap of paper with her number on it was tucked into a corner slot. The call was on its fifth ring. He was about to hang up.

"Hello…hello…is anyone there?" The voice on the other end was waiting.

Clay couldn't answer. He wondered who the male voice belonged to. If he asked to speak to Harriet, he might be questioned about who he was. He remembered her telling him, "There are things you need to know about me." Could this male voice belong to one of the things she was talking about? He did not know if she had told anyone about him. He couldn't take the chance on betraying her confidence until he knew for sure.

The voice at the other end of the phone repeated, "Hello, I'm still waiting. Is anyone there?"

Clay continued to hesitate. He really wanted to know who was answering her telephone. His hesitation brought the dial tone.

He returned to the hotel with a shopping bag containing two dresses, one in a size six and the other a size eight. Both when measured looked to be the same size; if neither worked, he was told he could return them.

The additional items he chose raised the clerk's eyebrows. Clay continued to shake his head at the saleswoman until she found exactly what he had in mind: the most outrageously revealing and skimpiest undergarments they sold.

The very pretty saleswoman was envious; it had been years since she was left wanting and breathless. Her days of ecstasy ended on the day she said "I do." Pleading, begging, and then demanding fell on deaf ears; her husband's style was now "slam, bang, thank you, ma'am." The woman who would be wearing these undergarments was sure to enjoy what that day or evening, or both, would bring. She was getting excited just thinking about it, and the man standing before her left no doubt he was the kind of specimen that was sure to satisfy.

Clay noticed the saleswoman's face was flaming, but surely not from what he had just bought; she must have sold hundreds of these undergarments. Well, maybe not hundreds, but then again, maybe none.

If Clay had not had his lover waiting on him, would he have tuned in to the saleswoman's need? Absolutely. She was at the right place, wrong time.

His last stop was at a beauty supply house to purchase a large number of hair supplies.

Sloan was sitting in a chair still wrapped in the bath towel.

Clay's brain was clouded with one thought, *God, she is magnificent.* When God created woman, Sloan was exactly what He had in mind. Clay refused to touch her; he didn't trust himself or her. They needed to keep their distance.

He tossed the bag to her, commenting, "We really need to get a move on, babe. My pilot is on standby. We have at least another hour of driving." But he wanted to have her, one more time. Did he dare? He glanced at his Rolex; time was getting away. It would be different if he had only himself to satisfy—that wouldn't take long— but he loved the effect he had on women. Quickies were not his thing. No exceptions.

When Sloan returned fully dressed Clay was astounded. The most expensive dresses in the shop had been disgustingly cheap at $49.95 each. He wasn't about to turn the town upside down to search for something that would put a dent in his wallet; he had to take what was available. If the garment industry could get a glimpse of what Sloan did to that dress, they would hike the cost. The dress, a cotton-rayon blend the color of a pomegranate, was cut low with a square bodice. It was sleeveless and belted at the waist with a straight skirt a minimum of four inches above the knees. No one could do to that dress what Sloan did. She appealed to his sense of style.

"Well, what do you think?" She turned slowly. If she were trying to entice him, she was succeeding. He refused to go to her.

"You are stunning."

Her smile brought the sun into the room. He was anxious to get her home to introduce her to his friends, but did he dare? Time will tell.

They gathered up what few belongings they had and made their exit. The next stop would be Chicago O'Hare Airport. In the car, Sloan rested her head on Clay's shoulder. She was happy and finally at peace with the death of her family. She slept through the remainder of the trip.

The airport manager took care of clearance for their departure. Andrew, his pilot, was leaning against Clay's personal aircraft reading the daily newspaper, his legs crossed, when Clay's Mercedes pulled up. Clay rushed over to the car's passenger side. This time Sloan waited for the car door to open; she was learning. He took her hands as she stood to face him. He looked deeply into her eyes, stating, "I can't wait to get you home."

She replied, "I can't wait to get there."

Their thought waves, if shared, would put lingering smiles on everyone's face.

"Andrew, I'm sorry for the delay—unexpected things kept coming up." Do we not know what that unexpected thing was? You bet we do.

"No problem, Mr. Clay. It gave me a chance to catch up on the news." Andrew folded the paper as he made his way to the rental car. He opened the driver's door, pressed the button to release the locked truck, and then loaded their belongings onto the aircraft. The car rental agency had a driver on standby to retrieve the Mercedes. Costs had been calculated when the rental arrangements were made, and monies would have to be reimbursed for overpayment.

Andrew was a tall black man in his thirties; hair kept short, eyes the color of coal and a small mustache above full lips with perfect white teeth. His smile turned up a little more on one side than the other. He was a woman's man. Handsome described him to a tee. He was married with two little boys.

Sloan took an immediate liking to Andrew. He had plenty of fine equipment for a woman to cheat on her husband, if given the chance. She thought he was a neat guy. Clay noticed her looking his pilot over; he was going to be a jealous suitor. She was told where to sit in the eight-passenger plane and to buckle up; she did as she was told. Clay took a seat alongside her.

Andrew was preparing for takeoff, waiting for clearance. Sloan had never flown, and she was frightened. She gripped the arms of the seat as the plane began its departure. Clay reached over to calm her.

"Babe, there is nothing to be afraid of; once we get in the air, it will feel as if you are sitting in your living room. Come on now, relax."

Sloan was really trying, but her stomach refused to cooperate. She began to quicken her breaths. "I don't think I can do this, I feel sick."

Clay recognized the signs; Sloan was beginning to hyperventilate. He instantly strapped an oxygen mask on her. Slowly she began to calm down. She was no longer fearful; the stomach upset was also fading.

He removed the mask.

"Feel better?" He still had his arm wrapped around her when she spoke.

"Yes, thank you. I've dreamt about flying many times, but like all dreams that's all they were, until now. Oh Clay, how do I ever thank you? I know absolutely nothing about you and yet I don't care. Isn't that strange?"

"Babe, you will come to know everything in time, but for now let's enjoy the flight. In less than two hours we'll be in New York, the place you will soon call home." On impulse their lips locked.

The plane landed without incident. Andrew retrieved their belongings as they made their way towards a waiting limousine. He would then return the aircraft to Clay's personal hangar.

Clay's own chauffeur, Gus, was sick with the flu, so a limousine service was called to assist in taking him and his passenger to his apartment building. He had at his disposal his grandmother's chauffeur, Maxwell, an unmarried and above-average-looking sixty-five-year-old, but the drive from the Hamptons to Kennedy Airport was at least an hour depending on traffic. Clay hated putting anyone out for his benefit; a limousine service would do fine.

Sloan was in awe; she was being led like a lost puppy. Suddenly she stopped and tugged on Clay's arm.

"Clay, what is all of this? The airplane and now a limo are too much. You surely can't afford all this. If you're trying to impress me, there is no need. I will love you no matter your status in life."

"Babe, you are in for the surprise of your life. Just hang in there and enjoy the ride."

Sloan shook her head but did as she was told.

A short and rotund uniformed driver quickly opened the car door as they approached. The luggage had been placed into the trunk, and they were ready to depart.

Sloan took Clay's offered hand as she slid onto the luxurious car seat. Was she in a dream? Would she awaken to find her life as it had been? Of course not, for that life was destroyed by flames. No sooner had Clay placed himself by his lover's side, than his lips searched for hers.

In less than a half hour the limo's driver pulled up in front of Clay's apartment. He double parked, then removed himself from the driver's seat, making his way to the last door on the car, allowing Clay and his passenger to exit. He then closed the car door and quickly removed the lone piece of luggage and a small bag, taking them to the entrance of the apartment building. Clay thanked him with a folded bill. The chauffeur tipped his hat in acknowledgment, all the while holding the entrance door open.

Clay had made his driver's day very worthwhile. Sloan never let a thing get past her. She watched as Clay reached into his wallet and extracted a bill; the denomination she did not know, but by the driver's expression, it had to have been a hefty tip.

Clay took both the lone suitcase and bag with one hand while his other pressed against Sloan's back guiding her towards the elevator.

Clay was about to introduce her to a place called heaven on earth.

CHAPTER TWO

Marc couldn't believe his luck. Sloan was alive. He needed to see her immediately. He ran to the sheriff's police car, pulling Ben with him.

"Where is she? Never mind, I know. She could be at no other house than her best friend Sunni's, right?"

"Marc, settle down, you need to think this through. She's in a grieving mode. She's going to need time to get her life back on track; to descend on her right now would be the worst mistake you could make. Marc, it's not as if she were in love with you. She could barely tolerate you, and you want to rush into her arms. I don't think so."

"But don't you see, Ben, she really needs someone in her corner, someone she knows beyond a reasonable doubt loves her, and that person is me. I'm going to see her whether you think it's appropriate or not."

"Fine, you do what you have to do, but let me put it this way: if she refuses to see you, you may never again have another chance to redeem yourself in her eyes. Come on. I'll drive you to your home so you can pick up your truck and destroy your life, whatever's left to destroy."

Marc's hand was about to open the car door, his thoughts totally on his beloved Sloan, when he hesitated. He caught Ben looking at him over the roof of his police car. Marc could read him like a book; he knew Ben felt bad for him, not only because of his mother but Sloan as well. He was taking on the role of a father giving him sound advice. What ever would he do without Ben? He was the father he never had but damn well needed in his life. Marc would not only take Ben's fatherly advice, he would thank him for it. This would turn out to be the worst advice Ben could have given, for tomorrow Sloan would be gone.

Marc could at least pay a visit to the Doc's office just to make sure his mother was doing all right. He would call ahead to make an appointment.

Ben and Marc reclaimed their seats in the patrol car. In a matter of minutes, Ben pulled into Marc's driveway.

"Ben, how would you like to have a cup of coffee with me? I could use some company for a while. You can also help me air out the house, okay?"

"Sounds great. I have plenty of free time now that I don't have to chase you down. Besides, I never refuse a fresh cup of coffee."

Their house really needed fresh air, if you could consider the month of July as bringing forth any kind of air, especially fresh. Marc went off to the kitchen to prepare some coffee. Ben had started in right away opening all the windows when Marc's phone began to ring.

Marc gave a yell, "Ben, will you get the phone? I'm putting some biscuits in the oven."

"No problem. It's probably the station tracking me down."

"Hello, this is the Andersons' residence. This is Sheriff Davidson speaking. Can I help you?… No, I wasn't anywhere near my car." Ben took notice of Marc sticking his head out of the kitchen opening, giving him a look like "is it for me?" Ben shook his head, then pointed to himself.

"Marc and I were at the cemetery. We just got back to his house. I'm going to indulge in some coffee and biscuits and then I'll return. Why, what's up?" The voice at the other end told him what he wanted to hear.

"Oh my God, this is incredible. My prayers have finally been answered. Halleluiah!"

Marc entered the living room when he heard the sounds of jubilation. He had never seen Ben so keyed up. The smile on Ben's face continued to stay minutes after he replaced the receiver.

Ben was unaware of Marc's presence.

"Come on, Ben, what's up? You can't keep me in the dark about something that apparently has you this excited."

Ben's smiling face turned to Marc. "She's talking, Marc. She's talking. Praise be to God."

It was like a thunderbolt striking Marc. "Oh my God, Ben, that's exactly the medicine I needed to put me back on my feet. To hell with the coffee and biscuits, let's make with the wheels. We have to get her out of that place and back where she belongs."

Ben would never have thought in a million years the words he used could have been referring to Marc's mother.

"Oh Marc, I'm sorry, I went to the extreme with my enthusiasm. The call was not about your mother, it was in regards to Cindy Bingington; she finally regained consciousness. Can you forgive me for acting out like that? You know better than I how badly I wish it had been your mother."

Marc's disappointment was pushed to the side. He knew Ben had being talking for years about Cindy. Ben felt Cindy was a victim of foul play and now he has the chance to prove her innocence and find the real person responsible for Timmy's death. He waited for this moment for a very long time. He will be much more excited in due time over Marc's mother. His patience paid off with regards to Cindy, and that same kind of patience will apply to Marc's mother. Ben relaxed with his cup of coffee and consumed more biscuits than he should. There was no need to start rushing around; a few more minutes would not make a difference.

Upon Ben's departure, Marc called to set up an appointment. He would be Doc's last appointment for the next day, at 5:00 p.m. Marc would indeed take notice of the Mercedes when it passed him, but that's as far as it would go.

If only he had known.

CHAPTER THREE

When the door opened to Clay's apartment Sloan's way of living would abruptly change. In the weeks and months to come, she will learn the ways of the wealthy. She will be a good student, one of the best. Sloan was entering a world not yet discovered.

Clay was her guide as she glided over the marble floors, indirect lighting providing the illumination needed throughout the entire apartment. Her family would never have known the meaning of the word *cramped* had they lived in such a place. The gourmet kitchen was something out of *House Beautiful,* the small appliances hidden within its walls made useable with a touch of a button. The gigantic room would have been a dream come true for her mama. But it was the bathroom that took Sloan's breath away; she then knew the meaning of paradise. She did not hesitate; her clothes went flying, as did Clay's. With a touch of a button water burst forth from every porthole in the whirlpool bathtub.

They made love as if it were their first time. Their lovemaking would continue once again after he carried his naked temptress to their king-size bed. He will never hear the excuse "Not tonight, I have a headache," as his many married male friends often spoke of. Sloan finally succumbed to sleep; she was exhausted from the traveling, but mostly from the hours of making love.

Clay had been awake for more than an hour. He missed her. The ending of Saturday came quickly; in a few days work would demand his presence. His longing and desire would keep him jogging back and forth from work to bed (well not exactly jogging, maybe a fast pace, maybe). If he could, he would tie her to his backside. As his need for her grew, she continued to sleep. It was time for a little persuasion. His fingers, light as feathers, began to caress her body, while his lips blazed a trail of kisses down her backside. She did not move or respond.

He shook his head; he would leave her be.

His time would not be wasted; he would make much-needed phone calls, first to his staff—their services would be on hold for a week, and they would be well compensated. If everyone had an employer like Clay, there would be hugs instead of guns.

He called his mother again, but this time neither she nor a male voice answered. He would call many times during his week home and beyond; the constant rings would become an annoyance. When he really thought about it, he knew nothing at all about his mother. Was she employed, the reason for no pick-up? Or could it be something much worse, like an illness; was that one of the things she would reveal later? He was making himself sick with such a thought. He would continue to call; eventually she would have to answer.

The time had come for some heavy shopping. Sloan needed a wardrobe.

Clay stood at the entrance to the bedroom. Sloan had thrown the top silk sheet onto the floor. Never in his life would he have thought a woman such as she existed. He was caught up in the splendor of the moment when she opened her eyes, locking onto his. She held out her arms. He hesitated, not because the need wasn't there, but other things were now a priority and lovemaking was not one of them.

"Come on, babe, we have to get you ready to meet the people that will consume your very existence. The first thing is to introduce you to the world of shopping. I've already called for my limo, so you need to get a move on."

He patiently waited, although he did keep glancing at his watch.

When Sloan finally did make her entrance into the great room, Clay's breath was put on hold, no one could do to a dress what she had done; she could don a burlap sack and all eyes would turn. She wore the second of the two dresses: a sleeveless form-fitting lavender knit dress with what Clay had thought was an acceptable neckline. He was sadly mistaken, for Sloan's breasts spilled over, revealing more than he thought possible. This woman, his woman, had more curves than a winding road.

"Clay, something must be wrong with this dress; the top won't stay up." The direct statement managed to evoke a response from him.

"No, babe, you just have the right equipment to fill it out." Did he dare walk her up and down the streets of New York? Would she be arrested for indecent exposure? This was New York, was he kidding?

As they stepped out of the apartment building, Gus, Clay's chauffeur, was ready to open the door to the limo. Clay greeted him from the door step, as did Sloan. He did not fail to notice Gus's reaction. Holding onto Clay's hand, she descended the steps.

Gus began to get aroused. This woman, soon to be a part of his life, was given life to bring ultimate pleasure to every male and female if she so desired. She moved as if in slow motion, the waves of her long dark hair in rhythm with the sway of her hips. She will disrupt many households in the weeks to come. Gus was thankful she was not his woman, for his boss was going to have a hell of a time keeping his friends away. That kind of a headache he could do without. It was time to focus on his job; never would he jeopardize his coveted position.

Clay was right; the body inside that dress was an attention grabber. He could trust Gus, but what about the others? Instead of being a doting husband, will he turn into a warden, allowing Sloan to enjoy outside activity only while in his presence? Will he trust Gus with his extraordinary cargo? You bet he will; Gus will be her protector.

Gus was buzzed. The privacy window slid down.

"Gus, we'll be going to quite a few shops. This could end up being a very long day for you, so be prepared. Our first stop will be Madison Avenue." Madison was in the heart of the Upper East Side, and many shops occupied the space. They catered to the very wealthy, offering clothing and accessories with price tags that would cause an ordinary citizen to go into cardiac arrest.

Gus was well acquainted with the areas frequented by the well-to-do.

He pulled in front of the first of many stores. Clay and Sloan patiently waited for the car door to open. Gus leaned down, offering his hand to Sloan; it was warm to the touch.

She replied with a smile while thanking him. Her touch excited him and he quickly moved aside, allowing her to pass. As she stepped onto the pavement, a couple of men stopped in their tracks. Each had different remarks.

"You are one woman I would gladly bring home to mother."

And then another.

"When you get tired of him, and you will, give me a call." A card was placed in her hand.

Clay tossed the card, shoving the man away. He pulled Sloan along, sidestepping the mounting number of gawkers.

Had she just entered a battlefield? She had never encountered so many people that appeared to be tied together; she wondered how anyone got to where they were going. Of course, she really had no idea, but thought this had to be worse than driving in traffic. She kept stumbling along as Clay continued his pull.

Finally the door opened, and he was greeted warmly. Everyone that knew anyone knew Clayton Chadsworth. Not only was he the most eligible bachelor throughout New York City, but he was also extremely generous with his credit card when it came to buying for his female acquaintances.

Sloan was caught up in a whirlwind, a never-ending day of shopping, although they did manage to grab a bite to eat somewhere in the middle of spending an obscene amount of money.

After Madison came Bloomingdale's, Bergdorf Goodman, Saks, Lord & Taylor, and then on to Barney's, high society's finest. Clay's credit card was well used with the understanding that all the purchases would be delivered ASAP. Daytime dresses, suits, evening gowns, skirts, slacks, blouses, shoes and coordinating accessories totaled in the high six-figure bracket, but he kept the best for last.

Sloan pleaded to the point of crying.

"Please, Clay, I cannot take another step, my feet are killing me. All I want is to relax in a hot tub."

"I have one more stop and then I promise we will return home, okay, babe?"

Sloan was seated in the limo. She had kicked her shoes off onto the floorboard and was hard at work rubbing her tired and burning feet. She was flippant with her answer.

"Do you have the stamina for carrying me? Because that is the only way I will enter another store."

She was beyond exhausted; her overwhelming excitement ended five hours into the shopping spree.

Clay managed to inform Gus out of Sloan's hearing range where his final stop would take place. Gus smiled knowingly.

Clay was out the door the instant Gus pulled to the curb.

"Scoot on over here, babe."

As Sloan slid across the seat, she began to make another flippant remark. "This doesn't look like… " Before she could complete the sentence, he had her up in his arms.

"Clay, what in the world are you doing?"

"Did you not say, you would not walk another step?"

"Clay, I was just being glib. I can walk. Please put me down."

"Babe, I wish I could, but the most incredible urge came over me, commanding me to sweep you off your feet." The look on his face was so utterly sincere, she could do nothing but laugh.

"Clay, I'm shoeless. Please don't do this, everyone is staring at us."

"Not us, babe, it's you, only you." He held her tightly and she surrendered, her head resting on his shoulder, her arm draped across his back, her fingers caressing the hair that barely covered the collar of his shirt. There was no mistake; this shared love was equal to none.

She was about to get the most incredible surprise of her life.

CHAPTER FOUR

Gus knew the steps to take when his boss had his woman in his arms. He ran ahead to open the door to Tiffany's. Clay did not put Sloan down until a seat was provided for her comfort. She was placed before a case with contents that amounted to maybe more money than even Clay made in a year.

The woman that waited on them was absolutely stunning. Sloan felt intimidated, out of her element.

Did she not remember her reflection in the Swimming Hole?

Clay had called ahead to have a specific tray of rings readily available for Sloan's viewing. She would be given the privilege of choosing her own.

She turned towards Clay, her hand cupped, covering her forehead.

"Clay, what are we doing here?"

"Babe, we are here to select your wedding rings."

Sloan dropped her hand and jumped from the chair, sliding her arms under Clay's, wrapping them around his back. Kisses swept over him, covering his entire face. She shed happy tears. He could not deny that he was overwhelmed with pleasure. She reclaimed the chair, heart pounding, thoughts limited to her wedding day. Clay stood alongside her as the many trays of diamond rings were presented. Kleenex was offered as the rain of happy tears never ceased. She could not see, for if it was not the fire of the diamonds, it was the tears that blinded her.

In the end Clay made the selection, for with every diamond ring shown to her, all Sloan could do was nod. The eighteen-karat white gold engagement ring contained an eight-carat square-cut diamond, its mounting carved high above two baguettes that graced each side of the center stone. The four baguettes were two carats each of diamond brilliance. The wedding band to complement held five baguettes of equal weight.

The staggering cost due to the grade was $642,000. Clay would accept nothing but the finest. The rings did not need to be sized; they were a perfect fit.

Was this a coincidence, or was destiny finishing up with what it intended?

Sloan refused to take her eyes off the ring, holding her hand high, enraptured with its beauty as they made their way towards the limo. Clay received his satisfaction from watching. He no longer had control over his life. He was caught in a web; never will he escape, nor will he want to.

Their second day of being together was nearing its end, the sunlight being tucked away. Clay finally realized what his grandmother and now his mother had been trying to tell him: "Unless you share your heart with someone, its beats are wasted."

His apartment, soon to be theirs, was looming ahead. If they thought the heights of their lovemaking were at their max, they were both mistaken.

The apartment door slammed shut and clothes were tossed about the room. Clay and Sloan were in a marathon to find the first rug available. Arms and legs entwined, mouths exploring, bodies thirsting for fulfillment. The rapturous minutes collided into an hour. Never in Heaven's greatest moment could there be anything to define what the two of them conquered. If they could, they would have devoured each other.

They awoke to the sound of a telephone ringing. The lone item of dress on either of them was Clay's watch. Sloan had discarded hers, wanting nothing to interfere with their lovemaking. The daylight was now in hiding; the darkness of the night would not have been evident if the lights within the apartment had been turned on. The voice at the other end sounded raspy. That voice could not be mistaken; it was his grandmother.

"Clay, did I wake you? The hour is late, but I need to talk to you. Do you mind the intrusion?"

"Grandmother, whatever the hour, whatever the day, I'm here for you."

"I was wondering if you had heard from Alexandria. The time for her arrival is almost upon us. Do you think I'm being foolish for being overly concerned?"

"Grandmother, foolish you are not, overly concerned maybe a little, but I'm trying my best to get in touch with her. Until then, please put all your worries to rest along with your body, okay?" It felt good to hear his grandmother laugh; she did not need a rock to fall on her head to understand the meaning of his words.

"I'll do whatever you say, and Clay, I am sorry for waking you." Sorry was also a word not found in his dictionary when it came to his beloved grandmother.

A few more words were spoken and their conversation ended. Clay found himself in a dilemma; the time for Ali to call was indeed nearing its end. His continuous calls to his mother also remained the same, unanswered. He had no alternative; he would have to return to

Sloan's hometown. He would conduct a so-called stakeout, for he surely could not ring his mother's doorbell; no telling who would answer, and he would not betray her confidence. He would give it another three days, and if he did not receive a call by then, he would make arrangements with his pilot Andrew to fly him back to Chicago.

But as fate would have it, Clay would not return to Mason's Mill.

It was time to introduce Sloan to his very small family, his beloved grandmother and his father. She had turned away, sleep reclaimed. He forced his naked body not to rejoin her; he could not sleep even if he tried. He would instead take a shower and definitely put on some clothes. He would be up for the remainder of the night and would not close his eyes again until the rising sun had again retired for the day. He removed his watch, noting the time, 2:45 a.m., as he stepped into the shower. Now he understood why his grandmother apologized. The shower was refreshing, but his mind was on Ali.

Now dressed in a pair of Armani slacks, an Armani polo shirt and a pair of Gucci loafers, Clay re-entered the great room. Sloan remained in the same position as when he had left her. He took a seat upon the sectional that surrounded his distinctive marble fireplace. He needed to clear his mind of the woman lying before him and think about the current situation with his grandmother. Although the fireplace was not in use at the present time, it was the first thing to be noticed when entering the room. He turned his thoughts towards the fireplace. With or without the pleasures of the glowing coals, it offered him time to pause and think. He again looked at the time, 3:30 a.m.

He could see his grandmother's face as clearly as if she were standing before him, this woman who asked but one thing of him, to bring home her Ali.

He understood why she couldn't sleep; she could rely on him to boost her confidence while waiting on the arrival of the daughter she had not seen in over twenty years.

Monday, a workday for many, would be the day he and Sloan started to make plans for their wedding day. When not thinking about what he should be thinking of, he stared at Sloan. Morning arrived at the usual time along with the door's buzzer. He glanced at his watch. Was he seeing right, 6:00 a.m.? Who could be calling at this time of the morning? There was no need to wake Sloan for she too heard the distinctive ring, and she ran naked, escaping to the privacy of their bedroom.

Clay opened the door to be besieged by a hoard of boxes and bags. When he said ASAP did they really think he meant within hours? Money does talk, no matter the time of day. The deliveries continued for the next two hours.

Clay stood among staircases of boxes, walking space eliminated. He needed help placing the boxes in the adjoining room, which was equipped with a massive amount of dressing closets, shoe racks, etc. All of the contents of the packages would fit comfortably there. He felt weighted down with what he was facing.

"Would someone be willing to help me place everything where it belongs? I will pay handsomely, not only for your time, but will reimburse your employers for the additional time away."

The four remaining deliverymen did not hesitate. Clay showed them the way to what would be Sloan's private dressing room.

Within forty-five minutes the clothing, shoes, handbags and jewelry from designers such as Roberto Cavalli, Gianni Versace, Gucci, Armani, Dolce & Gabbana, Christian Dior, Prada, Etro and G.F. Ferre, just to name a few, were distributed to their rightful places. The clothing now occupied cushioned hangers. All the useless tags that had been removed were added to the boxes and bags that would be hauled away. The many shelves that lined the room now held a mass assortment of shoes and handbags.

Two bureaus, designed and operated as one, contained many drawers. A side switch allowed the dual dresser to open. Each drawer would then slide out, giving the appearance of a circular staircase, allowing easy access. This was now filled to capacity displaying an enormous array of jewelry, scarves, undergarments and makeup; it would remain open to capture Sloan's attention.

Clay pulled out his wallet and removed ten $100 bills to be split equally among the four young men. He reminded them to inform their employers to send him a bill for the extended time away from other deliveries.

It did not take a genius to figure out that when Sloan escaped into their bedroom, it was not to get dressed, but to grab a few more hours of sleep. She had no idea what had just taken place. Clay's anticipation of seeing the look on her face was overpowering. One day she had nothing to wear and today she owned a department store.

She must have recovered from her loss of sleep; Clay could hear the shower running. When she made an appearance she was adorned with two towels: one for the head, the other for the body. Upon her feet Clay's slippers made a flopping sound as she walked. He was in the kitchen making a pot of coffee when she came up behind him. He was so much taller than she.

She wrapped her arms around him, laying her head on his back.

"I will never be able to thank you enough for all the beautiful things you've given me. But it scares me to be this happy. Clay, you have to promise me nothing will ever come between us."

He had his hands over hers when he turned to face her. His lips were what assured her. He picked her up; the towel fell to the floor, the headgear followed. She helped him remove his clothing while sitting on the edge of the bed, never once taking her eyes from his.

Their lovemaking would cease when the ongoing rings from the telephone interrupted them, his father was the intruder this time. They broke apart and started to laugh at the intrusion. They knew there was another world out there, and the telephone was proof. Clay rolled off the bed and made his way towards the persistent ringing. Sloan got the impression he would not be returning to pick up where they left off. She gathered the necessary garments and proceeded to the bathroom; this shower would be a quickie.

Clay picked up on the tenth ring.

"My boy, I'm sorry, but I couldn't stand it a minute longer. I've been pacing the floor waiting for your call doing as you asked, not to tell your grandmother Sloan has arrived, but how much longer must we wait?"

Clay started laughing.

"If you think you're excited, imagine what I'm feeling. But be patient, I'm going to give Gus a call and then we'll be on our way. Where are you calling from?"

"Home, why?"

"Aren't you supposed to be at work?"

"Not if you own the company." They both started laughing. This father and son had an extremely close relationship. Pandora's Box was waiting to be opened.

Clay could hear the water running. Sloan was taking yet another shower, and he would do the same in the spare bedroom. At the cost of water, they could well receive one of the highest bills ever mailed to a single residence. He earlier had allowed himself the luxury of a lingering shower; this one would not compare. He chose another pair of slacks and this time a button-down short-sleeved shirt and a pair of dress slip-ons; he was ready to go.

He was excited; he still hadn't shown Sloan her dressing room. She was startled when she opened the bathroom door to find him standing there. This time the towel would be removed only when she choose the dress she would wear for the day.

"Come, I want to show you something." Their hands locked together as he led the way, stopping in front of a double door. He released her hand to swing open the double doors to reveal the most astounding room that no other woman would ever lay claim to. She gasped loudly, her hands covered her mouth. Much time was taken touching the garments, closets full of clothing, shoes that would make decisions hard. She ran her fingertips over the array of fine jewelry, while her eyes swept over the entire room; its contents would stagger the wisest of minds, and it all belonged to her. Sloan collapsed onto the floor; her thoughts were of her mama. She covered her eyes, weeping for the loss of her family. All these things and more that were lavished on her, Clay would have done as much for her family. She hated God for taking away her only purpose in life.

Did God really think that replacing her prior life with a life of luxury would be acceptable?

Clay lowered himself to his knees and gathered her close.

"I pray those are happy tears. I don't know what I would do if they were not."

She would not disclose what was hidden in her heart; it would shatter this moment, his moment. "Oh Clay, of course they are happy tears—there are no other kind when I'm with you. I'm just completely overwhelmed. How did you manage to do all of this and escape my attention?"

"It's called sleep, babe." He allowed her a few more brief moments, for he could tell she was awestruck by the display before her. He shifted from his knees to sit beside her, continuing to hold her close.

"Babe, today you are going to meet the two most incredible people to whom I gave my heart many years ago."

Sloan turned to face him. "That has to be your mama and papa."

"Well, yes and no, but before I try to answer that question, I think we're going to have to work on some of your word usage."

"Oh, I'm sorry. What did I say that was wrong?"

"It really wasn't wrong. It's just that the words mama and papa are not used in the city. That's no reflection on you, babe—you were raised in the country and that's the language that's used there."

Sloan's feelings were sensitive when it came to her mama and papa. Tears tried to work themselves into her eyes, but she called them back.

"Oh, I see. I assume mother and father would be more in line with your way of living?"

His arm tightened around her. He had made a huge mistake, and it was obvious he was sorry. "Oh babe, I've hurt your feelings. I never meant to do that. I should have kept my mouth shut."

She would have been lacking in feelings had she not noticed his anguish.

"No, Clay, you are right. I'm a city girl now and I need to learn your ways. Will you help me?"

Clay was relieved with her reply.

"There isn't anything the two of us can't accomplish as long as we're together. No one is perfect, but we'll learn from each other." The two of them will learn many things; some would be better left unsaid.

Sloan snuggled further into his arms.

"Okay, tell me, who received your heart before me?"

Their laughter eased them into further conversation, Clay spoke first.

"My grandmother and my father are the ones that have held my heart all these years. I am who I am because of them."

Sloan shook her head.

"I don't understand. Your mother has to be in there somewhere."

"Babe, there are many avenues we have yet to cross. Until then, let us take one step at a time. The first thing is meeting my grandmother and my father. The second thing is to make arrangements for our wedding. I'm sure you're in agreement with at least the last one, are you not?"

"I'm in agreement with both of them."

"Okay then, I'll leave you. Make any selection you desire, though preferably something conservative. Grandmother's a little on the prim and proper side. I've already made arrangements with Gus to pick us up in about an hour. That hour is now on countdown; you have at the most twenty minutes in which to get dressed. Think you can manage that?"

"I can with minutes to spare." She blew a kiss, and he smiled as he closed the doors behind him.

Within two hours she would be introduced to a woman that her mama told her no longer existed; that woman was her grandmother. Had she known, would the words "I do" never have been spoken?

Never interfere with fate, sometimes it will show its cruel side.

CHAPTER FIVE

There was a notable change in the atmosphere when Ben stepped through the station's door.

"Well, we finally did it, Robert. I know you weren't around then, but that doesn't matter. You will now be a part of an investigation that should have taken place years ago. The phone calls finally paid off. You will see what you get with perseverance. Never, ever, give up on a case when you know the evidence that was lacking would materialize somehow, someway, someday."

He slapped Robert on his back, a show of excitement. Robert placed all his notes in regard to Mrs. Sarah Bingington on Ben's desk, and then went back to sweeping the floor. Ben took a deep breath before he dialed. He had waited far too long and now his hands began to tremble. He dialed the number that was staring up at him. Mrs. Bingington answered on the third ring. He felt bad for the Bingingtons; they'd had a fantastic antique business in town that they practically gave away when they were forced eight years ago to call Chicago their home.

"Mrs. Bingington, this is Sheriff Ben Davidson. I'm returning your call. God blessed this day, for this is the best news I've ever received. I'm extremely happy for you and your husband, and without question your daughter Cindy."

Ben remembered her well. Sarah was exquisite, tall with dark auburn hair, her eyes were almond shaped to the point of being oriental, her lashes were long, add to that a smile that grabbed a hold of your heart and refused to let go. Secretly, he'd had a slight crush on her for years. Whenever he came in contact with her, he could feel the heat rise in his face, and he always fumbled his words when speaking to her. She had quite an effect on him. His thoughts were, *You're not dead until the fellow below doesn't rise to the occasion.* His love for Harriet had nothing to do with his testosterone level.

He told Sarah he would get back with her when he made arrangements with his superior on the date of their meeting, and when it did take place, it would call for a celebration. But before he replaced the phone into its base, he had a favor to ask and to deliver the tragic news of the Parkers' deaths.

"Sarah, would you mind if I relayed this wonderful news about Cindy to the townspeople? They could do with a bit of good news." Of course Sarah had no objections, but she was mystified by his last comment and told him so. Ben then told her of the Parkers' deaths and how during her absence, Beth had given birth to three more children, all boys, now ages three, two and one. He could hear her sobs; he hated telling her, but felt she should know because of her and Beth's closeness years back.

Sarah was heartsick with the devastating news. Memories are a good thing when they bring a smile to your lips. She forced herself to remember only the good ones.

The best of the best was when she and Beth volunteered their time with food preparations for special occasions held in the church basement. They were grateful when volunteers did step forward. You would really be surprised at the number of busy lives, their rocking chairs always in motion. More often than not, it was she and Beth that did the huffing and puffing to stack the school desks against the perimeter of the room.

They would laugh when one or the other, or both, added the wrong ingredients in the food. Yeah, they screwed up a lot; conversation was their distraction. When they realized what they had done, they would stop, look at one another and as if reading the other's mind, would chime in: "Do you think anyone will notice?" Their high-pitched laughter would dance around the walls while they continued with the preparation of the uneatable item. When finished with the concoction, they attempted to show a compassionate side: "We'll just watch their expression when they chow down." This time laughter brought forth tears.

Sarah was besieged with grief. Beth was a unique person; she will miss her terribly, as well as the rest of her family.

She had yet to inform Ben that she and her husband would be returning to Mason's Mills. They were born and raised there; that was their home.

Cindy, their daughter, thought differently. Chicago was to be her stepping stone into the future and that will be her home. She just might be right, although for a different reason.

Ben offered Sarah his condolences and repeated he would be in touch with her soon. He was seated at his desk when he received the long-awaited news from his superior. He could now make the arrangements with the Bingingtons. He would take his leave on Friday, August 27. His length of stay would be one week and no longer.

The instant the phone found its cradle, Sunni came blasting through the door. She was out of control. She ran around his desk and grabbed Ben by his shirt, screaming hysterically.

"You have to do something. Sloan has vanished. Something terrible must have happened to her. She hasn't been home since Friday morning. I've been driving all over and she is nowhere to be found. Oh my God, what am I going to do? I can't believe this. She must have been kidnapped or maybe something worse. Oh God, what if somebody killed her?" Her hands slowly released her grip on him as she slid onto the floor, crying uncontrollably.

Ben was stunned. He mouthed his disbelief to nobody in particular. "What the hell is happening to our town?" He gently picked Sunni up off the floor and carried her to what he referred to as the holding tank. She would lie upon one of the jail's cots.

Ben spoke gently.

"Sunni, you must get a hold of yourself. You are not helping the situation. I need to know everything that happened on the day she went missing."

Sunni was not listening. She continued to shake and weep. Ben took a blanket that was folded at the end of the bed and covered her.

He needed the services of the Doc, Sunni's father. The Doc was at his office in town and quickly responded. The Doc's nurse informed the waiting patients that they would have to re-schedule. By the time of the Doc's arrival, Sunni had stopped her crying.

Sunni showed fear when she noticed she was lying on a cot behind bars. Ben explained the reasoning behind the cot and told her to remain calm.

"Sunni, you came to see me about Sloan, do you remember?" She nodded.

"We will find her. She couldn't have gone far. She's probably somewhere in the woods, confused and lost. We will conduct a search. By night's end I know we will have her safely home. Do you remember the areas you covered?"

"I inquired at all the neighboring houses. All I received were negative replies."

"Did you also check out the shopping center?"

"Oh my God…no, I didn't. How could I have overlooked something so obvious?"

"Don't worry, I'll check that out. But for now, what you need to do is to go home and get some rest. You will be the first to know when I find her."

Sunni had to believe what he told her was the truth, for he was the sheriff and he was supposed to know everything…well, almost everything. Ben asked her to be specific as to what took place between them the day before. She was now able to tell him how Thursday she and Sloan had gotten into a somewhat heated discussion, but by the end of the day, everything was back to normal.

Ben was taking notes as the Doc finished his assessment of his daughter's condition.

"Well honey, everything appears to be in working order, but I'm going to give you something to relax you."

Deputy Robert was never one to miss out on what he considered police business. He placed his broom against the wall and then leaned his body against the bars of the jail. If Ben required his services, he would be ready. An order for a cup of water was directed in Robert's direction. He rushed to the small refrigerator that held lunches, snacks and large containers of water. Attached to its side was a dispenser that carried disposable cups.

Sunni accepted the cup of water and didn't hesitate taking the medication. She prayed she would stay sedated until they found her best friend.

Doc tried to calm his daughter's anxiety.

"We're going to leave the worrying about Sloan to the sheriff, that's his job. He'll find her, and then all your distress will have been for nothing. Come on, honey, I'll take you home. You can pick up your car when you're able, or we can have Deputy Robert deliver it."

Sunni's car was a Jaguar; she trusted no one with her prized possession and told them so. Ben told her it would be safe parked in front of the police station.

The car's safety would last through the rest of that Saturday, but sometime during the night; someone drove it out of town. Not a sound was heard by the two rookies on the night shift. Sunni will soon have an additional thing to keep her mind distracted. She will never again see her car; seeing her best friend was a slim possibility.

In the early morning hours of Sunday, two seventeen-year-old boys were driving a Jaguar in excess of 100 miles per hour. A young couple returning home from their honeymoon was awestruck to see the driver enter a ramp the wrong way. They quickly pulled to the shoulder, praying that the road would stay clear of an oncoming car, but it was not to be.

A black minivan minus a headlight had no time to react. The Jaguar struck with such force the driver and his passenger joined the van as it sailed over the protective guardrail and ejected some of the unrestrained occupants. The vehicles were ablaze as they rolled several times, clearing brush and small trees in their path. The charred bodies of the boys who had previously enjoyed the speed of the borrowed car now lay amongst some of the van's passengers; others had body parts tucked among tree limbs and tall grasses that were left unattended. The husband, his wife, and their five children ranging in age from three months to seven years were within one mile of their home.

The young married couple rushed from their parked automobile to see if they could offer any assistance. Nothing could have prepared them for the carnage they stumbled onto. They will see those disassembled bodies in their worst nightmares for years to come. They remained on the scene as witnesses, giving answers to many questions. They also gave the detective in charge their names, address and phone number, should they be needed.

Was there something about God's Ten Commandments that the seventeen-year-old boys did not understand?

Ben posted a note on the church bulletin board early Saturday morning the minute Sunni was taken home. The note was highlighted. He prayed that whoever read it first would spread the news of the meeting.

Bible study was the only thing conducted on a Saturday. If attendance for church services was slight, it was nothing compared to Bible study. But Pastor Riley taught as if the pews were packed.

Sheriff Ben's note read:

A town meeting will take place Sunday the twenty-first of July after the 10:30 a.m. services. This meeting is of vital concern for all the townspeople. It is in your best interest to be present. Thank you, Sheriff Ben.

Ben thought Sunni had picked up her car sometime during the night when he noticed it missing early Sunday morning. He never worked weekends except when it was an absolute necessity. This time one of his rookies, in a juvenile act, fractured his collarbone while attempting to do a wheelie on one of the teenagers' motorcycles. Some of us never grow up.

Deputy Robert had just finished sweeping up the jail cell and was headed towards the bathroom to give it a good scrubbing. He performed this ritual religiously, on or off duty. He too was off weekends, but he thought of the station as his second home, preferring to be near the action.

Ben wished Robert had a warm body to share his bed, preferably a woman; maybe that would keep his ass at home. Robert was all about keeping things neat and orderly, moving or shoving furniture about the room, then standing back to see if its placement suited him. It never did, then he was off again doing what he loved to do. It was apparent this was his comfort food. Ben would get dizzy just watching him. He wondered if Robert had something hidden in his underwear.

Ben asked the rookies how the night went. Their reply was simple: "Quiet as usual." Their shift would end at 8:00 a.m.

When Sunni made an appearance she was shocked to find her car missing. She all but tore the station's door off its hinges.

"Where in the hell is my car?"

Ben stood, stunned, mouthing words she didn't want to hear. "I can't believe this. I thought you had already picked it up. Never in my career has this ever happened. I'm sorry, Sunni."

"And why do you think that is, Sheriff? Could it be because the low-lives that live in this town have never seen a car such as mine, let alone driven one? Do you have any idea how much that car cost? I trusted you and you let me down."

"Sunni, you need to calm down, we'll find it. Ranting and raving isn't going to do you a bit of good. I need for you to get your head on straight so we can dispatch the information throughout the counties." He pulled out a chair tucked close to Robert's desk. Sunni got the message and slumped into the chair. She was pissed and it showed.

"Robert, I know you're not on duty, but could you do me a favor and get the info we will need on Sunni's car?" Ben was grateful for an excuse to get Robert to play at being a cop instead of a housekeeper.

Ben was about to step out the door, then hesitated and retraced his steps. He touched Sunni's shoulder, repeating his prior comment. "Sunni, I really am sorry. I know how much that car means to you."

She just glared at him. She was incapable of understanding how her car was being driven by someone other than she, and how her best friend walked or drove out of her life. Something like this doesn't happen to those with money. There was no need for her father to place her on a pedestal; she managed to do that all on her own. She thought of herself as better than others and deserving of all that her parents had to give. Life as she knew it was beginning to unravel.

Ben for the first time in his life would have a multitude of crimes to solve. The first on his agenda was to see if he could find Saul's truck. Sunni told him that was Sloan's only means of transportation; she never left Sunni's home without it. His watch read 7:10 a.m. Robert was told if anything else were to come up, to notify him immediately. The rookies would have to stay around for another fifty minutes.

But just as Ben was about to exit, he came face to face with an elderly couple crying about their grandsons being missing. He was not only shocked, but bewildered by all the events that were occurring. It must be true: everything happens in threes.

Chairs were scarce, two per desk; never were four chairs in use at any given time. Ben would take a seat upon his desk.

The couple with their misery exposed were trembling. They welcomed the chairs while introducing themselves as Samuel and Marie Marconi.

Ben spoke gently.

"I need to know everything from the day of your arrival till now."

The elderly gentleman began the tearful story.

"My wife and I rented Cabin Number Three late Friday. We wanted to take our seventeen-year-old twin grandsons on a fishing vacation before they head off to college. We've been here before and really enjoyed ourselves. It took a lot of persuasion on our part to convince my son and daughter-in-law to let them go. They would never say it, but we know they think of us as incapable of handling two teenage boys. We're here to prove them wrong.

"Well anyway, we went to bed around nine p.m. We wanted to get an early start, beginning with breakfast in town, then on to the bait shop for fishing supplies. The boys, Vito and Luca, climbed into their sleeping bags way before we retired. I have no doubt it was because of the excitement of the next day that sleep beckoned them. When we awoke they were gone. We thought they were being considerate by not disturbing our sleep, and decided to get a head start looking at what the bait shop had to offer. They love to fish—it's their second passion, school their first. But Sheriff, we've been all over the shopping center and they are nowhere to be found."

Mr. Marconi, while giving the detailed information, kept dabbing at his face with his handkerchief. He and his wife appeared to be in their late seventies or early eighties. Mr. Marconi was a dapper-looking gentleman with a full head of snow white hair. He was clean-shaven and quite nice-looking. He was dressed in a white polo shirt, dark blue walking shorts and the ever popular Sperry white deck shoe.

His wife Maria had to have been a real knock-out in her heyday. Her blond hair was cut short and parted in the center. Diamond studs the size of peas hugged her pierced ears. She was a small woman with exceptionally good taste. She wore a white short-sleeved blouse with green piping around the collar; pale green slacks with a white sash completed the outfit. She wore white leather sandals, and no decent woman would dare be seen without a dash of color to her toenails.

The Marconis were a beautiful couple, well-mannered and apparently did not sweat bills, if indeed they had any at all, not while driving a Rolls-Royce.

When Mr. Marconi took a pause in his sorrowful tale, Ben casually glanced out the window of the station towards Cabin 3, eyeing their car. If given one wish, it would be to have a life such as theirs. He will find out in time that wishes are better left to those who can accept change.

Mrs. Marconi was having a hard time keeping her tears in check, tissues mounting. Robert noticed the mess and was quick with a waste basket; Sunni's information was put on hold. Maria was frantically searching for more Kleenex within her handbag.

Robert fetched an unopened box housed in a small storage cabinet beside the refrigerator. A supply was readily available in such a case; this was a first.

Ben offered encouragement.

"I'm going to send a couple of my officers to check out the woods. There isn't a boy that can resist such a temptation. Our forest is dense; they could easily have gotten lost. But for now, you need to return to your cabin, gather up a couple of folding chairs and enjoy the beautiful weather. In due time you will find your worrying was for naught."

They held onto Ben's hand, mouthing a thank you over and over. They departed with confidence, something Ben was great at providing.

Ben was not a gambling man, but if he were, he would bet his life on the boys being found safe. He hoped he would now be able to carry out his earlier plans, making inquiries in regards to Saul's truck and Sloan's disappearance. He told Robert that if nothing panned out he would be found at the church conducting the town's meeting.

The neighborhood search would not be necessary. Ben knew Sunni well; she would have gone over it with a fine-tooth comb. He had but one stop and that would be the shopping center. He decided to walk, his body screaming for exercise.

Several minutes into his walk, Ben noticed Saul's truck parked in front of the Laundromat. You would have to be blind not to see that thing; it was a derelict. He was excited. One case solved: Sloan was in town. A great weight was lifted. He was sure she would be in the clothing store. If not there, possibly the restaurant. Ben was about to enter the building when a light bulb flickered, the weight returned. She hadn't been seen since Friday morning and today was Sunday—just how stupid could he be? Sloan had definitely gone missing. He felt sick at his stomach. He welcomed the bench placed in front of the store.

How would he explain her disappearance to his sweetheart Harriet? He covered his face with his hands, his fingers rubbing his forehead, exhaling and inhaling rapidly as if he had just ran a marathon. He was extremely upset, wondering where Sloan could have gone and if someone had indeed kidnapped her. He was deep in thought when he was interrupted by his least favorite person.

"Sheriff, is there something troubling you?" It was Simon Sonderson, the gossip columnist with the *Happenings*. His shop was across the street from the gas station.

He must have had binoculars glued to his eyes, scanning the area for something offensive and worthy of print. He was not about to grab a headline from Ben.

"I'm fine; this heat would wear anybody down. Well, I guess I've rested enough. Have a good shopping day, Simon."

Before Ben started the area search, he needed to check out Saul's truck. He prayed he wouldn't find anything that would suggest a struggle, or worse, blood. The truck's interior was spotless, surprisingly in good condition, compared to the body of the truck. He removed the key from the ignition. He couldn't take the chance of the truck disappearing, for it might end up being part of a crime investigation.

He stopped at each store, pointing to where the truck was parked and inquiring if anyone was seen entering or exiting it. The replies he received were not helpful. You can always tell when someone hates their job: their attitude sucks.

"We are not paid to watch the comings and goings with the tourists. We were hired to push the sale of our wares."

Ben counted on similar comments, but still he had to ask. No one ever takes time to really notice the important things, such as a beautiful young woman by the name of Sloan who has gone missing.

Ben noted by his watch that he had nearly an hour before his speaking engagement at the church. He was grateful for the extra time; he wanted to see if the Marconis' boys had been safely found and returned to their grandparents. He was about to put his foot on the first step leading up to the police station when Robert came rushing through the door, missing the top step. Naturally he fell, bypassing Ben's outstretched arms. Robert didn't hesitate with what he had to say, even as he lay in the dust-covered road. Ben shook his head, worried about the workings inside his deputy's brain.

"Ben, we just got a dispatch from the state troopers about a terrible accident that involved two teenage boys and a Jaguar. The surrounding areas are being checked to see if any boys are missing. I told them to look no further after they informed me the car's registration was listed as belonging to Sunni. Ben, the Marconis' grandsons had to have taken her car. There is no other explanation with the car and the boys missing at the same time. Ben, they were seen driving well over one hundred miles an hour. They collided head-on with a van, killing all seven people aboard. Everyone died on impact. I have the number you can call for the complete report. God, Ben, how are you going to tell the Marconis? This is one time I'm glad I'm only a deputy."

Ben felt the bile rising in his throat. He had to verify it was the boys; he couldn't go on his deputy's word alone. This was something no grandparents entrusted with the care of their son's children should have to deal with. What was he to do? He glanced across the street and saw that the Marconis had taken his advice. They were seated in some folding chairs, waiting for their grandsons to return. Ben was reeling in anger. He had to find someone to take his frustration out on; it may as well be his rookies, though he seriously doubted they were still around.

"What happened to the rookies—did they split? Did we keep them past their checkout time? Did the door hit them in their asses in their rush to get the hell out of here?"

Robert could feel his anger. "No, Ben, they have yet to return. Apparently they are still searching."

Well, that's one way to make a person feel like shit. Ben couldn't have felt any worse. For years, every rookie that worked under him did nothing but complain. Now he had dedicated officers. He was grateful and would tell them so.

But he still hadn't climbed the remainder of the steps. He turned in the Marconis' direction and stared at the nicest couple he had ever met. He would now have to share with them the most devastating news that could possibly throw them into a world not of their choosing, not unlike that of his sweetheart Harriet. He needed the Doc. Ben thanked God it was Sunday; the Doc would in all likelihood be at home. He had started up the steps again when Mr. Marconi yelled out. "I guess they haven't found our boys yet, huh?"

Ben shouted back. "I'll be over in a few minutes to talk with you, but first I have a few things I need to take care of."

Mr. Marconi yelled back at him.

"That's okay, we're not going anywhere. Thank you."

At this very moment, Ben hated his job more than ever. He was heartsick and disgusted. He mouthed words only he could hear. "Why, oh why did I pick this dirty-dealing profession?"

Robert was talking on the telephone about nonessential nonsense when Ben took the phone from him. He dialed the number that would verify the grim facts told to Robert.

"Hello, this is Sheriff Ben Davidson over here in Mason's Mill. My deputy informed me you have a couple of boys who were involved in a tragic accident. By any chance did they have identification on them?" After several minutes Ben's hand began to shake. All he could manage was a meek thank you.

Doc's phone rang twice, he himself picked up.

"Hello, this is Doctor Harrison. How may I help you?" He always answered his home phone as if on call; frequently the calls did pertain to his profession.

"Doc, this is Ben. I need your services immediately at the station, and please bring your bag. Doc, consider this an extreme emergency."

The Doc pulled up in less than ten minutes, bag in hand. He rushed through the door expecting to find a body; instead he found Ben sitting at his desk with his head in his hands.

Doc hesitated.

"Ben, is there something wrong with you?" When the sheriff raised his head, his eyes were blood red and wet with tears.

"Oh my God, Ben, what has happened?" Ben relayed all the information on the Marconis.

Doc was teary-eyed when Ben finished.

"Ben, I will help all I can, but you have a job to do, and you have always conducted yourself accordingly. This time is no exception. My position in such situations is really no different than yours."

Ben nodded. He had enough on his mind without adding Sunni to his list. Doc would have to be the one to tell his daughter about her car.

Ben and the Doc stood by the door to the station for several seconds, Ben shaking his head while the Doc gripped his bag.

It was time to destroy numerous lives.

The Marconis were seated close together, each holding the other's hand. Nick's free arm was wrapped around his wife, her head resting on his shoulder. Did they already know something? Did they feel it in their hearts? Were they preparing themselves for the worst? Ben and the Doc approached them slowly, dreading every step that took them closer to the inevitable. They now stood before them.

Ben introduced Malcolm as his friend and the local doctor. Ben bent down on one knee, taking their hands into his.

"Mr. and Mrs. Marconi, I just received news of your grandsons' whereabouts. I know of no way to put this other than to just come out and tell you."

Mr. Marconi removed his arm from around his wife. He held his hand up in the air, as if to tell the sheriff to please stop. The Marconis grabbed a hold of each other and wept and wept and wept. They knew — how could they not? No one gets on one knee other than to propose marriage. Their unbearable anguish was felt by Ben and the Doc; they themselves could not contain their tears. Doc asked them if they needed any medication. They shook their heads. Before long they righted themselves; Mr. Marconi had something to say. He and his wife's hands were clasped together, drawing on one another's strength.

"Sheriff, we understand how hard it is to be the bearer of such tragic news. We know our grandsons are gone. I think we knew it from the very beginning, but we were desperately clinging to the hope that God in His mercy would bring them back safely. I guess He had other plans."

Mr. Marconi stopped talking; he couldn't go on. Ben gave him the time he needed to compose himself before he asked them if they were ready to know what had happened. They both nodded. When Ben finished, Mr. and Mrs. Marconi could not hold back another rain of tears.

Ben wondered how they would continue on with their lives. They were entrusted with their son's children and now those children were gone. Ben was still on his knee when he wrapped his big arms around them trying to offer some comfort.

Doc turned to face the road. He was feeling their agony. Many times he'd had to tell family members when a loved one died, but thankfully in his long career he was never faced with this type of situation. He wondered how the grandparents were going to tell their only son and daughter-in-law that their sons were gone.

Mr. Marconi was the first to break the link.

"When we are blessed with children we have to accept them on God's terms, for they are only on loan to us; they belong to Our Father in Heaven. God's will was carried out; we have not the right to question Him. I know all grandparents believe their grandchildren are perfect and can do no wrong. But these boys of ours truly were good boys. Vito was the oldest; it took his brother Luca an additional fifteen minutes to announce his presence. We were so proud that day, as they were our first grandbabies, but as time went on they ended up being our only." He hesitated, chocking on those words, realizing their days as grandparents were over.

Ben would hear the story of the young boys' lives.

Mr. Marconi shook his head, as if to clear his thoughts.

"Right before we came here, we had a huge party to celebrate their high school graduation, and their acceptance into Harvard. Did you know they both had IQs near genius level? How silly of me…how would you know that? It looks as if our bragging days are over."

He broke, grabbing at his wife.

"Oh God, baby, what are we ever going to do without our boys?" She tried holding on to him but she herself was not in control, and he fell to the ground. His screams brought many people to the site to watch in horror as the man before them clawed at the gravel and dirt while babbling nonsense.

Doc stepped in.

"Please, all of you need to go about your business. They don't need an audience."

Those that gathered took his advice and began to disperse in different directions, turning once or twice to take another look; this was the nature of the beast in all of us. Ben and the Doc managed to get the Marconis into their cabin, guiding them towards the bed. When they were seated Doc drew up two syringes of valium and injected them. Within seconds they were under control.

But Mr. Marconi had more to say.

"Our beautiful boys used extremely bad judgment when they took that car, costing not only their lives, but tragically the lives of seven innocent victims. We are beside ourselves with guilt over the loss the victims' family members will have to endure. And because of this dreadful decision, we will be held accountable for their actions, as well we should. But for now, we need to make arrangements to get our boys home to their parents. Do you think you can help us, Sheriff?"

Ben informed them of the steps that needed to be taken.

"Your grandsons were taken from the accident scene to the city morgue located in Franklin County. I was advised to tell you their remains are best not viewed, though positive identifications have to be made. Do you have any recent photos of them?"

Mrs. Marconi quickly answered with a magnificent smile. "Do we have photos? Is there darkness and light?"

She opened her handbag and produced a pocket-size photo album. Ben took the offered pictures. The first was without a doubt the Marconis' son, a replica of his father, and the woman seated alongside him had to be their daughter-in-law. Beauty was definitely not hard to come by in this family. Standing behind them were their sons. You will find no phony smiles here. This was one gloriously happy family, a beautiful family.

Ben turned the page. He was now staring into the faces of the people seated before him, standing behind their grandsons, hugging them tightly. The grinning boys' hands were clasped over their grandparents'. Never again would their smiles be captured on film.

Beginning to tear up, Ben turned away and moved towards the cabin's window as if more light was needed. He was a pussy cat when it came to showing his feelings. Vito and Luca were not only way up there in intelligence, but could have shaken, rattled and moved the earth with their looks. They had it all. Ben was feeling weak in the knees; his eyes began to hurt from the tears. If he was struggling with virtual strangers, what could be expected from the Marconis?

Picture after picture gave insight into the personality of the boys, making Ben feel worse with each turn of the page. He couldn't stop; he needed to see the ageless pictures. And then the most poignant of them all caused him to reach for a chair. Behind every picture there is a story, and this one told of high spirits and excitement with the boys' impending future.

Dressed in caps and gowns, the twins were facing each other, hands clasped in a handshake, their smiles saying what their hearts held, "No greater love hath thou." Ben thought it right and just they went together, for neither could have survived without the other. He couldn't focus; his eyes were clouding over. Before he turned away from the window to face them, he gave his face a dab with his handkerchief.

"With your permission, I will take the photo album to the morgue." Exceptions to the rule were made in the Marconis' case, their age being the factor.

"Once a positive ID has been made, you will be required to sign a form releasing them into the care of White Funeral Home to prepare their bodies for burial. You can then make arrangements for them to be flown home. I was also informed all the paperwork has been completed and you can leave at any time."

The Marconis were relieved twofold: because of the kindness of the sheriff they would not have to view their beloved grandsons' bodies and they could finally return home. But tragically, their last memory would refuse to depart, for in the years to come they would spend many sleepless nights thinking about the *if* word.

"Sheriff, we can't thank you and your doctor friend enough for your kindness and understanding. You have a town to be proud of. Maybe someday in the distant future we can return."

Their calendar will forever remain blank.

Ben sadly shook the Marconis' hands with final words of good-bye.

"I pray God will give you the strength to cope with the days that lie ahead."

Now it was Ben's responsibility to ID two very young boys who in their entire life had always lived up to everyone's highest expectations. The one time they journeyed off the straight and narrow it cost them their lives and the lives of many innocents.

The rookies returned and were informed of what had happened in their absence. They were saddened and shocked beyond belief.

Ben shook their hands and complimented them on their continued efforts in trying to locate the boys, and for staying way beyond their work schedule. This was the first time anyone higher up ever thanked them or shook their hands. This day brought them great sorrow and then rewarded them. Amazing how a so-called pat on the back can be one of life's simple pleasures.

When the drapes covering the boys' bodies were pulled back, Ben tried to grab onto the gurney but instead fell to his knees. The bile rose quickly and he didn't make it to a bathroom; the vomit spewed out onto the floor. He made a vow: never again would he allow his eyes to view the likes of the char-burnt mangled bodies that were now displayed in front of him.

That vow will soon be broken.

CHAPTER SIX

Ben quickly regained his composure after leaving the morgue. He forced himself to empty his thoughts as he looked at his watch; it was past 11:00 a.m. He had to get to the church; he had a speech to present. He couldn't remember a day in his life as being so unbearably sad, long and tiring, and it wasn't even noon. He wondered how he could do a ground search for Sloan without falling asleep standing up.

Again the attendance was overwhelming, again Pastor Riley shook his head. He looked at the crucifixion of Christ hanging on the cross and softly said, "These people really need Your help. Would You be so kind as to give them a shove in my direction? Thank you."

The pastor was noticed, quite frequently, talking to himself. Those that noticed thought maybe he was getting senile, though he was barely forty years of age. Stranger things have happened. He was a little on the heavyset side, standing five-foot-nine. He was considered quite good-looking with a full head of curly dark brown hair and very blue eyes. He had a very engaging smile. His vow of chastity apparently was wearing thin, for he was often seen winking at some of the younger women. Maybe that was why many of the townspeople wondered why he had chosen that particular profession. A few of the women in town would have gladly pulled back the covers, while removing his collar, to welcome him into their bed. These women were worse than the men when it came to sex. Some were seen licking their lips whenever a male newcomer happened into town. These women definitely needed to take up some kind of hobby, other than training their eyes on a man's crotch.

When the pastor finished with the services, he turned the pulpit over to the sheriff.

Ben was tall, but appeared much taller when standing at the pulpit.

"Thank you again for your attendance. I think what I have to say will probably astound each and every one of you. But first, I am grateful that I never heard one word of protest when I released Marc from jail. I think you all knew deep within your hearts he could never have done something so appalling. Some of you are also aware that Sloan has gone missing."

A gasp was heard from many of the congregation that did not know. They too would wonder in the weeks to come what had happened to her. They would also start locking their doors. They would talk to no strangers. Their community was returning to a town of fear.

Ben did not hesitate with what he had to say; he had other things to take care of.

"According to Sunni, Sloan left her home on a Friday and has not yet returned. An all-points bulletin has been put in place. We found Saul's truck in the shopping center after Sunni made us aware of Sloan's disappearance. The keys were in the ignition and nothing in the truck seemed out of place. We need volunteers to make and hand out posters and place them in all the shop windows. Everyone's help would be appreciated in searching the woods and surrounding areas. I pray you will have the stamina to withstand what could turn out to be many hours. But before we begin what will be an intense search, I have a few things that demand my attention. So to those that are willing, please be at the station in about two hours. I have additional news, but Marc also has something to say, and I think I've kept him waiting long enough."

Ben turned the pulpit over to Marc.

"I want to thank all of you for trusting your heart in matters that could have destroyed my life. I loved the Parkers. They will continue to live within my heart. Sloan has always been the love of my life. We need to find her. She managed to escape the fires of hell, and by the grace of God she will escape her captor and find her way back to us. Someone out there knows of her whereabouts; she would never leave the one place she knows she is loved."

Marc stepped away happy with the sounds of applause.

Ben smiled as he shook his hand, then he was again back at the pulpit.

"With everything that has befallen our community, I feel it's only appropriate to reveal some great news. Cindy Bingington has regained consciousness and is talking and walking again. Her parents just called, informing me she had been released from Alshore Nursing Home eight months ago. If you all remember, the Bingingtons moved to Chicago where the nursing home is located. They chose to live in an apartment close to the home, thinking that Cindy would be her old self after a short stay, but as you all know, that stay lasted eight years. But I'm happy to say she is again living on her own and has returned to college. She is due to take another bar exam in the upcoming months. Her life may have been put on hold, but she hasn't given up her dream of becoming a lawyer. God in his mercy truly does perform miracles. I will be making arrangements to visit with her and her parents in a matter of weeks."

Again the applause was deafening. The pastor should think about offering Ben a partnership with him and God. Ben could do the sermons and the pastor could save their souls.

It was too bad no one took notice when one individual did not applaud.

The night caller was quite upset. Cindy's recovery should never have happened. The caller had a huge task to embark on. The caller would have to make plans. This job required air transportation, something the caller was unaccustomed to.

Ben again thanked everyone as he turned the pulpit back to its rightful owner, the pastor.

"We must all feel as if the hand of God reached down and touched the face of Cindy, awaking her from her extended sleep. Her journey back to us has been long. But God has always had her in his keeping. Let us now bend our knees in prayer for the safe return of our precious Sloan. This community has seen enough sorrow; we must believe that God also has her in his keeping. Praise be to our Father in the Highest."

The parishioners knelt, their heads bowed, thanking God for Cindy's return from the unknown while praying for Sloan's safety.

Ben organized an intense search for Sloan. Everyone from town and beyond gathered together as Ben instructed how the search would be played out.

Groups of fifteen would search different areas within the woods and fields. They were to cover every square inch; nothing could be left to the imagination. The last thing on the agenda would be to drag the lake.

The Swimming Hole, which had a depth of more than twenty feet and a circumference of two hundred feet, would be dragged last. This undertaking took more than two weeks. They were now conducting a search for a body instead of a rescue. The townspeople blessed themselves when no body was discovered. Ben thanked everyone who participated.

It was time to call off the search.

CHAPTER SEVEN

Sunni hated the sheriff with every breath in her body. He made a promise to her. He told her he would find Sloan. She wished nothing but horrible things for him.

She would cry herself to sleep. The time was fast approaching for her to return to school. She would continue to cry nightly for a very long time over her loss. She had never loved someone as much as she loved Sloan, and that included her parents.

Her father had plenty of time to book her flight. She had her bags packed before Sloan went missing; now she had to begin a new life, one that would exclude Sloan. Her chosen profession would provide a better life than that of her parents. She planned to complete her four-year course in interior design and then open her own studio. It would be called Ni's House of Design. She would open a shop in Manhattan for it is known to be one of the most expensive cities to not only shop, but to live in. She would make Manhattan her home.

As the days passed with still no word on Sloan, Sunni was turning into someone no one could stand. She yelled at her parents for everything little thing they did for her. Nothing they did pleased her. She needed to return to school before their home turned into a house of hate. Her mother was seen crying all the time. Her father tried everything possible to put a smile on his daughter's face, but nothing seemed to work. His last attempt was to replace her Jaguar.

She screamed she didn't want it.

"What don't you understand? That car reminds me of Sloan the day she went missing. Just how stupid are you? You both just need to get out of my life and stay out of it."

She just might get her wish.

Doc thought it best for Sunni to return to school earlier than necessary. School might be the answer to regain her sense of stability. He would give her enough money to stay in a hotel if she wasn't able to get into her dorm room. She would be driven to the airport the next day. Arrangements were made quickly by her father. He instructed his nurse Ethel to cancel appointments for his patients that day. Doc and his wife needed to be free of the constant yelling and items flying through the air from Sunni's fits of anger.

The car was empty of conversation on the drive to the airport. Sunni's mother sobbed the whole way. The Doc turned up the radio to drown her out. Sunni just held her ears. Their family was falling apart. Now the Doc understood what Saul meant when he said Sloan was building her life around Sunni. Apparently his daughter was doing the same.

The airport was never crowded during the week, since most travelers booked flights for the weekend. Doc pulled up to the loading area. He gathered three of the suitcases to be tagged. Sunni already had her carry-on swung over her shoulder. The ticket gripped tightly in her hand would show her anger. Her mother, still sobbing, tried to hug her only child. Sunni shoved her aside; her father stayed his distance. There were no good-byes. There would be no phone calls. There would be no letters.

The Harrisons' world had collapsed around them.

CHAPTER EIGHT

Sloan chose to wear her hair swept to one side, secured with a mother-of-pearl comb; the natural waves flowed freely down her backside. She wore little makeup: just mascara, blush and lip gloss. She chose a short-sleeved pale grey Versace dress with a circular neckline, bloused out and fitted at the waist. A single strand of pearls lay upon her neck. Earrings were the finishing touch. She wore three-inch heels, steel grey in color, with a matching handbag. Her birth certificate as always was with her. Unbeknownst to her, when she walks through the doors of the Chadsworths' mansion, she will be entering the very home her mother was born and raised in.

Clay stood when Sloan strolled into the room. He felt as if he should bow; she was that exquisite, and the throne would be hers for the asking. He had to sit; he was that weak in the knees.

She approached him slowly.

"Do you think what I'm wearing is suitable?"

"Let me put it this way, I will never question what you wear in the future."

Sloan was more than happy. She had accomplished what she thought would be the impossible: pleasing the man in her life.

Clay rose, taking her hand.

"Come, it's time to meet the people that will come to mean as much to you as they do to me."

Gus arrived with the limousine. He remembered his station in life, but he couldn't help himself, his breath refused to release. This was a woman that would draw people to her like a magnet. He was standing by the now opened car door as Clay guided her in, but not before she greeted Gus with cheerful hello and a smile to melt frozen butter. He would casually glance into the rearview mirror, but never once did he not see their lips compressed.

The day was full of sun, the best day ever. Even if it had not been such a beautiful day, in the eyes of lovers there is no other kind.

Gus pulled up to the same stone pillar that many years ago, a young girl by the name of Jena had visited; the same black box was still tucked inside. Gus did as the other chauffeur years ago had done, pressed a button, said a few words and waited until the gates swung open.

He pulled to the front of the estate and parked. Knowing his grandmother might not be up to a lengthy visit, Clay instructed Gus to stay around.

Sloan had the same reaction as that of Jena many years past. She staggered along as Clay led her to the steps, her eyes trying to take in all that was before her.

If she'd spoken her thoughts aloud, she would have said, "This is not a house but a castle. Do people actually live in such a place? How much is their electric bill, and what about gas? The house payment alone would give a person nightmares." She could utter only one word as she mounted the steps to the entrance: "WOW."

Art, the butler, was the one to welcome them when the doorbell sounded. Clay didn't need to search his father out; he knew he would be in his favorite part of the house, his study. He had yet to release Sloan's hand, his need strong for her touch.

Phillip, his father, was seated in a massive brown leather chair, his eyes closed, a pamphlet of papers laid across his lap.

"Father, you can open your eyes, the waiting is over."

Phillip didn't just jump; he flew out of his chair. Papers totally forgotten found their way to the floor. His strong embrace for his boy did not go unnoticed by Sloan. She had known that kind of love. The formation of a tear was wiped away with her free hand. Phillip was the same height as Clay. Would everyone in her new world tower over her? That would be a first.

"So, you are the one that now occupies the space in my boy's heart. Would you mind terribly if I hugged you?"

"I would be greatly disappointed if you did not." Clay released her into his father's arms.

Clay knew his grandmother would give Sloan the same warm reception. He could not reclaim her; his father had already taken her under his wing.

The three of them exited Phillip's study and made their way to the grand circular staircase. Phillip and Sloan led the way, Clay followed. Phillip could have used the elevator, but that would have meant less time spent with his boy's girl. Many steps later, they stood in front of the doorway to Lydia's room. Phillip had yet to visit with his mother this day; he was waiting on his boy.

Clay took the initiative, knocking gently on the door. Doleanna, Grandmother's round-the-clock nurse, opened the door smiling, whispering the words everyone longed to hear. "This is a blessed day; Lydia is as fit as a fiddle. God has set aside this day as her day, Halleluiah."

They were the ones blessed. You could go to the ends of the earth and back and never would you find another Doleanna.

Grandmother was sitting up in her bed, a slight touch of makeup applied to her face. She was reading her favorite classic, *Gone with the Wind.* Phillip was the first to make his way to his mother's bedside; Clay and Sloan would wait their turn. Lydia looked up and smiled; she slid the book off to the side and held her arms open. She was ready for her son's embrace. Neither Phillip nor Clay in the last six months had witnessed what was now being played out before their eyes. The love of their universe was not only sitting up and smiling, but was without pain. How could this be, other than by God's intervention?

After the intense hugs by Phillip and then Clay, attention was given to Sloan. Clay took Sloan's hand, guiding her towards his grandmother's bed.

"Grandmother, I followed your suggestion, I listened to my heart. I would like for you to meet the woman I'm soon to wed. Her name is Sloan Parker."

Could there have been a happier day for Lydia, other than the return of her daughter? Never in a million years.

"Come, child, kneel beside me—my eyesight is beginning to fail."

Sloan will come to love being called child, but only by Lydia, for she will come to love her almost as much as her mama.

Lydia took hold of Sloan's hands with a comment. "These are strong hands, working hands. You have had a hard life but you are a survivor. Your name suits you—it's beautiful and powerful—but it's the eyes that reveal who you are,; they are the windows to your soul, do you know that?"

Sloan did not know what Lydia was talking about. Was she expected to answer?

Lydia did not give her a chance to respond.

"Your eyes are all goodness and light. And now that I have seen all I need to see, it's time to celebrate. I believe a hug is in order."

Sloan rose from her kneeling position; she was desperate for the warmth of a mother-like-figure. She gently wrapped her arms around this wisp of a woman who had just stolen a huge hunk of her heart. The hug was long and sincere. When they separated their eyes locked; the bonding began.

"Draw up a chair, child; we must make plans for your wedding day."

Phillip drew his boy to his side. His mother and soon-to-be daughter-in-law were deep in conversation, out of their hearing range.

"My boy, what's up with your mother and Ali? I haven't heard you mention them in a while. Is there something going on that I should know about?"

"Father, I know nothing. I have called numerous times with no success. I have so much to deal with at present, I just don't have the time to investigate it thoroughly."

"My boy, I didn't mean to upset you; I would never do that. It's just that since you have found them, I can't think of anything else."

"Father, it's the same with me. I can't get them out of my mind, and I refuse to let them go. The only alternative I have is to return to Mason's Mill—and trust me, this will happen, though exactly when I have no idea. At present, I have a woman I love and want to marry. Once that's out of the way, I will then make arrangements to fly out of here."

Phillip hugged his boy, understanding his logic; he too will endure.

They now turned their attention to the women and their continuing conversation.

"Now tell me, child, what kind of wedding do you see in your future?"

Sloan first focused her eyes on Clay and then moved on to Phillip, finally resting on Lydia.

"I would like a simple wedding with only family in attendance." She did not wait for a reply.

"Please don't get me wrong, I have always dreamt of a huge wedding with a cake as tall as the Statue of Liberty and gifts that would take a lifetime to open. But those visions were seen in the eyes of a child. Today, I desire no fanfare, just the presence of the people that mean the most to Clay. I pray this doesn't offend anyone?"

Lydia was right; this child carried her heart in her eyes. Clay was more than delighted. Phillip's take was that he always stood by his boy. Clay strolled to his grandmother's bedside and took Sloan's hand into his own, feeling proud of her for speaking what was in her heart.

Lydia now had the floor.

"Pray tell, child, you failed to mention your family. Will they not be attending?"

Eye-to-eye contact was made; a mist began to form over Sloan's. She was a quick study, but Lydia, the wisest of the wise, spoke again.

"Well then, let's get a move on. Time waits for no one." They once again made eye contact, Sloan smiled in gratitude, and Lydia nodded. They will become the best of friends, expiration date, less than three months.

Clay put in his two cents' worth. "We will have to call our family priest. My greatest desire is to be married in my father's study." This time, it was father and son making eye contact. Phillip's chest couldn't expand any further; the pride in his boy was that great.

Phillip added a few of his own cents. "The walls of this great old house will once again vibrate with happiness."

Clay was getting anxious. "Okay then, it's time for us to take our leave. We need to apply for our license before we can be married. Grandmother, if you feel up to it, I would like for you to make arrangements with our priest, the sooner the better."

"I will call him immediately with a rush order." His grandmother was at it again; he knew there would never be a replacement.

Gus was waiting when Clay and Sloan, grinning like fools, rushed out the front door. You would have thought they had already taken their vows. He held the car door open.

Five words were spoken: "Take us to City Hall."

Clay and Sloan arrived just in time; according to the sign posted inside the swinging door, the office was to close in less than an hour.

With hands joined, they stood in front of the city clerk. Clay had his eyes fixed on Sloan when he spoke.

"We need to apply for a marriage license. What are the requirements?"

The clerk leaned slightly; her hand retrieved the necessary papers stored beneath the counter.

"You must fill out these forms and return them to me promptly; our office closes in fifty-four minutes. Are you aware there is a twenty-four-hour waiting period, and this application is only good for thirty days? After that you must re-apply."

"The thirty days will not pertain to us; we will be married tomorrow by night's end."

The couple sat side by side, heads positioned together looking over the form. Clay's eyes hurriedly scanned the form. He filled in the spaces that applied to him, while asking Sloan the questions that pertained to her. There it was: proof of birth required. She felt instant relief. Never underestimate the power of Destiny.

"Damn it all to hell, I forgot about the birth certificates. I'm sorry, babe; it looks like our marriage will have to be put on hold for a while. I have mine at the apartment, but we will need to send off for yours."

Sloan sat there as Clay rattled on about his disappointment. He stopped when he noticed her devilish smirk.

"What are you smiling about? Did you not hear what I just said?"

He was overly stressed; he'd thought he had everything worked out. This was the worst setback to his plans. But Sloan had already removed the required document from her handbag, and she now held the opened paper in front of him. He turned his eyes from her, taking in the typewritten words.

He was stunned. "Where…?"

She held up her hand to quiet him. "When you asked me to marry you, I knew I would need proof of my age. It's been with me from day one." Clay's world had not shattered after all. Their lips locked together.

The clerk tapped a container of water on the counter. She had no time for their foolishness.

"You have no time remaining. I must have the form and all the necessary papers if you plan on marrying, as you say, by night's end."

"I'm sorry; we will have to return. We failed to bring some of the required documents," Clay replied.

The clerk shook her head. The day had been slow, way too slow; she could have left early had they not arrived. It wasn't as if she ignored the posted times. The majority of couples wanting to get married were camped out on the steps way before the doors opened. The couple standing before her was the exception.

The next morning the same clerk moved back quickly when she unlocked the door, for Clay and Sloan stepped forward; the last arrivals from yesterday were now the first. They had the papers that were required, including proof of one year of residence from at least one of the parties.

They were on their way. By tomorrow noon they will be in all aspects a Mr. and Mrs.

Lydia had spoken with her priest the day before. He would deny her nothing; she had supported his parish for more years than he could count. Money aside, he would still have granted her request, for she was highly respected not only by him, but by society in general. His thoughts were, *The Gates of Heaven eagerly await her arrival.*

Gus was informed that morning that he would be taking them to Barney's. Sloan needed a wedding gown. She may not have that huge wedding cake as tall as the Statue of Liberty, but she would have that wedding dress. She and the exquisite gown she will be wearing will dazzle the minds of all the people of New York City when their wedding photo is released to the papers. When that certain gown is chosen, the most sought-after designers will be greatly disappointed that it is not one of theirs.

Sloan was again exhausted, one gown after another, nothing seemed right. Clay waited patiently; he would not see the dress until their wedding day. Periodically he sent in sales clerks to check on her progress, but they always returned with the same reply.

"She has tried on countless gowns, but nothing seems to please her. We are not discouraged and neither should you. There is a gown here and we will find it; you just need to have a little faith."

He stretched his body on the chair; he would attempt a nap.

This exceptionally long day suddenly ended when Sloan came rushing out of the dressing room. She dropped down beside Clay's chair, her hands grasping his.

"Clay, I found it. There is nothing that can compare. I wish you could see it now, but I know that is out of the question. I'm…I'm so happy." She burst into tears.

"Babe, I've resolved myself to always expect tears when something pleases you. But this time you need to put them aside. You must tell me if the dress needs alterations or can it be delivered immediately?"

"It's perfect, like everything since I met you."

"Okay then, we'll have them deliver your gown as well as my tux to my grandmother's house ASAP. Tomorrow we have a wedding that will require our presence." Happy tears were now replaced with laughter.

Gus drove a jubilant Sloan and her grinning partner directly to their apartment with the following request, to pick them up no later than 6:30 a.m. the following day.

Dog-tired was the best word to describe their condition. They badly needed sleep. They could not get out of their clothes fast enough. The jets within the bathtub burst open expelling the steaming water. Their weary bodies absorbed the luxury of the bubbling water, reducing their pain to a tolerable condition.

Clay was the first to exit, towels within his reach. The pleasures of lovemaking were placed on hold. He was desperate to make a phone call; the need to speak to his mother was great. As before, the sounds of the rings became deafening.

He spoke aloud, frustrated.

"God, where is she?"

On the third ring, Doleanna answered with a buoyant hello. This was his grandmother's private line, only Clay and his father had access.

"Well, you're in high spirits. That must mean my grandmother is following your lead."

"I've already hit my knees this morning in prayer thanking Our Lord for granting her another day without pain. She awakened before me, making a to-do list. I've never seen her so upbeat. Would you like to speak with her?"

"No, I'll just let her do her thing. She is in her element doing what she loves to do, taking charge. I'll see you both very early in the morning. And Doleanna, please keep praying; God is definitely hearing you."

"Oh Mr. Clay, Our Lord listens to everyone's prayers; it's just that sometimes His reply saddens our heart."

"Well then, I guess it's my turn to give the knees a workout. Thank you, Doleanna."

"Why Mr. Clay, you shouldn't thank me; it's Our Heavenly Father you should be thanking."

"You are absolutely right. And Doleanna, my thanks this time rightfully belongs to you for taking such great care of my grandmother."

Clay's eyes began to tear when she gave her reply.

"I love her, Mr. Clay."

"I know you do. Until tomorrow…take care." He replaced the receiver, and then fell to his knees.

THE WEDDING DAY

Sloan had awoken way before Clay, the time 5:10 a.m. She rolled ever so gently as not to disturb her lover. She stepped softly across the hardwood floor, her silk nightgown lightly swishing against her body as she made her way to the great room. She made herself comfortable on the sofa. The ringed finger on her left hand was placed into the palm of the other. In a matter of hours the ring will be joined with its mate.

Clay was lying face down upon the mattress when instinct caused his arm to reach across the bed, his hand searching. His reflex was quick. If a stopwatch had been set no one could have leaped faster from a bed. His naked form ran from room to room calling Sloan's name, yet he received no reply. He stopped short, holding on to a doorframe. He was gasping for breath. He had but one thought: *She changed her mind. There will be no us.*

But there she was, no more than thirty feet from him. She was in her own world, her hearing turned off. He remained where he was. *There will be vows.* After several minutes Sloan left her world to join his. She turned her head in his direction, aware of his presence.

"Clay, this is it…this is the day. If you want to change your mind you better do it now."

He walked over and took hold of her arms, pulling her up towards him. "I could say the same for you." No other words were spoken; they held each other for it seemed an eternity. He was the first to pull away. "I think it's time we get a move on, or they just might start without us."

The warmth of laughter was shared as they made their way to their respective dressing rooms. Neither would be wearing wedding apparel. Her gown and his tux had hopefully been delivered as promised.

Gus smiled as he waited; he was more than happy for his employer. His boss found his heart and she was a beauty. He didn't have to wait long. Clay and Sloan burst out of the entrance, hands clutched together; the door hinges would surely need to be readjusted. Greetings were shared, followed by laughter.

Gus was startled when he pulled up to the mansion entrance; the black steel gates were already opened. Clay also took notice. Should he be concerned? Gus pressed hard on the gas pedal, afraid of the unknown. A barricade of trucks surrounded the driveway. Gus, Clay and Sloan all exited the limo at the same time. It was then Clay noticed the logos on the trucks: Barney's, The Flower Shop, Laci's Bakery, Sounds of Music, Too Good Catering and Peter & Paul's Photography.

He stood with his hands on his hips shaking his head. He began to laugh. He then turned to Sloan and Gus.

"Grandmother's to-do list has just been taken care of."

The door to the grand house stood ajar. Clay and Sloan entered. It was as if they were arriving for a wedding that had taken months of preparation. The house was abuzz with activity. The rails of the circular staircase were blanketed in Point de Gaze lace that was gathered every three feet and tied with silk ribbons and bows.

Caterers were busy setting up the buffet table in what was called the great room, similar to a ballroom, while the musicians were arranging their instruments. Two round tables were covered and draped to match the stairwell, one made more beautiful by the seven-tier wedding cake, while the other with a calla lily centerpiece was reserved for the wedding party: the bride and groom, the family priest, Grandmother, Phillip and the jewel Doleanna. A banquet table was set up for the cooks, servants, butler and two chauffeurs. Thirty-six would be attending. Tripods were put in place by the photographers to capture every single moment.

To say Clay and Sloan were shocked would be an understatement; they were without words and would remain so for most of the morning.

Phillip claimed Clay. "Come, my boy, we have to dress for a wedding." Clay followed his father like a pup follows its master.

One of Lydia's maids was instructed upon Sloan's arrival to take her to a room that was made ready for her special day. Sloan stepped through the double doors, awaiting her were two women, one to dress her, the other to do her hair and makeup. Who was she, that she deserved such an honor?

Time was gaining speed. A gentle tap on Sloan's door gave welcome to Lydia; another blessed day of freedom from pain. The bride was ready, the last-minute touches completed. Her back was facing Lydia when she was told to turn.

Lydia started to cry. Her thoughts turned to her beloved daughter Alexandria. *Oh my sweet Ali, this should be you standing before me. Where are you, my baby girl?* The weeping could not be controlled. Sloan ran to her side, falling to her knees. Her attendants were aghast; she could possibly undo all they had done, although they dared not say a word.

"Grandmother, please do not cry, you will upset everyone." She looked at Doleanna, during their brief relationship they had acquired an understanding. Doleanna stepped aside, turning the control of the wheelchair over to Sloan. Sloan began to push Lydia's chair towards a full-length mirror while commenting on Lydia's stunning dress. Sloan's soon-to-be husband was always talking about his grandmother's fantastic sense of humor; she prayed he was right and she wouldn't hurt Lydia's feelings.

"Look at you...you are so beautiful. If you continue to cry, those tears will wash away your face. Surely you do not want that to happen."

Lydia giggled.

"You are so right; it took skilled hands to fill in these cracks." Laughter sounded the cure for all ills.

Doleanna reclaimed her patient. She and Lydia would use the elevator to bring them down to the main level, while Phillip rode up to guide his boy's soon-to-be bride down the grand staircase. Clay earlier had asked his father if he would honor him by giving away his bride. Again Phillip's chest expanded.

It was time to present the bride.

The Wedding March echoed throughout the mansion. Clay was standing at the foot of the stairs ready to receive what will be his lifetime partner. The priest with hands folded in front was waiting in the background, Lydia and Doleanna close by. Servants were huddled together; they would be given the honor of attending what will be classified as a wedding like no other.

Sloan appeared as if she floated down from Heaven, a halo as her crown.

Clay took a hold of the railing to secure himself. Standing at the top of the stairs, a vision unlike anything he had ever seen began descending towards him. Phillip guided her gently. Her hair was twisted and curled within a band of pearls high upon her head; a shorter version of the attached lace veil covered her face, while the remainder flowed freely, joining the spirals and ringlets down her backside. The makeup artist took painstaking care to apply just the right amount of makeup, paying a great deal of attention to Sloan's captivating green eyes.

The designer dress by Valetino had cap sleeves with a square-cut, hand-sewn pearl bodice; the folds of the white silk gown flowed from an empire waistline. The wedding dress barely touched the floor; the gown was simple and elegant. The bridal bouquet, given to her by Lydia, was chosen with great care, white garden roses were a symbol of love and stephanotis represented marital happiness. Sloan would be bombarded in the coming weeks for personal interviews and she would be the featured column in many magazines. She will take Manhattan by storm.

The cameras were in motion and would continue long into the evening.

Phillip took hold of the veil and folded it back; he kissed Sloan and placed her arm into Clay's. Doleanna wheeled Lydia over to reclaim the bouquet until the "I do's" were said.

Clay and Sloan's arms entwined as they took a few more steps to stand in front of the family's priest.

"We have come here this day in the presence of God to join together this man and this woman in holy matrimony. Who gives this woman to be married to this man?"

Phillip smiled, his chest ready to burst with pride.

"I do."

The priest continued with the ceremony.

"Clay and Sloan, with your right hands joined together, please say after me: I, Joseph Clayton Chadsworth II, take thee Sloan J. Parker, to be my wedded wife, to have and to hold from this day forward, for better for worse, for richer for poorer, in sickness and in health, to love and to cherish, till death us do part, according to God's holy ordinance; and thereto I give thee my troth."

Sloan was then instructed to take Clay's right hand and repeat the same vow. The priest proceeded forward.

"Clay, you may now place the ring on Sloan's hand and say after me: With this ring I thee wed. In the name of the Father, and of the Son, and of the Holy Spirit. Amen.

"Sloan, you will now place Clay's ring on his finger and say after me: With this ring I thee wed. In the name of the Father, and of the Son, and of the Holy Spirit. Amen."

The priest then joined their right hands together. His final ceremonial words spoken were: "Those whom God hath joined together let no man put asunder. I now pronounce you husband and wife. You may kiss the bride."

Rice that had been distributed to the servants was now being thrown. Cheers, claps and laughter followed. They were excited to be invited to join in the festivities and to share a dinner with the Chadsworth family. The servants would be treated as equals; they would not know their place that day. Their pictures would also be on the cover fronts of all tabloids, each paper trying to outdo the other with such captions as:

"Are the eyes deceiving or were the Chadsworths' guests servants?"

"Servants being waited on at the dinner table: What is this world coming to?"

And in yet another magazine:

"Servants including the matriarch's and the groom's chauffeurs attending the wedding of the year: Have the Chadsworths no dignity?"

The long day finally came to an end. Lydia retired shortly after dinner, as did the servants. The maids were live-ins and shared sleeping quarters in a wing specifically for the hired help. In the morning would be back to normal; clean-up would commence first thing.

The wedding party now consisted of a modest four. The musicians, caterers and photographers had exited long ago.

Phillip and Gus felt like intruders. They tried to carry on a conversation, but between two different people from two different walks of life, conversing is almost impossible. They decided to call it a day. Phillip attempted to bid good-night but received no response; the bride and groom had retreated into a world that allowed no outsiders. Gus returned to the limo.

The light tap on the driver's window awakened him. Gus immediately opened the door and climbed out, apologizing to his boss for not staying alert.

"I should be the one apologizing; the hour is late. Your wife will never forgive me for keeping you long into the night. Tell her I will make it up to her with your next paycheck, although she will probably tell me where to put it. Those would be my words if someone tried to keep me away from my wife. Did I just say wife? Who would have thought? Gus, I do need one more favor from you, it's huge and I pray it isn't too upsetting, but it will require your services for two full weeks, morning, noon and night."

Gus was crestfallen. Clay was right on target; his wife sometimes did get upset with his long hours, but never had his boss required him to work two full weeks. He wondered if his wife would tell him to take his job and shove it.

Clay and Sloan were still standing outside their limo, Gus beside them, when together they shouted with excitement, "You and your family are going on a two-week all-expenses-paid vacation of your choice. Our aircraft is your aircraft and our credit card is your credit card. Andrew, our pilot, will be calling you tomorrow. So, let's get the wheels spinning. You have plans to make and we…well, never mind about that, just get us to our apartment."

Gus the gabber lost his ability to speak, but thankfully he did not lose his ability to drive. Was his wife pleased? Let's put it this way, he had more orgasms in one night than he thought possible.

While making arrangements for Gus, Clay also notified his household help that their services would be on hold for another two weeks; their paychecks would be in the mail.

Clay repeated his grandmother's phrase, "time waits for no one," and the hiatus for them was nearing its end. Their honeymoon bed would finally find relief. Now all phones will be turned back on; life on the outside will begin.

During Clay's time away, he never once thought of his mother or Ali. It was now time to make a few calls. The first to his mother; his annoyance would begin again. The second to his grandmother, who had begun to slide back into the world of pain. God's reply to all prayers would sadden their hearts.

He called his father, telling him of his plans to return to work. Money only flowed when Clay put his nose to the grindstone. He needed to make a lot of money to cover the expenses he planned on lavishing on his new bride, for is it not true, "you are considered a bride for a full year"?

Help returned, Chef Sonja and housekeepers Joanna and Mya. Sloan now had servants to do as she ordered. It would take some time to accept her position as the wife of the wealthiest man in New York City.

Clay pulled Sloan to him. A deep penetrating kiss would have to last them the day.

She held on tightly, not wanting him to leave.

"Clay, please don't go."

"Babe, I have to work; there is so much more I want to give you."

"I don't need anything, you are all I want. Besides, my dressing room is full. You bought out the stores, all available space is taken, there's barely enough room for me."

"Then we knock out a wall, problem solved." She shook her head; he again took her into his arms.

"I'll miss you, babe, but I need to focus on work. Were you not the one to insist we use our apartment as our honeymoon hideaway? Well babe, the honeymoon has seen its last day."

Sloan was already depressed thinking about being left alone. The sure way to take care of that problem would be Clay's presence. She dropped her head, showing her disappointment.

He touched her chin, bringing it upward.

"You need to make me a promise: keep everything warm, for when I step through that door that warmth will flare to boiling."

Sloan tried to laugh, but could she wait? She was already to that point.

Clay was about to shut the door to their apartment then thought better. What would Sloan do all day? He peeked around the almost closed door.

"What's your take on spending the day with my grandmother? She would be thrilled to see you." He never got a direct answer; her lips were all over his. He placed the call. Gus will find out in short order; his chauffeuring days will be turned over for Sloan's use.

After yet another lingering kiss, the door closed; it was the best way to start a day. Clay whistled as he walked to work.

In no time the two and a half weeks of honeymoon clutter that was left behind was removed and order was restored. Sonja was busy making a list of the food items needed for the week. Preparations for dinner would then be taken care of. Sonja never left the apartment until her employer had been served; she would continue, but it would now be for two.

Sloan stood at the door, again feeling overwhelmed with the wealth of the family she had married into. She rang the doorbell. Art smiled as he welcomed her.

"Mrs. Sloan, there is no need for you to ring the doorbell, you are now family. Would you like for me to announce your presence?"

"That is not necessary, Art. Clay called ahead; Mrs. Chadsworth is expecting me."

He offered his guidance to Lydia's room.

"Thank you, Art, but I'm acquainted with her room."

Sloan rested her hand on the railing, remembering the touch of elegance that graced the staircase just two weeks prior. She was now a married eighteen-year-old woman; the mound of diamonds covering her ring finger confirmed that. She could use the elevator but never would;

that was for Lydia's use. She also knew that, if Lydia could, she would use the stairs.

Outside Lydia's door Sloan stood staring at the doorknob. She had spent but a few minutes with this woman since they'd met, and today she would spend hours. What would they find to talk of? The knock was a gentle tap.

Doleanna's hearing was sharp. Sloan was welcomed with a hug. She was surprised; was everyone this friendly? She could feel the very essence of the house. If these walls could talk, would they reveal all? Would they tell of love, joy and laughter? Or was there more than the eyes could see?

Lydia tried to shout out but had to settle for a murmur. Doleanna gave Sloan a little push; she knew Sloan had not heard her.

"Come sit beside me, child. I was not feeling my best until I received Clay's call. When he told me of your visit, I instantly felt a rush of adrenalin. You are just what my doctor should prescribe."

"Then I will have to visit with you every day…of course, with your permission."

Doleanna was also happy with Sloan's visit. Lydia had been feeling poorly, and the nurse noticed tears frequently being wiped away. She was free from pain for the time being; Doleanna was her relief donor. She also wished she had the capacity to soothe the soul, give relief to Lydia's anguish. Lydia now wanted to sit up in the bed, Doleanna complied, gathering and fluffing her pillows. Lydia had enough. She shook her hand, waving Doleanna off, but this was done with a smile.

"Well now, is my grandson making you happy, seeing to your needs in and out of bed?"

Sloan could see how Lydia would mesmerize her audience, more likely causing them to be shocked. This woman was a work of art; never will there be a carbon copy.

"We are extremely happy in and out of the bed,…more so in bed."

Hearing the conversation, Doleanna giggled, hiding her head. Lydia and Sloan's laughter rang out and down the stairs.

True to her word, Sloan visited with Lydia daily. She also met most of Clay's close friends, married and unmarried, and in the months ahead they would also become her friends. But for now Lydia had all her attention.

They would sometimes talk at length about Sloan's expectations of married life.

"There will definitely be children; hopefully we will have a home far away from the hustle and bustle of New York City. But of these, my priority is to always be happy."

The daily visits sometimes held silence, hand holding being the pleasure of the day. Lydia had to bite her tongue many times wanting to know if Clay had told Sloan about his mother, but their conversations never mentioned anything in that regard. She would not take it upon herself without Clay's approval.

Sloan refused to leave Lydia. Clay never had to second-guess where his wife disappeared when she was a no-show at the apartment. He would spend many evenings not only with his wife, but his grandmother as well, except for one night.

Lydia was fading away. Sloan refused to accept this; she would get on her knees to be as close as possible, pleading with Lydia to hang on. She could not bear to again lose someone who had a stranglehold on her heart.

Doleanna was replacing the tissue boxes frequently. The calendar pages were turning; September paid a visit.

Lydia was resting quite comfortably, Sloan as always holding her hand, when Lydia spoke.

"Child, would you please tell Doleanna to take a break? I need to talk to you in private."

"Yes, of course, Lydia. Doleanna…"

"I heard her, Mrs. Sloan. You call me if you need me, okay?" Sloan nodded.

"Child, my deadline for departure time is fast approaching; there's no time to waste. I need to know something and I think you have the answer I've been seeking. It is extremely important for me to know where you came from and the family you never speak of."

Sloan was taken aback; she wasn't expecting what came out of Lydia's mouth. She could not tell another lie.

"Lydia, from the very beginning I lied to Clay about my family, and it's been dreadful, and I don't know how to clean up the mess." She dropped her head, weeping. Ashamed of what she had done, she begged for forgiveness.

Lydia reached out, bringing Sloan's bowed head upward.

"Child, there is no need for forgiveness; you did what you had to do." Lydia brushed away the tears.

Sloan was thankful for her understanding. She also knew the time was fast approaching to say a final good-night. Lydia was asking for her last request to be granted, how could she refuse?

"I told Clay my papa refused to give us his consent to marry, and the only way for us to be together was to run away. That was a horrible untruth. It's difficult to talk about. I try to forget, but it refuses to let go; it's with me every waking moment, crippling my life. I should have been with them. Why God chose for me to stay, I have yet to figure out. I pray nightly to Him to help me forget—it's just not working. What I'm trying to say is that I no longer have a family; they perished in a fire."

Lydia maintained a sitting position, but fell back onto her pillows, shocked and saddened. Sloan was grabbing tissue after tissue, her nightmare holding on. Lydia may have been weak, but not so much as not to comfort her beloved grandson's wife.

"My beautiful child, I am deeply sorry for forcing you to relive your past."

It took several minutes before Sloan was able to return to her former self. She felt an enormous weight thrown off her shoulders. There will be no more lies.

"What is it that you wish to know about my family?"

Lydia delicately asked what she hoped would not bring on another flood of tears. While at the same time, praying her suspicions were not true.

"Tell me about your mother. Was she as tall as you?" Lydia's fingers were crossed.

"Heavens no…my mama was petite like you, and also a blond. There are things you do that remind me so much of her. You have two of the exact habits. You tilt your head to one side when someone asks you a question, and when deep in thought you look upward, as if the answer is floating in the air. That was so my mama. Strange…but I never realized until this very minute how much you two resemble each other. The only real difference is she had brown eyes and yours are blue…amazing…" Sloan was caught up in the moment, and then tossed it aside with no further thought.

She continued where she left off.

"She had a heart of gold, my mama; she never knew the word 'unkind,' and was so generous with her time, she would do anything for our church. But with all her spectacular qualities, it was her smile that drew people to her like a magnet."

Sloan stopped talking; Lydia appeared to be going into shock. Sloan looked around for help.

"I'm going to call Doleanna." Lydia refused. She struggled to sit up in bed, pulling on Sloan's arms.

"Were you an only child?" Lydia prayed she was; her fingers stayed crossed.

"You may not believe this, but I had seven sisters and four brothers younger than I." Sloan did not understand where all this was going. Lydia persisted with the questions.

"How old was your mother when she perished?" Lydia prayed she was older than thirty-six; if she was, Lydia would then uncross her fingers — she would then believe in its power.

"My mama was thirty-six."

How much more confirmation did she need? When Sloan mentioned her siblings, she should have known. The tears came rushing forth while she violently shook her head.

"Oh my God, Lydia, what did I do? Did I say something wrong? Please talk to me."

She could not speak, she started gasping. Sloan had to struggle to remove her arms, her grip was that tight. She ran to the door screaming for Doleanna.

Doleanna within seconds was at Lydia's side. She did an assessment and gave her an injection of liquid valium. Lydia finally settled back, although a stream of tears flowed steadily. Sloan had her body pressed against the door. Although upset and shaken, she asked Doleanna if she could stay. Doleanna nodded.

"Lydia, please forgive me. Had I known this would trouble you so, I never would have told you."

Lydia now understood the delay with her daughter's arrival; her baby girl must have died shortly after Clay had found her. She closed her tear-coated eyes. Her baby girl died along with her babies, the exception her firstborn. She would never hold and cuddle with her grandbabies. The grief was unbearable. She felt a mounting pressure within her chest. She wanted to die…she needed to die to extinguish the agonizing pain.

Cancer could not lay claim to the pain she was suffering.

Lydia opened her swollen eyes to look into the eyes of her remaining granddaughter. Her thoughts were of her beloved grandson. She was extremely concerned for it is *illegal* to marry a relative. *What would Clay do if he knew the truth? What are the ramifications of marrying a cousin? Could he be arrested and charged with incest? Would he have to do prison time?* Lydia had to secure her grandson's future; Sloan must continue to live her life on a lie. Lydia was defeated; the lies will continue.

Sloan never took her eyes off Lydia, she was that concerned. Lydia could barely speak. Sloan removed herself from her seated position to kneel at her bedside.

Doleanna again was asked to leave; she complied, nodding at Sloan. Sloan understood its meaning: call on her if needed.

"My precious child, I have a great favor to ask of you and you must trust my judgment to never ask why; do you think you can do that?"

"I will do whatever you ask of me."

"You have to promise."

"I promise."

"All right then, I will take you at your word. You must never tell Clay the truth about your family; you must keep to the story you have told him."

"But…"

"No buts, you promised."

That night Lydia begged for forgiveness from God. And Sloan, she vowed never to break her promise.

Clay in due time will know all there is to know, but long before the facts come from the lips of his wife.

That night Lydia entered into a semi-conscious state. Sloan refused to leave her side.

Doleanna made the necessary calls. Phillip and Clay were to take a client out for dinner when they got the call. Loved ones began to gather around Lydia's bed. Dr. Frederick Marshall, the family's doctor, began checking her vitals. All eyes focused on him. He stood back, said a few words to Doleanna, and then he began to take the family members' hands one by one, pulling them aside far enough that Lydia would not hear.

"I'm sorry; it's a matter of minutes, an hour at the most. I would like to say a prayer for her; will everyone join hands in reciting the Hail Mary?"

They reclaimed their prior positions, but this time they knelt in reverence to the woman that had been the backbone of their lives. And then the friend, mother and grandmother opened her eyes. Heaven had to have descended and placed a kiss upon her lips, for she smiled a smile like no other. She rose to a seated position unassisted. She held her arms out and slowly began to rock while patting someone she undeniably loved. Everyone looked about thinking the impossible, and yet the scene before them left little doubt. She was holding on to something, to what they had no idea. Unbeknownst to all present, Lydia's baby girl Ali had come to take her mother to their new home. Lydia died happier than she had been in life. Clay felt extreme remorse for failing to keep his promise. Everyone in attendance knew they had witnessed a miracle. Life continues no matter the form, whether it be here or on the other side. Each in time will reflect back on this moment, when Ali's death is uncovered.

Phillip called the newspaper, alerting them of his mother's death. Lydia would grace the front page of not only the newspapers, but all magazines and tabloids.

Her funeral was kept private in accordance with her wishes. The mourners' attention was drawn to the claps of thunder that sounded one after another, similar to a twenty-one-gun salute showing reverence for someone so highly respected. With solemn faces her family walked slowly away from the mausoleum, umbrellas held high as the rain splattered across their shoes. The servants followed, their tears a match for the raindrops.

This day will not end until the reading of Lydia Diane Chadsworth's will.

CHAPTER NINE

Marc was beside himself when Ben called off the search. But he knew Ben was left with no recourse. Marc didn't have time to dwell on Sloan's disappearance; he had to prepare for his return to school.

He still had four more years to complete before he could begin his career in architectural design. His desire to be an architect started when he was just a little boy drawing all kinds of weird designs; his mother couldn't buy enough paper. Marc would not be considered merely good; he would in time be recognized as one of the greatest.

His greed for money was not for himself, but his beloved Sloan. She was entitled to all the riches of the world and he would make sure she had it all. And when she did return (for he would never believe she was dead) he would show her his accomplishments and she would welcome him with open arms. But for now, he was concerned about his mother. There was no change in her condition. He visited her daily. He worried; she wasn't getting enough exercise, although the nurses in charge of her care worked with her daily. She was gaining way too much weight; surely Ben must have noticed. Marc wondered why he never said anything. He would ask the Doc.

His call was answered immediately.

"Dr. Harrison's office. May I help you?"

Marc recognized the high-pitched voice as belonging to Ethel.

"Ethel, this is Marc Anderson. I need to make an appointment to see the Doc."

"Is this an emergency, Marc?"

"No, it's a private matter. But I would like to see him as soon as possible."

"Well, how about today? He has an opening at four-thirty."

"That would be great. Thanks, Ethel."

"See you then, Marc. Bye."

Marc was a little early, like thirty minutes. He thumbed through the magazines, impatient for he knew not what. He started pacing. No one was seated in the waiting room. He wondered what was taking the Doc so long. Finally a neighbor he knew slightly made an appearance.

"Howdy, Marc. How's things going now that you're a free man?" The man gave a little chuckle. Marc never considered himself anything else. He looked to the person making that comment and thought it best to ignore it.

Doc told Ethel she could leave for the day. She removed herself from her desk, took up her handbag and proceeded towards the door, hesitating just long enough to turn the open sign to closed. She bid good-bye to them both.

Doc welcomed Marc into his office.

"Have a seat, Marc. I know it's a sad time for you. I would have thought by now, we would have had some kind of reaction from your mother. But she'll come around eventually, I'm sure of that. As to the disappearance of Sloan, that has me puzzled. But I've always believed in the saying 'no news is good news.' My feeling is she'll turn up when's she ready. She just needs time to sort through all that has happened. I think she took to the highway, probably hitchhiking her way to wherever she feels the need to go. That's not the safest means of travel; I surely wouldn't want Sunni to travel that way. But Sloan has to make her own decisions now that her family is gone. So what is it that is troubling you? Ethel said it was of a personal nature."

"First of all I want to thank you for bringing up the possibility of hitchhiking. I would never have thought of that. You just gave me more reason to believe Sloan will be back. Thank you."

"You're quite welcome. So what's on your mind, Marc?"

"Doc, I'm really concerned about my mother. She seems to be gaining a lot of weight, yet her face is so thin and drawn. She would be embarrassed if she were aware of her condition."

Doc knew this would happen eventually. He was hoping Harriet would be the one to convey the news. Now he had no choice. It was true; she was indeed gaining way too much weight. He was planning on doing an ultrasound to make sure her pregnancy was progressing as it should.

"Marc, she is aware of her condition, even in her present state of mind."

"What? Doc you're not making sense."

"Marc, your mother is pregnant."

Marc jumped to his feet shouting, "What the hell are you talking about? There is no way she could be pregnant. She's doesn't even date. Doc, I really hate to tell you this, but you have made a mistake. You would have had to examine her internally to come to that conclusion, and my mother going into shock wouldn't justify that kind of exam. I think you better explain your reasoning behind that."

"Marc, your mother came to see me the day of the fire. She was concerned something was wrong with her. It was then I confirmed her pregnancy."

"I can't comprehend my mother doing something so vile as giving herself to a man."

"Now hold on, Marc. I can't believe you would use that word in regards to your mother.

You must know your mother and Ben have always had feelings for one another. He spends as much time at your house as you do. His love for your mother runs deep. He's always wanted to marry her. He now has great expectations that she will accept his proposal of marriage. You have her so high on a pedestal that you cannot conceive the fact she has desires and needs like the rest of us. You surely wouldn't deny her those perks in life. Marc, she was happy with the news; please don't destroy that happiness."

Marc's thoughts were spinning. How could he condemn the Doc and speak to him that way? He was their friend and he was only looking out for his mother's best interests.

"Doc, I'm really sorry for saying what I did. All I can do is ask your forgiveness. I'm blown away with the news. I'm really naïve, aren't I? I think of my mother as being too old to do anything other than hold hands—stupid, huh? I know she loves Ben. I've caught them in the act many times…ah…kissing, that is. She would quickly pull away from him; she was embarrassed that I had seen them in that compromising position. Oh my God, it just dawned on me, I'm about to be a brother. I can remember from my early years, how I was always asking for a baby brother or sister. She always told me this couldn't be accomplished without a father. Well, it looks like I acquired a father today, doesn't it?"

"Marc, I'm excited for you and Ben. You really need to go and see him. I think he's concerned you will think ill of him."

"I'm on my way. Thanks, Doc." They rose from their seated positions, shook hands and said their good-byes.

Marc would look at his mother in a different light. She now has someone else in her life, has always had. He had been blind to that fact. Doc had to bring that to the surface. He no longer has to worry about her well-being. Ben would take good care of her. Marc could now make a life for himself.

It was early evening when he left the Doc's office. Ben in all likelihood would be on his way to visit Marc's mother. He never missed a day visiting her. Marc drove by Ben's trailer home and noticed his patrol car missing. He had thought right; Ben already left for the nursing home. Marc would also visit with his mother.

As he drove into the nursing home lot, he noticed Ben's patrol car. He parked his car in the area for visitors and immediately went to the receptionist's desk to sign in. He, like Ben, never missed a day. Alayna welcomed him. She was a people person, very sociable and always upbeat. She was in a striking two-piece pale blue double-breasted suit. Her earrings, necklace and bracelets were sterling silver with insets of aqua stones. She wore silver pumps. This lady knew how to put herself together.

Marc was leaning over to place his required signature when she spoke again.

"I know it's none of my business, but your mother is really lucky to have you and the sheriff to visit with her. Many of our patients have no living relatives. My heart goes out to them. Thankfully, we have organizations that donate their time, entertaining and bringing them small gifts to unwrap. It's uplifting and brightens their day. Everyone needs someone in their lives, especially the elderly who totally depend on someone to take of their needs. I hope I didn't talk your ear off. I also yearn for someone to talk to. Like I said, there aren't too many visitors."

"It's a pleasure to talk to you. And no, you didn't talk my ear off. How's my mother doing?"

"I visit with her when I can, usually on my lunch hour. She is so pretty. I hope it won't be much longer before she awakens." Marc appreciated the word she used to explain his mother's condition. He stopped at the door to her room.

Alayna had failed to tell him Ben was here. He was kneeling in front of her wheelchair, his hands tucked into hers. Marc could not help himself; he was going to eavesdrop. He slowly retraced his last two steps, placing his back against the wall next to the doorframe of her room. He acted nonchalant, as if he were waiting for someone.

"Sweetheart, I'm here again. I think it's time for you to wake up. My heart aches with missing you. I nibble at my food and I'm lacking in sleep. The days drag on and on. You need to awaken, if only for our baby. He will be here soon. He will need his mother to comfort him and feed him. I can't do this alone. I need your help in raising him.

"I haven't told Marc about our baby, I want to tell him together. I know he will be as excited as I am. Sweetheart, your son needs you desperately. His days are miserable. He has depended on you his whole life. He now needs your help to get him through the trauma he's experiencing.

"Sweetheart, I pray you can hear everything I'm saying. If you need more time to recover, that's fine with me. I'm never going to leave you. Our baby will never be without a father. I'm here to stay. So long for now, sweetheart, I'll see you tomorrow."

Marc heard it directly from Ben's lips: the sheriff had impregnated his mother. He felt like an intruder. How could he stoop so low? He couldn't let Ben see him. He hurried down the corridor. The men's bathroom was four doors down. He rushed inside, waited a couple minutes, then reopened the bathroom door and came face to face with his mother's lover.

Marc spoke first.

"Oops, I guess we're here for the same reason."

"Yes, I think so; I'll be with you in a second. Would you mind waiting? I would like to talk with you, preferably in the visitors lounge." They both laughed as Marc stepped through the bathroom doorway, allowing Ben to enter.

Marc waited patiently. He considered Ben a good friend and hopefully a father. Within minutes Ben was facing him in the guest's quarters. He pulled a seat out from against the wall. He wanted to face Marc as he spoke.

"I just was visiting with your mother. Her condition remains the same. I wish there was something I could do to bring her out of the nightmare she is living. I am forever hitting my knees; they're beginning to get calloused." Ben's eyes were beginning to tear up. He was sick to death of all the never-ending tears. He wanted his Harriet back.

Marc rushed up to the plate before he backed out of what he had to say.

"Ben, I went to see the Doc. I was worried about my mother's weight gain."

Ben's heart started to pound. He should have told Marc himself. He shouldn't have heard it from the Doc. Ben began gripping the arms on the chair, preparing himself for an ass chewing.

"Ben, he told me my mother is pregnant and that you are the father. I love you, Ben. You have always been good to us, and I know my mother loves you—how could she not? You have always been there for her as you are now. And Ben, if I were to have a father, you would be my choice. But I do have a problem. I don't think I'll have the patience to wait out our little one's arrival."

Ben reached for him, tears visible, a hug making everything all right. His fears were unfounded. He should have known better. Marc by definition was his son. And when he and Harriet married, he would legally adopt him. Marc would then be by all legal intents and purposes Ben's biological son. Ben was heard whistling as he excited the front door.

Marc strolled down to his mother's room.

Harriet was staring straight ahead. He hated to see her like this. She had always been so vibrant and happy.

"Hi, Mom, it's your one and only come to see how you're doing. Do you know that you are entering into your fifth week here at the care center? Wouldn't you like to come home? I miss you and our conversations. And eating out is becoming a drag; the food critics are about to stamp me as one not likely to survive.

"But enough about me, let's focus on you. I guess by now you've noticed your weight gain. I'm told babies can do that. I bet you never thought in your wildest dreams something like this would happen, but surprises always come when least expected. We are going to have to make a huge adjustment to our way of living. I for one am looking forward to it, but I think it will take Ben a while to adjust. At present, he's playing a role acting as if everything is hunky-dory. But he's never been married, let alone fathered a kid; he has the right to be scared. But knowing him as we do, in time he will be giddy with happiness. I don't need to see into the future to see if you and Ben will make suitable parents. This kid of yours is going to be a dynamo. Look how I turned out, and that's with one parent—can you imagine being raised with two? I am so looking forward to being tagged as a big brother, but I'll have to rely on your expertise in teaching me the steps to taking care of a baby, although diaper changing will be better left to its mother.

"Mom, I can't stand it, I need you desperately. I will be leaving for school in a matter of days and you were always there to see me off. All I'm left with is the belief in the possibility. Well Mom, I think it's time to put a zipper on my mouth and give your ears a break; besides, my stomach is calling out for that killer food, yuck. I love you, Mom." He wiped his eyes as he left her room.

Marc was not the only one concerned about his mother's weight gain. Doc was also concerned. Harriet was a very tiny woman. Her weight was ballooning out of control. It could well be because she was getting no actual physical exercise. The nurses walked her but she tired easily. She was given food the consistency of baby food without much success. They needed to keep up her strength; intravenous feedings were given nightly as well as vitamins for the baby.

Doc was thinking of having her transferred to the hospital to perform an ultrasound. But before he could do this, he needed to get Ben and Marc's permission. He started dialing as soon as he entered his home. He acknowledged his wife Miriam, while avoiding his daughter Sunni, who was poring over her books; she would be leaving for school in a matter of days.

Ben answered on the first ring. He too had just arrived home after stopping at the restaurant in town for something. Each time he stopped there it reminded him of his sweetheart. "The way to a man's heart is through his stomach" definitely applied to him.

"Hello. This is Sheriff Davidson's residence."

"Ben, this is Malcolm. I guess by now you've talked to Marc. How did everything go?"

"It couldn't have gone any better had I planned it myself. Thank you for your help. I know it had to be difficult for you. I should have told him myself. I just thought Harriet would have come around by now. I really wanted her to tell him, but circumstances being what they are, we really had no choice."

"Ben, now that everything is out in the open, I was wondering if you and Marc could drop by the office tomorrow. I need to discuss something in regards to Harriet. Would tomorrow be okay? I can squeeze you in around my lunch hour, say 12:30 p.m.?"

"Should I be concerned?"

"No, no, I just want to go over a few things."

"That's fine by me. You needn't call Marc, I'll take care of that. If for some reason he can't make it, I'll call you; otherwise, plan on us being there." Ben had no idea how long Marc would visit with his mother. He thought it best to call later in the evening before he closed his eyes.

They were seated in the waiting room at the Doc's office precisely at 12:30 p.m. No early arrival this time. The next scheduled appointment wasn't until 2:00 p.m. Doc welcomed them into his private office. They took a seat facing one another. Doc started the conversation. Ben and Marc listened intently.

"I want to transfer Harriet to St. Mary's Hospital in Franklin County. I know the driving time is an additional twenty minutes, but if by chance I have to admit her this hospital is one of the best. Marc, you mentioned her weight problem. I am a bit concerned about it; that's part of the reason for the transfer. I would like to do an ultrasound to check on the development of the baby. Now, I'm expecting no surprises and neither should you. The second test is a blood work-up, which would have been done if the unexpected hadn't happened. That's about it. Will you agree to have her admitted to the hospital?"

They were relieved Doc suggested the transfer. Marc wanted him to keep his mother there until she came out of her present state.

"Marc, we can only keep her if we find a problem, and I seriously doubt that we will. The care she's receiving in the nursing home is the very best. A hospital setting would not be in her best interest."

"When are you planning on doing this?"

"As soon as I see my last patient at 3:00 p.m., I'll go to the nursing home and sign the necessary papers. Why do I notice a look of concern on your faces? There's no need to worry. I have everything under control. Now both of you skedaddle. My lunch is waiting." He gave them each a hearty handshake. His demeanor was upbeat, giving them further confidence.

Ben trotted off in the direction of his police car as Marc made his way to his truck.

Very soon they would be in for the shock of their lives, in more ways than one.

CHAPTER TEN

Doc's plan on leaving at 3:00 p.m. for the nursing home was not to be; instead he would not depart until after 4:00 p.m. He had an unexpected visitor, his wife Miriam. She was clearly upset, eyes red from crying. Ethel opened the door to the waiting room, giving Miriam access to the office. The Doc had just finished with his last patient when his wife approached him. She was tearing at tissues held in her hands.

"Malcolm, I'm really sorry to burst in on you like this, but I'm beside myself with worry over Sunni. I've been on the phone for hours trying to get a hold of her and she's not answering her phone. I just know something is wrong."

He reached out, taking her hands into his.

"Honey, you need to calm down. Sunni hasn't been herself since Sloan went missing, you know that. It's apparent talking to us is not high on her priorities. She needs time to get over the grief of losing what she considered the sister she never had. Until then we can do nothing to help her. If she wants or needs us, she will call. Trust me."

"I have always trusted you; I think that was part of the problem. In the beginning, we agreed that we would give Sunni a sister or a brother. I remember like it was yesterday when the lawyer called about a six-month-old baby girl that was available for immediate adoption. Sunni had just turned one. I was excited with the prospect of having two little girls so close in age; they would've been like twins. I never pressured you for an answer, but with each passing day my hopes were dashed, which brings us to the here and now. Why, Malcolm? Why did you not agree to that adoption? I think I'm entitled to an answer."

"Miriam, have you lost your mind? I have enough on my plate with our daughter possibly losing hers. Now is not the time to bring up our past. Some things are better left unsaid, and this is one of them."

She jumped from her seated position and began to scream, tears once again finding their way.

"I refuse to let this go. I need an answer to my question. Why didn't we adopt that baby girl? Why? God in heaven, please tell me." This was not the calm, sweet and soft-spoken woman he married. She was out of control.

"All right, you want to know the 'why' —

here it is." He was forced to show his true colors. Colors no one had ever seen, including his wife.

"I didn't want another girl. I wanted a boy. I didn't even want Sunni. You forced her on me. I was weak. I should never have given in. I yearned for a boy, a son to carry my name. But no, you had to have the first baby that was made available. I hated you for taking her. And the problems we are now faced with, I turn over to you. I'm finished with her. Now, would you please leave? I have a patient to see."

Miriam was in total shock. Something was wrong. This was not the man she fell in love with. He had never shown such anger; hate was riding on his backside. All these years it was a façade; Malcolm only pretended to love his daughter. Was he also pretending to be a compassionate and caring doctor? What kind of man had she married? He was holding open the door to his office, more or less booting Miriam out. When she passed through, he slammed the door, shutting her out of his life.

Ethel was on the telephone, taking no notice of the Doc's wife as she stumbled out of the waiting room in a state of bewilderment. She was swaying back and forth, as if on a drunk. Finally she made it to her car. She began driving, exceptionally slow. Some of her neighbors waved as she passed, receiving no acknowledgment. Rage set upon her as she gripped the wheel, head bent forward until it almost touched the steering wheel. She would never again look into the face of the man she had once loved.

Sunni had no idea of the damage she had inflicted upon her parents, and she really would have cared less, even had she known.

Doc arrived at the nursing home at 4:53 p.m., an hour and a half later than planned. He had arranged for Harriet to be picked up the minute Ben and Marc walked out of his office. His late arrival, thankfully, coincided with the arrival of the ambulance. He had a fetish; it was to be present when a patient of his was admitted to the hospital, their comfort a high priority. He talked for a few minutes with the nurses that would see to her care. He informed them in writing of the tests he wanted and then departed for home. He arrived at his home at precisely 8:52 p.m. Miriam had already retired for the evening in a bedroom other than the one they shared.

In the early hour, before darkness turned to light, one explosion after another rocked the foundation of the Harrisons' home. The series of explosions started in the three-car garage, attacking the Doc's neatly placed containers of gasoline. The townspeople were again running towards what sounded to them like the end of the world. If only they were more observant, they would have noticed a dark figure running towards the fields that stretched out behind the Harrisons' home. The night caller took a surgical instrument and a ring belonging to the soon-to-be-departed residents.

The raging fire rapidly consumed what was left of the Doc's home. Fire trucks were once again heard in the background as the townspeople screamed for someone to help the Doc and his wife, the only people known to be in the home. Everywhere you looked residents were lying in the road crying, some comforting others, but this time no one attempted to enter. The flames had already swallowed the home's contents; one brick wall after another blew outward with each explosion.

The fire continued in its haste to destroy. Mayhem started to erupt. Everywhere you looked anger was taking over the inhabitants' lives. They were confused. They knew the Doc had stored gasoline in his garage for years. Why did not someone notify the fire marshall to have them removed? They were striking out at their neighbors, each blaming the other, when no one was really to blame, although time will tell.

Unbeknownst to them, an unthinkable evil was wreaking chaos in a small town barely noticeable on the map. The night caller in the beginning only intended to remove one candidate, but excitement and anticipation of the next was not to be denied. As time moved forward, so did the caller.

Ben heard the explosions as he arrived at the scene before the fire trucks. He fell to the ground covering his face with the palms of his hands, the fire illuminating his fallen body.

Marc also heard the explosions, but because he lived closer to the Harrisons, he arrived a little before Ben. He remained standing choking back his tears. His mind centered on his mother. Who would take care of her? Marc and Ben entrusted her care to only one man, and that man no longer existed.

The townspeople were showing signs of fear, wondering when this ongoing nightmare would end. There was nothing anyone could do. Tears in the early dawn hours could not help put out the flames.

Two fire trucks sounding their sirens pulled to a stop, and firefighters began rushing about, taking to the hoses like they were pieces of string. They were running towards yet another fire. This time their attempted rescues would save neither the Doc nor his lovely wife, Miriam. They could not fathom how there could be two fires so similar in nature within weeks of each other. Something was not right. The firefighters would not be the only ones wondering if this was just a coincidence.

They would never recover over the loss of their beloved doctor. His wife Miriam, whose helping hand had benefitted so many, would also be greatly missed. Their remains were burned beyond recognition. They too would be put into cold storage at the morgue. The plans for their burial would be put on hold.

Sunni, their only living relative, had to be notified. It would be days before news of her parents' death reached her. When no one seemed able to get in touch with her, she was finally notified by certified mail. Three days after signing a receipt for the letter she arrived in her hometown and set about making arrangements with the same funeral home as the Parkers.

The caskets containing the Doc's and Miriam's bodies would remain closed. Again the residents gathered to pay their last respects, though this time the services were held in church. Hundreds lined up to offer their condolences. Sunni accepted their tearful sympathy hugs. Suddenly, nearing the end of the procession, she collapsed. Ben knelt at her side, placing her head in his arms.

He spoke loudly to the people in attendance.

"The church services are over and most of you are aware the burial will be for a select few, and they will be there to see to Sunni's needs, should they arise. Please let us respect her privacy. I'm sure if she could, she would thank each of you."

Sunni was beginning to show signs of recovery. Feeling Ben's arms around her, she glared at him, although he was unaware of it. She removed herself from his arms, scrambling to stand. He offered his help, but she pushed him aside.

"I'm all right. I just want to get this burial over with. I need to return to school."

Ben was shocked by her actions, and then thought better. She had just lost her parents; she hadn't had enough time to grieve. It was apparent that Sunni was not the type to show her true feelings in front of so many, although she had known these people her entire life. Ben felt extremely sorry for this young girl, one he watched grow from a toddler into a fine young woman, thanks to the loving support of her parents. If only he knew. She stood by as her parents' coffins were being lowered into the ground; not a tear escaped those close-set eyes.

Mr. Hewlett, the bank president, was on a search for Sunni, up one road then down another, with important news that could not wait. He was about to give up when he noticed her standing among the ruins of her home. He hated to intrude, but he was there for a purpose.

"Miss Harrison, I'm sorry to interrupt you, but I need for you to come into the bank. There are some matters that need to be taken care of."

As Sunni took in his comment, her thoughts were, *God, don't tell me I owe money on this dump.*

He'll have to wait until hell freezes over before he sees a dime from me.

"Miss Harrison, would you mind terribly coming into the bank right now? It really is a matter of great importance."

"Are you an imbecile? Can you not tell that I'm grieving? You'll just have to wait." She wasn't about to go to his bank. She was planning on skipping out of town immediately, never again to be seen or heard from.

Mr. Hewlett continued as if he had not heard her comment.

"Miss Harrison, I really hate to conduct business out in the open. But I see I have no other choice."

Sunni shook her head. She could run to her rented car. It was parked at the edge of her blackened driveway. She decided to hear him out. It wasn't as if he could handcuff her and take her away for money her parents failed to pay.

She noticed the banker looking around.

"Mr. Hewlett, what the hell is your problem? Let's get this over with. I need to catch a plane."

"I was wondering if there is a place we could sit down and conduct business the proper way; standing is not appropriate for you to sign papers. I was also entrusted with a letter that was to be turned over to you in the event of your parents' deaths. You know, I really would prefer to do this at the bank."

She was thinking while screaming on the inside, *This man has a serious problem with details.*

"Okay, okay. I'll go to your damn bank." She glanced at her Rolex. Only the very best would grace her body. The time was 12:20 p.m. She would grab a bite to eat in town after they "conducted business the proper way." She followed Mr. Hewlett, the man that brought forth a flood of tears to her beloved Sloan. She hated him and wished he had been the one to die.

Would this wish be granted?

Sunni parked her car directly in front of the bank. The shopping center was busy as usual with tourists. She took one final look at the town that once held her heart, and had now torn it out.

She was welcomed into the bank. Mary, Mr. Hewlett's personal receptionist, was seated at her desk.

"Good afternoon, Miss Harrison. May I help you?" Everyone knew her; after all, was she not the Doc's daughter? She ignored the greeting and the offer of help. She wasn't there to pass the time of day or to be gracious. Mary stood, trying to get her attention. Sunni bypassed her and went straight to Mr. Hewlett's office.

Mr. Hewlett was seated, arranging the papers he was to turn over for Sunni's signature.

He stood as she entered; he was quite the gentleman. He was gracious to the point of being obnoxious. He knew the benefits should Sunni want to be a new addition to his collection of bedding partners. She wouldn't be his first choice; well, not his last to tell the truth, but what the hell, when you have needs like his, a piece of ass is a piece of ass.

"Please take a seat, Miss Harrison. I was made the trustee over your parents' estate. I have everything ready for you to sign. The first thing on the agenda" — *There he goes again with details,* Sunni thought — "is the reading of the will." She never gave it a thought that her parents would have a will.

"The will reads as follows: 'I undersigned, Dr. Malcolm Edward Harrison, now residing at 50137 Redding Road located in—"

Sunni interrupted his speech.

"Could you just get to the gist of the damn will? I don't need to hear every little detail. As I said, I have a plane to catch." Her sighs were not contained.

He was gruff with his response. So much for acting as a gentleman.

"As you wish, Miss Harrison. There are actually two wills, one for each parent. Everything they owned was free of debt. They were sensible to carry the maximum insurance. Everything will be replaced as if the fire never took place, including the extensive collection of diamond jewelry. Your mother was wise to the fact that gold and diamonds rise like the cost of inflation. She followed through each year with appraisals. This alone will put hundreds of thousands of dollars in your pocket. It was a wasted effort trying to convince your mother to store them in a safe deposit box, her comment being, 'I don't intend to drive to the bank to wear a specific piece of jewelry when a special occasion warrants it. My jewelry stays with me.' I'm sure the insurance company will send an agent to sift through the debris to recover what they can of her jewels."

Sunni knew her mother's obsession with diamonds. She could have cared less, but in time she too would have her own collection.

Mr. Hewlett continued. "They also had stocks, bonds and CDs worth an exorbitant amount of money. If you would like to know the market value, I have that information. But that is not all; they each carried a million-dollar life insurance policy. You are their only living relative and sole beneficiary. You are an extremely wealthy woman, Miss Harrison. The man that marries you will indeed have something to smile about."

Sunni couldn't believe his comment and told him so.

"You, Mr. Hewlett, are an ass. I don't intend to ever marry. No man will do to me what you have done to your wives." She grabbed the wills out of his hand.

She needed to read them for herself. Her eyes quickly scanned the paper. Every word he said was true, she was indeed a millionaire twice over, plus she had "an exorbitant amount of money in stocks, bonds and CDs."

"What dollar amount are you talking about?"

The banker rustled with a few papers, looking for the list that separated each by its amount. His fingers started tapping on the calculator.

"If it's okay with you, I'll give the amount in a rounded figure." He slid the written amount over; he couldn't wait to see her reaction.

Sunni nonchalantly picked up the piece of paper. She stood so quickly, her chair fell backwards. She didn't hesitate with a response.

"Oh my God in Heaven, is this for real? This is totally beyond belief. I had no idea my parents were worth this kind of money." Her eyes roamed over the amount, seventeen million dollars. She quickly responded with an unbelievable request.

"I'll take that all in cash."

Mr. Hewlett started laughing. He was sure she was joking with him.

"Would you like that in one-dollar bills?" He continued to laugh.

"What is so damn funny? Do you think I'm kidding?"

He stopped laughing with a single thought, *This is one crazy broad.* He wondered what she would be like in bed.

He needed to explain further. "Miss Harrison, there will be no need to cash all that in. You will shortly have in your hands two million dollars. If I were you, I would let the stocks, bonds and CDs continue to make money for you as your parents did. It's not as if you will ever have need of that much money."

"Mr. Hewlett, you are not me, and you certainly are not my parent. I will do with my money what I choose to do, and that is, I want it all in cash as soon as possible. Do you understand?" Her tone of voice stunned him.

His attitude should have shocked her, but she took no notice.

"Well, Miss Harrison, I hate to tell you this, but you cannot get actual cash. Besides, no one in their right mind would carry that degree of money on their person—in your case in hordes of suitcases. The monies you request will be in the form of a cashier's check. Once you place that check into your personal banking account, you can withdraw any amount you wish within reason.

"But if you really wanted all of that in cash, no bank actually carries that amount on its premises. You would have to give them sufficient time to make these funds available. What you really need is to hire a financial advisor to take care of your affairs. All I need now is your signature on the documents in front of you; it takes time to process the paperwork."

Sunni reclaimed her fallen chair and placed her signature at the spots marked with an X.

"There is one more thing I will need from you, and that is notarized copies of your parents' death certificates. Once I receive them I will turn them over to Mutual Life Insurance. In a matter of weeks you should receive a check for two million dollars. The only other thing that needs to be taken care of is for Harding Home & Car Insurance Co. to finalize their paperwork. As soon as that is taken care of, you will be notified as to the amount you will receive. There's no question your welfare was your parents' main priority. Soon you will have everything your heart desires. What a grand feeling that will be."

Sunni's feelings for Sloan surfaced.

"The one thing I wanted, I lost. So no, Mr. Hewlett, I will not have everything my heart desires."

He was finding out he had a knack for putting his foot in his mouth.

"If my father was so cautious, then why did he have all those containers of gasoline stored in our garage? He knew that was an extreme hazard. I'm sure you are aware that our house fire is under investigation? They came right out and told me it was arson, which is utter nonsense. No one would deliberately cause the death of my parents; they were loved throughout their community.

"In the meantime, do whatever you have to do to make it easier on me. I just don't have the time to deal with this. I will call when I have settled in a permanent residence and have contracted a financial expert. If you encounter any problems I will leave a number where you can reach me, and Mr. Hewlett, I expect you to expedite this matter, or you will be seeking employment elsewhere."

She was feeling the power. Mr. Hewlett would trip over himself in his rush to comply with her wishes. He was thinking of his next paycheck.

Sunni stood, gathering all the copies of the documents she had signed.

The letter with her name scrolled across the center of the envelope was from her mother; she recognized the writing. It would take residence inside her handbag. She strolled out of the banker's office. No thanks were given, nor were there signs of remorse over her parents' deaths.

Sunni put her rented car into reverse and then into drive, gunning the engine as she tore out of the small town. She vowed never again to return; she was taking her money and running. She was headed towards Chicago, then a flight to New York, the place she would eventually call home. She would not read the letter from her mother for several weeks. Sunni was now in a hurry; she had a new life to live and live it she would. The suitcase bearing the weight of the documentation declaring her wealth would stay locked and stored in her dorm room closet. She would continue with her schooling. She desired her degree; she needed to prove now more than ever she was somebody without a show of her parents' money. Three more years till graduation; she had the patience to endure. She will not spare any expense when she opens the doors to what will be called Ni's House of Design. In time, Sunni will have a waiting list for her services.

CHAPTER ELEVEN

Simon could not get his paper out fast enough. This town was boosting his creativity in writing. If this continued he might have to hire someone to run his antique business while he devoted all his time to the *Happenings*.

Would he dare the heading to read: "The Doc and his wife went out in a blaze of glory"? Yeah, if he wanted to be run out of town. Oh well, so much for the greatest headline that was sure to have been his best seller. The front page would instead read:

Heartbreak again strikes Mason's Mill

Simon was again counting his money.

When the news was received about the death of the Doc and his wife, the staff at both County Valley Hospital and St. Mary's Hospital went into mourning. Nurses were seen running from various stations repeating what they heard. Sobs were heard up and down the hallways. Some of the nurses requested time off, their grief overtaking them. Many of the residents who had worked hand-in-hand with the Doc and held him in the highest regard wondered what they would do without his support. Doctors were seen shaking their heads in disbelief; some appeared to be hiding their tears, ashamed to show that they too were human.

Mason's Mill needed a doctor immediately. Word spread quickly. Was there a resident doctor looking to take over a well-established private practice? Within two days, that position was filled.

Doctor August Rolan had been renting a house in Franklin County and was looking for a permanent home. He was made aware that Doc Harrison's home was to be rebuilt in a matter of two months. The arson investigation ended with no positive proof. Dr. Rolan jumped at the chance to own his own home that was reasonably priced and close to the hospitals. He was forty-two years of age and single, tall with broad shoulders and thick, medium-length sandy hair that just touched his collar. His eyes were a dark bluish green, and his well-defined lips hungered to be kissed. Name a nurse, any nurse, married or single, that would not give it her all, locking her lips onto his, tossing his body into a supply room if necessary, just to get that fantastic body of his to unite with hers as one.

It did not take long for the townspeople to welcome Dr. Rolan into the fold. The Doc's office was business as usual. No one was aware Dr. Rolan kept himself hidden in a closet. Wishing upon a star would not help change his preference.

Henry White needed Dr. Rolan's services, medical for now. He had twisted his ankle and could barely walk when, with the assistance of crutches, he hobbled into the new doctor's office without an appointment. Dr. Rolan was bent over Nurse Ethel's desk filling out a narcotic prescription for a patient pick-up when a tap on the closed frosted window signaled someone's arrival.

Nurse Ethel slid the small window open and then commented, "Mr. White, what a surprise. How are you? Are you here to make an appointment?" Everyone that knew anyone knew Henry White the coroner; he was the only known gay guy residing in Mason's Mill. That was about to change.

"Ethel, I had a mishap and I know it's late in the day, but I need to see the doctor immediately. I think I might have broken my foot or ankle."

Dr. Rolan was finishing up for the day and had just turned away when he heard the sound of distress. He turned back, moving closer to the still opened window. The instant Dr. Rolan's and Henry's eyes made a connection, the sparks flew; Ethel was caught in the cross fire. She then knew why Dr. Rolan was not married. She was stunned, but not appalled; things are as they are. She was not judgmental. Henry was helped into one of the examination rooms by none other than the doctor himself. Nurse Ethel was told she could take her leave. Scheduled appointments were over for the day. She would not be the one to spread the word; she refused to be Simon's partner in crime.

Another weekend was here. Many days had passed since the death of the Doc and his wife. Harriet was being seen daily by a resident doctor waiting on Marc and Ben to assign her care to the new doctor in town. It was Ben's weekend off. He called Marc to ask if he would like some company. He felt the need to console him as well as be consoled. He was about to knock when Marc opened the door. Marc immediately wrapped his arms around Ben. Ben was right about displaying his feelings. They took turns comforting one another. It was Marc who brought up the subject of his mother.

"I guess we turn Mother's care over to Dr. Rolan."

"I'm sure he's a good doctor, Marc. We really don't have much of a choice. He's already taken over the Doc's practice; from what I've been told, everyone seems pleased with Doc's replacement. We really shouldn't put off calling him; his answering service can relay the message. What do you think?"

"Absolutely, and I want to make sure he does the tests the Doc initially signed for."

Marc hesitated a moment, shaking his head.

"I still can't believe he's gone. Mom is going to miss him terribly. I hate having to tell her how he died. When she awakens, this news could put her back where she is now."

"We will not tell her until we know for sure her recovery is complete. When she asks 'Where is Doc,' we simply say he's away on vacation. I hate to lie to her, but I'll do whatever it takes to keep her safe."

"I agree. Let's give the new doctor a call."

Dr. Rolan returned their call immediately. Marc answered, telling him what his relationship was to the patient in question. He told him everything he thought was important and about the tests Dr. Harrison had already put in a request for. The doctor's voice was crisp and seemed concerned about Harriet's present condition and the pregnancy, but above all, the tone in his voice seemed genuine and very caring.

"Mr. Anderson, I'm presently at the hospital. I will review your mother's records and all the tests Dr. Harrison ordered will be carried out. I will do a follow-up on her condition the minute I'm through talking with you. The tests Dr.

Harrison had arranged will need to be rescheduled. Other than that, everything will remain the same.

"I'm going to put in a rush order on the ultrasound only because of her present state. Let us plan on you being at the hospital around 7:30 a.m. Monday, but if for some reason this test cannot be carried out that day I'll let you know. The blood test results will take a few days, but the ultrasound will tell me what I need to know immediately. And Mr. Anderson, I want you to be prepared to see what the wonders of technology have given to us. You will be given the privilege of actually seeing for the very first time your baby brother or sister in action."

"Dr. Rolan, this is one appointment that will not be cancelled."

"How about the father, will he also be coming?"

"Are you kidding? You could padlock the doors, bar the windows and send in a posse, he'd find a way in." Marc managed to extract a hearty laugh from Dr. Rolan. This doctor was a keeper.

"Then I'll plan on seeing you both at the appointed time. Until then, take care."

Marc liked the doctor's attitude and his seemingly happy disposition.

Marc and Ben continued their nightly visitation with Marc's mother, her condition not showing any improvement. Monday morning couldn't come fast enough. They arrived early: 7:13 a.m. to be exact. Ben had asked for time off; his request granted, his shift would be covered. They were shown to the waiting room and told they would be called when everything was set up and Harriet was made comfortable. Minutes passed, then an hour. They were seen pacing the room.

A nurse approached them. She was a young girl probably the same age as Marc. She was a tiny pretty blond with a french braid that draped past her waist. Her complexion was milky white. In the more than an hour in her presence, she was seen smiling all the time. This girl had a happy soul.

"Dr. Rolan wanted me to inform you that your mom is sleeping and that he is attempting to wake her. He thinks if she's awake and hears her baby's heartbeat for the first time this could trigger her awareness. It's just a trial run. He asks for your patience until she comes around."

Ben and Marc continued with their pacing. Another thirty minutes passed. Finally the smiling nurse escorted them into the room containing the ultrasound equipment, and their beloved Harriet. She had her eyes opened, although it appeared she was still lost within herself. Marc approached her first, gently placing a kiss upon her cheek and telling her who he was. Ben did the same, only his kiss was upon her lips.

The technician was a woman of large proportions, age somewhere in the thirties, short frizzy hair and pitted, rough skin. Her outward appearance was not pleasing to the eye; her personality was what won them over. Her name was Tina.

Tina raised Harriet's gown to expose her stomach; a sheet tucked below her abdomen was secured from her hips down. Marc and Ben's sharp intake of breath when her belly was exposed caught the attention of Dr. Rolan.

"I'm guessing by the look on your faces you've never seen a pregnant woman's stomach?"

Ben was the first to speak out. Marc's mouth continued to hang open.

"Dr. Rolan, there has to be something wrong. She's huge, almost to the point of being grotesque."

It did not get past Dr. Rolan that Harriet did appear much larger than she should be considering her expected due date, but he did not want to cause any undue alarm until proved otherwise; after all, Dr. Harrison was strictly going by the readings on the machine, which can sometimes be faulty.

"What the two of you fail to take into account is her size. She is, according to our records, five feet tall. If you were to put her belly on an average-size woman she would appear small."

Ben could envision his sweetheart's belly being stretched on the frame of a tall woman. Dr. Rolan's explanation was reasonable. Marc finally closed his mouth, for he too had been listening, and from the doctor's point of view that seemed feasible.

Ben and Marc's world was about to be turned upside down.

Tina squirted a gel onto Harriet's stomach. She then placed a handheld device over the goo and started making circles on different areas of Harriet's belly, all the while watching a screen that looked like a television, only this picture was totally different. Dr. Rolan never took his eyes off the screen. Ben and Marc did not know what they were looking at.

Dr. Rolan finally spoke. "Ben and Marc, I want you to take a look at your baby—. Wait a minute, go back. Yes, right there…. Oh my, what have we got here?"

Ben and Marc looked at one another. No matter what the doctor said in reference to Harriet's stomach, they now knew something was wrong and Dr. Rolan was about to confirm it. They held onto each other, ready to offer comfort.

The doctor began pointing out a previous site.

"Go back a slight bit…yes, there it is. This is unbelievable. Let's make a confirmation on this.

Repeat the process, only slower this time. I want to make sure I'm seeing what I'm seeing. Do you agree?"

"I agree, Dr. Rolan."

Dr. Rolan and Tina moved closer to the screen, moving their heads back and forth. They looked at one another, nodding their heads. It was finally confirmed.

Dr. Rolan told Ben and Marc to take a chair. They had been standing throughout the test, now they were being told to sit. No one is ready to hear bad news. They couldn't take much more tragedy in their lives, and yet what does a person do but accept the inevitable?

"I want you to watch the screen carefully. I will tell you what you are looking at; after a while you too will become aware of what you are seeing."

More goo was added as Tina repeated the process. Images began to appear. She turned the ultrasound machine over to Dr. Rolan. She found many of the doctors liked playing (her selected word) with the machine, although they were always asking for her help, as their knowledge of the workings of the machine was very limited. Dr. Rolan started pointing out the various pictures on display.

"This here is Baby A. Do you see the face?"

Marc and Ben both replied they did, smiling broadly. Their baby was sucking its thumb. Everything was okay. They were relieved.

"Now do you see this baby's face?" They again replied with a yes. "Well, that's Baby B."

Marc and Ben glanced at each other. Shock was written on their faces. Ben couldn't speak; he was dumbfounded.

Marc took the initiative, leaving no room for doubt in his mind. He wasn't thinking about Ben. "Dr. Rolan, are you telling us we are going to have twins?"

"Before I answer that, I want you both to look at the screen again. Do you see this baby's face?" Again they both nodded their heads, they thought they were looking at the face they had just seen, and their baby appeared to be waving at them.

"Well, that face belongs to Baby C." They couldn't comprehend what they were being told. Dr. Rolan was smiling broadly. "Congratulations, you are going to have triplets."

Ben was not saying a word. His face took on a shade of ash. Marc was ecstatic. He jumped up laughing and shouting, thanking Tina the technician, and shaking Dr. Rolan's hand, while Ben was being ignored. Marc then realized Ben was in a state of bewilderment. He began to shake him, bringing him out of his stupor.

Ben finally acknowledged him.

"I can't believe it; I'm going to be the daddy of three babies? Boy, is Harriet going to need us."

"You bet she will, but oh, what a joy this is going to be."

Dr. Rolan gave them the necessary time to gather their thoughts.

"If I can detect the sexes, would you like to know?"

Spoken as if rehearsed, they both reacted with the same response. "No, this is one surprise… oops, three, that we want to celebrate as a family."

"Okay then. Are you ready to hear their heartbeats for the first time? The volume will be turned up, to hopefully get some kind of reaction from their mommy. I'm going to talk to Harriet first; I want to see if I can get her hyped up over the news. I would like to use her first name, if that meets with your approval? It seems as if patients are more responsive if they think of me as a friend."

Marc and Ben nodded their heads, giving their approval. They were taking a liking to this new doctor more and more.

"Harriet, I have some fantastic news. Are you ready to be a mommy three times over? Yes, that's right, you are expecting triplets. You are definitely going to have your hands full with three babies to care for. Their daddy is standing right here by your side, grinning from ear to ear. He's waiting for you to acknowledge his presence. Marc your son is also here. He can't contain himself. You talk about happy…he has a smile never to be erased. Everyone is waiting to hear your babies' heartbeats for the first time; I pray you can also hear them."

Ben noticed a slight hand twitch from Harriet. Was he about to witness a miracle? Dr. Rolan, the technician and Marc had their attention focused on the screen.

Ben was the only one to notice. Then it happened again. He tugged on Marc's arm, using hand gestures to refer to Harriet's movement. Marc noticed. Ben was not imagining his sweetheart's movement.

The heartbeat from Baby A sounded loud and clear. Marc and Ben positioned themselves on each side of Harriet's bed, each taking a hand. Dr. Rolan moved the machine slightly to accommodate Marc as he took his place beside his mother.

The heartbeat from Baby B sounded slightly louder. Harriet began moving her eyes back and forth, up and down, and her head turned towards the rhythm of the heartbeats. Dr. Rolan was astounded; the babies' heartbeats were forcing their mommy to acknowledge their existence.

Baby C's heartbeats were possibly the loudest, and with those beats Harriet began to come around. She continued rolling her eyes back and forth until at last she managed to focus on Marc. She then turned her head towards Ben when he spoke her name. The two people she loved most in the world began to cry. She tried to reach out, but it was an impossible task. She will manage to overcome that obstacle with help and determination. Marc and Ben could not have gotten any closer had they been in bed with her.

Harriet spoke, but barely above a whisper; it was quite an effort.

"Marc, where am I?"

"You're in the hospital, Mom, but everything is okay. You've been in sort of a dream state. I know about the pregnancy, Mom, and I am thrilled. It sure took you long enough to make me a brother."

Harriet smiled that one-dimpled smile of hers, causing Marc and Ben to again cry. Marc's mother was back. Ben's soon-to-be bride had returned from the land of the lost.

She was now giving her full attention to every word spoken.

"Mom, you were given an ultrasound. We just found out you are going to have triplets. It's a blessing three times over. Do you understand what I'm saying?"

Her voice would remain but a whisper for several days. "Three babies…I'm carrying three babies?" She turned her head, looking into the face of the man she had loved, it seemed, for a lifetime. Tears were collecting in her eyes. Ben brushed her tears aside.

"Sweetheart, do you think you will finally say yes to my proposal of marriage? We can't have all our babies being raised without their daddy underfoot, now can we?"

Harriet's vast amounts of tears were not wasted.

"Oh, my darling Ben, I have loved you from day one. Yes, my love, I will marry you."

Marc turned his head, giving them a moment to embrace and kiss. All these years he must have been wearing blinders not to recognize the signs. The years Ben practically camped outside their driveway in his patrol car. When leaving his home Marc would always give a wave, never really understanding. How many times is someone allowed to be stupid?

Dr. Rolan was enjoying their moment. Harriet was told she would be staying the remainder of her pregnancy at the hospital. She was told this was only a precaution because multiples usually come early; how early there was no way to tell.

"The babies will be monitored around the clock. Any changes that we feel would endanger their lives as well as yours, and we will take immediate action. According to the ultrasound you're twenty-four weeks into your pregnancy. I would like for you to carry the wee ones for another nine weeks; in my opinion, thirty-three weeks is their safety zone."

She continued to nod her head along with her lover Ben and son Marc.

"Harriet, Ben and Marc have already been given the grand tour; I think it's now time for mommy to pay her babies a visit."

The technician moved the machine closer to her bed. Tina felt privileged to be given such an honor, to show this woman the happy side of life in the face of what she had gone through. The tragic circumstances surrounding Harriet's admittance into the nursing home had become well known when bits of information leaked out of her small town and spread into the adjoining communities. Tina and thousands like her read the tabloids.

Tina again applied the goo and with the hand-held device began to search out the babies. They maintained their prior positions; it was getting to be a bit crowded. When Baby A appeared, she was still sucking her thumb. (Yes, it was a girl.) A precious thumb sucker caught on film. Harriet managed to bring her hand to her mouth, choking on her tears. She could not speak.

When Baby B appeared, its face was closer to the screen, the eyes were open and this baby was smiling. (Sex unavailable.)

Baby B's magical smile brought forth that captivating smile of Harriet's, her face still wet with tears. Was that a lone dimple matching its mommy's? A further look left no doubt, another treasure on film. Ben would be held captive in his own home.

The final blessing was Baby C sound asleep, although making movements with its lips as if sucking from a baby bottle or nipple, whichever will be Harriet's desired choice. Knowing Harriet there will be no doubting Thomases in her town; her breasts will see much action.

Harriet could not take her eyes off the screen, nor could Ben and Marc. This was a matinee never to be forgotten.

"I asked Ben and Marc earlier if they wanted to know the sexes. They declined, not wanting to make any decisions without you. I think we're past the point of determining their sex, they're starting to lose space, but with a lot of cooperation from them, I could try, if that is your wish."

All three looked at each other, reading the others' thoughts. They chose to be surprised. Baby A's announcement would also have to wait. Dr. Rolan would have said the same thing if his selection of a partner had been different. The countdown to delivery would now begin.

It would take another three days before Harriet would ask that all-important question, "What brought me to the hospital?"

CHAPTER TWELVE

Harriet's mind had erased the memory of the night she lost her beloved best friend Beth and her family. Ben and Marc were visiting at their usual evening time. They decided they would accompany each other on their nightly visitation. This would greatly help Marc, school already in process. Harriet was now sitting up, slowly being introduced to soft foods. She was regaining her strength. She was beyond happy. That smile would leave her face very shortly.

She wanted to know what had happened to her. Ben and Marc thought again about lying, but hiding the facts would not alter what had happened. They decided to come right out and tell her. They each took one of Harriet's hands. She knew at that moment something dreadful had happened, but what? She was a psychic, why did she not know? Had she lost her abilities to see the past and predict the future? Did her pregnancy remove that power?

Ben and Marc decided earlier on which of them would be the one to break the news. A coin toss would decide which of them would tell her: heads would win, tails would lose. Ben won, if you would call that winning. He prayed he would find the words to lessen the pain, if there were such words.

"Sweetheart, tucked inside that dreaded place you chose to enter is an unbearable sadness that took you away from us. That grief is shared by all, but because of the special bond between you and Beth, no one can measure up to your pain."

Harriet's hands twisted tightly into theirs, she let out a piercing scream. Her memory of the horror of that night was brought forth; she was reliving the nightmare. She returned to the living only to face the Grim Reaper. Two nurses and one doctor came rushing into her room. The resident doctor yelled out an order for Demerol; a low dosage would not harm the babies. He needed to bring some calm to the patient.

She surrendered to the shot, but not to sleep. The doctor and the nurses, secure with the knowledge Harriet had returned to her somewhat former self, took their leave, telling Marc and Ben to alert them immediately if another episode occurred. Harriet continued to weep. Ben and Marc allowed her this time. Loving someone deeply stabs away at your heart when that special person dies, but that kind of love is a gift, for without it, there are no memories. Her weeping would not stop; maybe this was the time to give her the good news.

Ben had his arm tucked around the babies, feeling their constant thumps; their space was growing smaller with each passing day. "Sweetheart, I do have some great news; it might help to lessen some of your pain."

Harriet wiped her eyes with the offered Kleenex; she would welcome any kind of relief from her unbearable grief.

"Sweetheart, Sloan is alive. God spared her. A part of your beloved Beth will continue to live on through her daughter. But for the time being she has gone missing. This happened shortly after the burials. I think she's running away from herself, trying to escape the horror of that night. She needs to lose herself before she can again find herself. Do you understand what I mean?"

"Oh Ben, yes, I do understand, but I also need to know if she is safe and where she has taken herself. Do you understand me?"

"There isn't a town that doesn't have her poster hanging from its windows. She can't stay away indefinitely. This is where she belongs, and when she does return, our home will be her home."

"Oh yes, Ben, we will love and care for her as if she is our own. Beth would be so pleased." She again started weeping. She would shed more tears than the worst of storms.

Ben and Marc would not continue with a tale of woe, the tragedy of Doc and his wife Miriam will have to wait.

CHAPTER THIRTEEN

The knock on the door startled Cindy Bingington. She had been concentrating intently on reviewing her studies for class the next morning. She had received her law degree years ago, but because of her confinement to a sanitarium eight years prior she needed to take refresher courses. She was now a student at Northwestern University here in Chicago.

She noticed the time—9:37 p.m. No one had ever knocked on her door at this time of the night. She was in her nightgown and wondered if she should answer. She remembered well the advice from her mother, "Never take chances if there is a possibility harm could come to you." Cindy brushed the thought aside and rose from her chair, setting her reading glasses down on her paperwork. She retrieved her housecoat from the hook on the backside of the bathroom door and wrapped the colorful lightweight garment around her, making sure to pull the collar close around her neck and to secure the belt before she answered the door. The peephole was damaged by the last tenants and had yet to be replaced.

She edged the door open ever so slightly.

"Can I help you?"

"Yes, please. I am really sorry to interrupt you, but I seem to have lost my apartment key. I live in building two. Would you mind if I used your telephone to call my friend who has a duplicate key?"

Cindy had acquired an apartment near the loop off Michigan Avenue near the school. Two apartment complexes sat side by side; she was on the main level of building one. This apparently was one of the residents. She had yet to make friends with any of the other tenants, since her schooling demanded her full attention. She welcomed in the night caller.

The instant the door was again secured with its deadbolt, the caller's rubber-gloved hands shoved a gun into Cindy's back. She was told not to scream; if she did not heed this advice, she would not see the night end. *Mother knows best,* she thought—she should have listened. She started to cry. She had just reclaimed her life and was getting it back on track, and now this, whatever "this" was.

"You are expecting the sheriff to pay you a visit, are you not?"

Cindy was puzzled with that question. "I have no idea what you are talking about."

"Don't play stupid with me, lawyer woman. Yeah, I know all about your rehabilitation, your return to society, your deep desire to help people with problems. Well now, tell me, how are you going to help yourself?"

"I am expecting Ben Davidson who is a friend of mine, but I don't know how it is any concern of yours, and I have no idea what you mean by helping myself."

"Let me tell you how it concerns me, and how you cannot help yourself. You remember Timmy, don't you? Of course you do. I'm proud to say I was the one that murdered that little retard."

The caller took a bow. Cindy gasped at that degrading word. The caller's high-pitched laugh rang out. She knew this person. She tried to put a name to the face standing before her, but drew a blank. She continued to look deeply into the caller's eyes, the windows to the soul. She jerked back; those eyes drew her into a whirling mass of darkness where the worst kind of evil dwelled. Satan in comparison would have been a friend. The bell rang; she had a name. Cindy had never forgotten that day and everything that transpired. She should have told her parents when her memory returned; she should have told someone, anyone. Although not yet known, she would die with that knowledge, never knowing the bodies that would continue to pile up. A single gloved hand reached out. Cindy didn't have time to react before she was forced down upon her sofa.

"For all your smarts, you really were rather stupid in one regard. You should never have put your address in the phone directory, for without that I never would have found you." The caller's explosive laughter made Cindy nauseous.

"I am not going to enjoy this. I usually torture my victims. I cannot do this to you. Do you want to know why?"

No comment was forthcoming from Cindy's mouth. She was afraid for her life, as well she should be. She allowed what she thought was a resident neighbor into her home, but instead evil came knocking and would leave no calling card.

"You are going to take your own life. Now don't shake your head no. I'll tell you what; I'll give you a choice. How about that? I usually don't do that with my victims. My method is to bash, strangle, burn, or whatever I deem appropriate at that moment. This is my proposition: I can kill your parents or you can take your own life. Which will it be, parents or you? Come on, come on. It's a toss-up, isn't it, but the decision is entirely yours."

Cindy was face-to-face with a person whose sanity was not in question. The gun was pressed close to her face. She could not risk her parents' lives; she loved them dearly. They gave up their lives to save hers. She would now have to give up her life to save theirs. She gave the caller her answer. The caller was excited with her choice.

"You are to write a letter of confession and a good-bye. The letter will be addressed to your parents."

The caller then grabbed a mass of Cindy's hair and pulled her into the kitchen. She cried out in pain, holding her head in the direction of the pull to try to reduce the stress on her scalp. The caller shoved her down into the chair, punching her head repeatedly with a fist. Cindy continued to howl in pain, pleading with her attacker to stop. Her sobs for help went unheard; she was alone in her agony with a lunatic.

A piece of paper carefully torn from Cindy's writing pad was placed in front of her along with a pen. Cindy threw the pen to the floor. The caller grabbed the hand that threw the pen and proceeded to bend back the fingers. The excruciating pain brought forth a scream like no other. The caller stopped, shoving a hand over Cindy's mouth. The victim's bloodshot eyes bulged from the intense pain.

"The next time you pull a stunt like that, I will break every finger, starting with this one." A hard yank on Cindy's thumb brought forth a flood of tears. She couldn't believe the pain endured with just a finger. She continued to cry, she couldn't stop.

"What you are going to write must match the handwriting in your notepad, understood?" Cindy nodded; what choice did she have?

"How do you address your parents?"

Cindy tearfully answered, "I call them Mother and Father."

The severe punch directly into her spine forced her to fall face forward onto her kitchen table. She again screamed out in agony.

"You lying bitch."

A letter in the works with the heading "Mom and Dad" had been placed within one of her law books. Cindy planned on placing the letter into a safety deposit box when it was finished. When she attained the title of attorney-at-law, she intended to mail it. The contents of the letter were to be a never-ending thank you. But now parents will never know the extent of her undying love and gratitude.

Cindy began begging for her life.

"I should never have deceived you, I am sorry. Please don't hurt me; I can't take the pain. Have you no heart?"

The response was another slam to the back. Piercing screams sounded out. Cindy was on the verge of collapse. A hand was immediately placed over her mouth.

"If you scream out like that again, I will be forced to gag you, understand?" The hand was removed. Cindy tearfully mouthed "yes." The caller noticed the eyeglasses and asked if she needed them to write; Cindy knew better than to lie. She continued sobbing as she began to write what she was told.

Dear Mom and Dad, I cannot think of anything harder than what I'm about to tell you. I want you to understand it had nothing to do with either of you; do not lay guilt upon yourselves. You raised me beautifully, but something evil was brewing inside of me over which I had no control. I can't continue to live a life of deceit. Tell Sheriff Ben to stop looking, I was the one that killed Timmy. Yes, it was I. I can visualize both of you shaking your heads, but what I'm telling you is the truth.

That terrible, terrible day that Timmy died, my nerves were in shambles. I could not get my mind off my upcoming position in the law firm. Would I be what they expected? Would I crumble under the pressure and disappoint you both? Timmy was at his worst; he was in one of his mood swings. I could not control him. He refused to do what I asked of him. I felt the need to punish him and punish him I did.

I remember on that day the questions put before me, but I felt as if I were in a haze. At some point reality jumped in when Sheriff Ben told me my little Timmy was dead. My honorable self returned long enough to realize the gruesome act I inflicted upon my little friend. That must have been when my body shut down and I went into shock.

When I finally awakened all these years later the evil that resided inside me had vanished. I knew I was back to being me. I felt cleansed and happy. I was ready to confess, but each time I saw you both I knew that confession would destroy your lives. Never again would you have peace or happiness. There would be scorn everywhere you went. People would grow to hate you for loving me. I decided to forget that hideous act of murder and go on with my life.

I was planning on telling Ben when he did call on me, that I had no memory of that day, then last week daily headaches erupted along with nightmares. I couldn't go on. I had committed a monstrous crime. I needed to be punished, but what punishment would be good enough? None, absolutely none. Suicide was my only option. Mom and Dad, there is no way I could put you through a trial lasting months, maybe even years. I don't believe God in all His goodness will ever forgive me. To ask for the Fossolds' forgiveness would be disgraceful.

Please tell Ben to forgive me for not telling him years ago — this had to have weighed heavily on his shoulders. All I ask of you is to remember the good times, forgive the bad.

P.S. If you still have doubt, I was never told how Timmy died or where his body was discovered. The tool I used was a large rock and the damage done to his head was extreme. When I finished with him I threw his body into the Swimming Hole.

Please love me, for God cannot.

Cindy

The caller was giddy; the letter was refreshing, for Cindy did as she was told. The next part would leave the caller anticipating more torture in the future. Cindy's prints on the letter and the envelope addressed to "Mom and

Dad" would convince the authorities they need not look further for another source; it would be determined to be Cindy's handwriting.

"Come, we must not leave a bloody mess behind on such nice carpet. The bathroom is the appropriate place to perform surgery."

Cindy's sobbing had not let up, but when the word *surgery* was used, she started to scream for help. She was again silenced with a hard slug to her back, forcing her to fall forward onto the tile floor in the bathroom. She scrambled to stand up. The caller allowed this; Cindy needed to be in the tub.

The caller turned on the faucet, considered using hot water, but thought better; no need to scald before the slice.

"Remove your clothes and climb in the tub." Cindy remained standing.

"You must be aware that this is your hour of death." A raging laugh erupted from the caller. Cindy was frantic at this point, again begging for her life. Tears and snot were pouring forth, covering her face. She gave the appearance of someone deranged.

"Please don't do this; I beg of you, I don't want to die. The eight years I lost can never be recovered; please don't take the remainder please…please…"

Her death wish was ignored. "Please, I want to live." Bloodshot eyes bulging, Cindy watched the caller take her razor from the medicine cabinet and carefully remove the newly replaced blade. Her eyes could not have opened any wider had someone stretched them to their full extent. She finally realized there would be no more tomorrows, no more birthdays, no more holidays, and no further dreams about her future. She wanted one more minute, one second to hold her Mom and Dad. Her life had but a few minutes.

The caller twisted and tugged on her hair, forcing her into the bathtub. Water splashed onto the floor as Cindy collapsed into the nearly full tub. She no longer cried. She began to pray the Hail Mary.

The caller's laugh raged on.

"I want you to place one palm up, then the other, until you have sliced through both wrists. You must cut deeply; otherwise I will use the razor to turn your face into hamburger. It would not be a pretty sight for your parents to identify. Now cut."

Cindy looked upward, leaving earth behind. She did not feel the pain, for her God was with her as she sliced deeply into her wrists. Only a slight amount of blood appeared at first, but when she applied an excessive amount of pressure, first to one wrist and then to the other, the blood poured forth. Cindy slowly began to descend into the crimson-colored water. She would never again be awoken with the nightly horrors that tormented her over the death of her sweet Timmy. Her eyeglasses would never again frame the face of a soon-to-be lawyer when facing the judge in preparation for her first trial; they would be the caller's keepsake. It was time for the caller to catch a plane.

The habitual ring of Cindy's phone call to her parents' house each morning at precisely 6:15 a.m. would never again be heard. They knew something was not right when their daughter's black-rimmed eyeglasses were not among her belongings. They decided against telling those in charge of the investigation, choosing instead to confide only in someone they totally trusted. Cindy's burial would be very small and private; those in attendance would be her parents and a priest.

Mr. and Mrs. Bingington would not be moving back to Mason's Mill; they would remain close to their daughter, very close.

CHAPTER FOURTEEN

Ben had just pulled in front of the police station when Robert, on the lookout for his patrol car, came running towards him. On the way he side-swiped a dog's dropping and shook his head in disgust. He knew he would be the one cleaning up that mess. Robert liked things kept neat; having a dog would not provide that.

"Ben, you got a call. I think it's an emergency."

Ben also shook his head, although for a different reason. *Good grief, enough with the emergencies.*

Tomorrow, Ben would leave for Chicago. His suitcase was packed, the ticket tucked in his wallet. He could not wait. Cindy would reveal the killer responsible for little Timmy's death. Soon Ben would be credited with putting the murderer behind bars. This would be his first big arrest. This investigation that was thrown to the wind would be recalled. Finally Ben's day had come.

Harriet was now gaining strength with each day and was agreeable with Ben's departure. She too was excited for him, knowing he was proud of his profession; all he ever wanted was to follow through and be completely satisfied with an investigation, any investigation. It would be his day to prove not only to the residents but his superiors as well what a great cop he is and always will be.

Ben climbed out of his car, tucked in his shirt, pulled up his pants, straightened his tie, adjusted his hat, walked up the steps and proceeded through the door.

This would end up being the worst day in his career in more ways than one.

With a flick of his wrist, Ben tossed his hat onto the metal hat rack. He never wore his hat inside the station; for some reason it didn't feel right. Oh well, that was his quirk.

The receiver was lying on its side, waiting for the proper person to pick it up. Ben felt a foreboding. If not, then why was his gut starting to cramp? He could not help himself, he hesitated, giving way to his thoughts. *What if I don't answer, and then whoever is on the other end gets tired of waiting and hangs up? Bad news averted. But what if it isn't bad news, but good?*

"Hello, this is Sheriff Ben Davidson speaking. Sorry to keep you waiting, there was a bit of an emergency." Emergency, what emergency? Did he not just say "enough with the emergencies"?

"Sheriff Davidson, this is Police Chief Roger Walker with the 23rd District in Chicago. I regret to tell you that I have some bad news. Had it not been for the discovery of two letters I would not be making this call. One of the letters was addressed to you personally from Mrs. Bingington, the other was in reference to you and some information you were seeking in a murder case.

"Cindy Bingington and her parents, Ken and Sarah Bingington, were found dead of apparent suicides. The day after the Bingingtons buried their daughter, we sent an investigating officer over to see them. We needed to clear up a few details so we could close the investigation. They were aware of our visit, so when the officer received no response to his knock, he called the apartment manager to unlock the door. Their bodies were discovered, side by side, holding hands. They each had their own revolver; all it took was a single gunshot to their mouths. Their daughter's death without doubt caused them to end their lives. We have a few loose ends to tie up, and then I will forward the letters over to you."

Ben was a man of many words, but his response belied this.

"I'll be waiting."

He felt as if the world had slid out from under him. Something was dreadfully wrong, his gut was screaming. He needed to start another investigation… Yeah, right. He couldn't get an investigation going in his own town, and he expected the authorities' full cooperation in a case out of their jurisdiction. This would be deemed a hopeless case. He lost the ability to control himself; the telephone went flying across the room. He pounded his fist on his desk and let out a howling scream, his anger no longer contained.

Ben's words to God were sincere.

"Please, God in heaven, tell me what is happening."

Robert ran to his side, but not before he picked up the telephone and replaced it in its rightful place, making sure the connection had not been disrupted. Neatness was always a high priority, no matter the situation. Ben had his head positioned between his hands, fingers working circles on his forehead, his elbows stationary on his desk.

"Ben what happened? Can I help?"

Ben dropped his hands, shaking his head. "No one can help. You know, Robert, there's an old saying, 'It's not over until the fat lady sings.' Well, I guess she just sang her last song."

He stood up, gave his deputy a slap on the back with an announcement.

"I'm going to the hospital. If the station blows up, a dog gets hit by a car, or if you see Willie boy running, don't call me, because frankly I just don't give a damn."

Robert had never seen such behavior from his superior. Should he call the chief of police? Was his boss having a meltdown? If he reported him, would Ben lose his job? Would Ben hate him, if he did? Robert started pacing back and forth, this was definitely a dilemma. This was not a neat situation. He stopped pacing. He could be king for a day, be in charge. He never thought his moment would come. Robert claimed Ben's chair of honor and began to smile. He prayed for the day to never end.

Should he be careful what he prays for?

Ben pulled into the designated spot at the hospital and hugged the steering wheel. He needed to hear the words he was thinking and if someone noticed him talking to himself, he could care less.

"How can I dump all of what I just learned onto my sweetheart's lap? She's been through enough. But God, I need to talk to someone other than You. I need to see an actual face and hear an actual response. Sorry, no offence, but that's the way I feel."

He opened the patrol car door, pulled himself together, shut the door and headed straight for Harriet's room. Her eyes were closed; she was doing what the doctor ordered, complete bed rest. Though she was now walking, her only chore was bathroom duty.

Ben's thoughts poured forth while basking in his lover's beauty, stomach and all.

"My beautiful sweetheart, you have given to me far more than I deserve. You are my universe, the other half of my soul. When death does come calling it will not lay claim to that love, for it is rightfully yours."

Harriet's eyes opened. She could feel her lover's presence, she could imagine his breath upon her face, and his very essence filled the room. She raised her arms, welcoming her lover into them. Ben was not casual with his walk from the doorway; he ran into her arms. He buried his head onto her chest, stomach preventing a head lap. He starting weeping; he needed Harriet's comfort and confidence. She would put his world back into perspective. She gently stroked his head, knowing that whatever was wrong, he needed this release. When Ben's weeping slowed to a sad sob, Harriet gently pulled his head upward, looking deep into his eyes.

"Oh my darling, I can't bear to see you in such distress. My heart feels like a hammer and with every beat struck, it wants to pound out your anguish and despair. Please let me help you."

Ben raised his hand; his fingers began stroking the wrinkles in her concerned forehead. "It seems as if the world has collapsed around me, and I can't put it back where it belongs. Everything is falling apart, and no matter how hard I work at trying to fix it, it never seems to be good enough. I just want an out."

"Now you listen to me, Sheriff Ben Davidson, I didn't fall in love with a quitter. You have more guts and determination in your one finger than all the men in Mason's Mill. You would go to the ends of this so-called collapsed world and mend what is broken if it took your entire life — you are that kind of man. Your strength is the glue that binds our town together. Without you to guide the townspeople, Mason's Mill would cease to exist."

Ben knew that without Harriet's love and guidance, he would cease to exist. He had a sad tale to tell. She listened. When all was said, they embraced, their arms providing a great measure of relief and comfort.

He pulled up a chair, giving his sweetheart her much-needed room upon the single bed. She took both of his hands and placed them onto her stomach; one hand would not suffice. She was careful not to disturb the babies' heart monitors; they would remain secured until delivery.

The babies were having the time of their lives, activity in full swing. Ben and Harriet's joyous laughter rang out at their antics, something they desperately needed in their time of grief.

Ben left his sweetheart's room with a spring in step. He would return to work.

Murder would end his day.

CHAPTER FIFTEEN

Ben returned to the station and was about to park when Robert came tearing out the door, missed a step and tumbled down the remaining steps, letting out a howl of pain in the process. Ben quickly put the patrol car in park, turned off the engine, and ran to his deputy's side. He knelt on one knee, his hand touching Robert's shoulder, showing his concern.

"Are you all right?"

"Oh God, Ben, I think I might have broken something. The pain is God-awful."

"Don't move. I'll see if Dr. Rolan is available."

Robert grabbed a hold of Ben's arm as Ben started to rise. "Ben, I was running for a reason. Norman just called. Frantic would best describe his tone of voice. He said the next-in-command at the bank called and told him Mr. Hewlett didn't show up for work this morning, and because the cabin was Willie's second home, he asked him to check it out. I told him to do nothing until he hears from you. I feel sorry for Norman, he was crying nonstop; he thinks he's going to lose his job for letting Mr. Hewlett live in the cabin."

Robert noticed the look on Ben's face and responded, "Those are Norman's words, not mine."

Ben had a hard time believing anyone of average intelligence would entrust the responsibilities of managing sixteen cabins to someone whose mental capacity was that of a ten-year-old.

But for now, Ben was more concerned about Robert's fall than "Willie boy." He figured Willie got a hold of something really good last night and decided to stay around for an encore.

Ben had previously advised Willie to stay away from the cabins, but he knew it went in one ear and escaped out the other; once a Casanova always a Casanova. Sugar Daddy he was not, the lining of his pockets hanging out.

"Mr. Hewlett can wait. I'll see if Dr. Rolan is available. I'll be right back; don't you dare move."

"I don't think I could if I wanted to. I'm just sorry I have to put you through this alone."

"Don't you worry about this other nonsense. If anything comes out of it, which I doubt, I will call in another deputy."

Ben ran up the same steps Robert ran down, checking to see if anything was amiss, but everything appeared safe.

Fortunately Dr. Rolan was at his office in town. He would be arriving within minutes. Ben secured a blanket and pillow from the jail's cot. He would not see Norman until his deputy was taken care of.

Dr. Rolan's diagnosis, although without an x-ray, was a fractured ankle. A crowd was beginning to form while they waited on the arrival of the ambulance. It would be a fruitless effort to send them away; for some reason people enjoy the misery of others, God help us.

Robert kept apologizing over and over. Ben was deep in thought trying to come up with a way to shut him up. He was sure Robert was on his hundredth apology when at last the ambulance pulled to a shrieking halt. Surely the paramedics had been informed of the condition of the victim. There was no need for them to burn rubber. Ben was thankful they hadn't collided with another car en route; that would have caused more stress upon his ears with Robert's continued apologies. Ben glanced up into the heavens, thanking God for the ambulance's safe arrival to take Robert away.

Ben was worn out; *done in* was really the correct phrase. Robert had the capacity to tire him out at the start of a day, making the ending downright miserable. But Ben had to admit,

Robert was an excellent deputy; he would stand on his head if Ben so ordered. He was not only dependable, but would work a double shift if he had to use toothpicks to hold his eyelids open. He was never one to complain… well, maybe a time or two; nobody's that perfect.

Ben waved Dr. Rolan and Robert off as the ambulance pulled away. He then trotted over to the cabin's office.

Norman Woodstaff, cabin manager, was fifty-six years of age, nearly bald with a handlebar mustache and full beard. What does not grow on the head, grooms the face. He was short, five-feet-six or -seven, and was thin to the point of being skeletal. No one knew where he came from, nor did they care. Norman wandered into town as a young man years ago and was given his current job and a place to live; he was here to stay. With no friends, he had only himself to chat with. He occupied the living space attached to the office, having all the comforts of a regular home. This was not given with a heart; it was part of his salary as he worked around the clock. During his free time, Norman was given the honor of cabin cleanup.

Ben happened to be standing in line at the bank one day when Norman popped in and instantly began waving. He stood side by side with Ben. He had his weekly payroll check with him, holding it opened with both hands for everyone to see. Ben couldn't help but notice the amount…well not really, but he was curious to see how much Norman was being taken advantage of. The net amount was a measly $31.43. Ben felt badly for the man, but who was he to criticize the owner of the cabins? He gave him credit for providing a roof over Norman's head. Norman had been manager of the cabins for as many years as Ben had been on the police force.

Norman was a nice enough guy but had the annoying habit of constantly rubbing his nose. If someone were deaf and their only means of communication was the reading of lips, that person would have to hold onto Norman's hand to receive his message. He was sitting in the office behind his desk, rubbing away, when Ben strolled in. Norman stood to welcome him.

"I stayed far away from the cabin Mr. Hewlett rented. He told me last night not to disturb him, he needed his sleep. The bank thinks he lives in the cabin. Does he?"

Ben also had a habit of rolling his eyes. He shook his head at Norman's lack of common sense; night was long gone, and daylight had but a few hours remaining.

"Well, it looks like we'll just have to remove that 'Do not disturb' sign, won't we? After all, Mr. Hewlett does have an hour or two to finish up his workday."

Norman laughed. He was going to enjoy this; he never really cared for Mr. Hewlett. He knew Mr. Hewlett thought of him as slow and stupid. But Norman had eyes he used for seeing; he was aware of the women that often snuck into Mr. Hewlett's cabin. If the woman was also tired and wanted to sleep with Mr. Hewlett who would care? Certainly not Norman.

"What cabin did you assign him?"

"He told me he wanted a cabin as far away from you as possible. He said you make too much noise while he's trying to sleep. I put him in Cabin Fourteen. Cabin Fifteen and Sixteen were used. He told me he was okay with that."

Ben shook his head again; he knew the one making the noise.

Ben mouthed out an order, stern he was not. "Get the master key to the cabin just in case he refuses to open up."

They strolled down the road, neither of them in a hurry. If "Willie boy" got wind of their impending approach and tried to make a run for it, Ben could quickly nab him, the daylight in his favor.

Ben did not knock, but nearly pounded his way through the door.

"Open the door, Willie, there are people scanning the globe for you." When no response came forth, Ben was not about to give him a chance to escape through the back door. The key was not necessary; the door was unlocked.

Failure to lock up was not in Willie's best interest. Was he that excited? Did this woman have something more to offer than the ones before her?

Ben pushed Norman back, telling him to step away, this was police business. Norman continued to step back until Ben told him to stop. He was without question rather slow upstairs.

When Ben was about to enter the cabin, he called out again, "Willie, if you're in here, it's time to make it known." He received silence. Ben strolled in. Willie was there lying on the bed. A heavy burgundy cover was tucked around him, his face the only thing visible. The air conditioning was running full blast, and the room was ice cold. A chill swept over Ben, but it was not from the cold of the room. His dependence on his gut did not let him down. The cramp tightened; something was definitely wrong. Ben's hand reached for his holster, unbuckled the snap, and removed his revolver. He again called out to Willie, again no response. He had no alternative. Ben retraced his steps, his back pressed against the now closed front door, revolver now in hand.

"This is the police. You are surrounded, please come out with your hands held up." Not a sound could be heard, the air conditioner refusing to shut off. With both hands clasped to his revolver Ben worked his way towards the only other room, the bathroom. The only thing moving in that cabin was the shower curtain, the air conditioner performing the way it should.

Ben made his way to the bed. Mr. Hewlett's exposed face was a ghastly grey. Ben pressed his fingers to his neck; there was no pulse. He already knew he was looking onto the face of death, but a confirmation was called for.

He stood back with his hands on his hips, revolver now safely tucked away. Ben had little doubt that Willie's heart took its last beat while in the act. He wondered what woman was the last to be pounded, and was she present when he took his last breath? If so, she didn't stay around. She was probably one of the married ones.

Ben continued to look at the sixty-five-year-old man who was above average in looks and height with a full head of dark hair and a carefully trimmed mustache. Mr. Hewlett was known to frequent the gym in Franklin County, and he had a body to be envied by all who saw and knew him, including Ben. But surely it was not the body that attracted so many women to him? Was it because of his position at the bank? Or was it just the thrill of getting it on with someone other than the woman's husband or boyfriend? But above all, how in the world did he manage to support twelve kids while also supporting his cabin habit? Ben had all these questions and many more. Would there be someone to answer them?

No one was in hearing distance when he voiced his comment—certainly not Norman, who was probably still backing away; although he'd been told to stop, his mind sometimes got confused with orders.

"Well, Willie boy, we meet again. This is one time you finally managed to get away from me, although I don't think this is exactly what you had in mind. But like the old saying goes, no good deed goes unpunished, unless your nightly sex sessions were not considered a deed."

With Willie already dead, there was no need to call in the paramedics, but the coroner needed to be called. Henry was recovering from a sprain in his foot, according to Dr. Rolan. Would everyone be limping around town? Henry's foot had been wrapped, he was given a cane, and within days he was able to perform his duties.

Ben removed himself from Cabin 14, locked the door and told Norman to return to his duties.

"Is everything okay, Sheriff? Is Mr. Hewlett missing?"

"Everything is going to be okay, Norman. Thank you for all your help."

Norman liked people that were nice to him; the sheriff always had kind words for him. Norman would always wave and say hello to every passerby, but no one bothered to look his way. Sometimes he would look in the mirror to see if he was there.

Ben would make the call to Henry from the station. He took his time walking the rocky road; it wasn't as if Willie would be going anywhere.

Henry was on the scene within a half hour, aware of a likely heart attack. He pulled up in front of the station in the hearse. He thought Ben might as well grab a short ride, his theory being "why walk if you can ride." He was not keen on exercise, probably because he was gifted with genes that never required a workout. He had quite a knock-out body for a man in his fifties.

When the hearse appeared, Norman stepped out of the office waving excitedly at Mr. White. Ben yelled out to Norman as he climbed into the passenger seat, stating he would return the master key as soon as possible. Norman said it was okay if it was okay with Ben. Did he understand? Ben wasn't about to stay around to pick at his brain, although he was curious to see if it was working at full function. God help us if it were. Norman continued waving long after the hearse made its stop at Cabin 14.

Ben unlocked the secured door, allowing Henry the hobbler to enter. There was no hesitation. He did as Ben had done, felt for a pulse. Having confirmed the absence of a pulse, Henry then pulled back the covers, something Ben should have done; why he did not would cause Ben to have nightmares doubting his abilities as a dedicated police officer.

"Ben, I hate to tell you this, but I think you better think about another profession."

Ben was standing with his back against the front door, arms crossed, waiting to be told his unmedical diagnosis was correct.

"Why, did I miss something?"

Henry continued to hold the cover away from Mr. Hewlett's body.

Ben walked over quickly, taking his place alongside Henry. What he saw made him gasp, placing his hand across his mouth. He ran to the bathroom; this time he managed to make it to the commode before relieving his stomach of its contents.

No medical examiner would be needed. Henry officially pronounced Mr. William Hewlett dead. His diagnosis would not be questioned. Mr. Hewlett expired as a result of blood loss from a partial genital removal. He was naked and the blood that drained from his body had already soaked into the mattress. His penis was severed at its base.

Ben rejoined Henry, apologizing for the race to the bathroom and also for not following through with his initial examination. Henry shushed him; no apology was needed. His slip-up, if that is what you would call it, would remain between the two of them; after all, no harm was done.

They looked at one another. Their thoughts on Mr. Hewlett's penis removal may have been somewhat different, but both agreed that this was savage brutality brought on by pure hate. They did not want to contaminate the crime scene any further, but it appeared Willie's penis had gone missing. They looked as best as they could without disturbing the body. The penis was a no-show. It was time to call in the investigators that handle murder cases on a regular basis; they would photograph the crime scene, collect and tag items for evidence.

Ben walked over to the night stand to use the telephone; rubber gloves were provided by Henry. Ben had to be careful not to disturb any prints the killer may have left behind. Henry stepped outside while Ben made the necessary calls. In a matter of minutes, Ben was seen securing the area with yellow crime tape. Henry had to stay around; he would be the one to remove the body and take it to the morgue.

The cabin now surrounded with yellow tape grabbed the attention of the other cabins' renters. As word spread the townspeople gathered in numbers, desperately seeking the identity of the person or persons to be carried out. Henry stood at the door while Ben tried to control the mob.

Ben shouted to the oncoming crowd, "If any one of you attempt to cross beyond the secured area, you will be arrested, understood?" Many heads started bobbing.

He stepped back from the taped area with a request. "Henry, would you mind keeping an eye on the ones who don't have their ears on? I need to make sure Norman doesn't open his mouth about Mr. Hewlett."

Henry raised his eyebrows and pursed his lips before making a comment. "Good luck with that one."

"Yeah, it's like wishing on a star, but that never works either. I'll just have to give it my best shot. Be back in a flash."

Ben entered the office. Norman was at his desk rubbing away and pretending to read a book. Ben knew he was an illiterate; he signed his name with an X. But with all his faults Norman was a genius at keeping tabs of the money collected from all the tenants. His boss could have cared less about the workings of Norman's mind; his main interest lay in the folds of his money.

Norman jumped; he'd been unaware Ben was standing before him. "Sheriff, I didn't see you. Are you here to give me back my key?" Norman remembered the key and Ben had forgotten. Sometimes you have to give credit where credit is due.

"I forgot about the key. Thank you for reminding me."

Norman ran around his desk and gave Ben a big hug and a huge smile. He was thanked; today was a happy day. Again, it was such a small thing to put a smile on someone's face.

Ben was just about to discuss with Norman what he had come for, when who should appear—none other than Simon Sonderson. He had been running towards what was now common knowledge about a death or deaths in one of the cabins when he caught a glimpse of Ben entering the cabin office.

Simon rushed in, his lips flapping.

"Well, well, Sheriff, it looks like this town is finally catching up with the real world, yellow tape included. Did someone just happen to drop dead or is it something more sinister, like murder?" Was he playing games with Ben or was he really that lame?

Norman's expression was vacant when Simon spoke. Ben prayed he would stay that way.

"Simon, I have better things to do than furnish your paper with what you perceive to be entertainment. What you ought to do is run down the road to where all the commotion is taking place. I'm sure someone will jump at the chance to be included in the scoop of the day."

"Thanks a heap, Sheriff; I never would have given that a thought."

Ben loved to send someone like Simon on a wild goose chase. He would find out that no one really had any answers to all the questions he would put forth. He would be barking up many wrong trees.

Norman was still smiling at Ben.

"Norman, I would like for you to do something for me. It's called pretending. Do you understand?"

"It's like make-believe, right?"

"That's right. Let's make believe you don't know who got into Cabin 14. Let's pretend someone snuck in without you knowing. And if anyone asks you who is in that cabin, what will you say?"

"I don't know who is in that cabin, somebody must have broke in. Is that okay?"

"Norman, that is perfect. You must remember those exact words; do you think you can do that?"

"I can do that. But will I get into trouble with my boss for not keeping an eye out for people that break in? He would really be upset if I don't get the money before he sneaks in."

Ben for a minute was struck dumb, shaking his head with Norman's absurd reply. Ben could not help but stare, trying not to believe the words that continuously fell out of Norman's mouth. The makeup of Norman was beyond understanding; he is who he is. Acceptance, no matter the faults, is what separates the man from the child.

"Norman, your boss couldn't do without you, you are his man. Besides, we are playing a game, and he is not one of the players. He won't know a thing about what we are doing."

"Yeah, it's just the two of us. Are you going to tell me when to start, or is it a secret?"

Ben began to doubt he could pull this off.

"It's only a secret between us and we are going to start the game right now. When the game is over, I will let you know." Norman started to giggle, he was happy someone was going to play with him.

Ben rushed back to the cabin. Norman came with no guarantees, but neither did life.

The investigators with the crime unit pulled up at the exact minute Ben was thanking Henry for his help in controlling the townspeople. Patrol cars began lining up bumper to bumper. Ben had all the help he would need. He would be assigned extra officers to his station until Robert, who indeed had a small fracture in his ankle, got back onto his feet. He would be placed in a cast and sent home, although that would not keep him away from the station.

If Simon thought he would get information from the cops with his phony reporter's ID, he was sadly mistaken. But he was determined. He strolled nonchalantly around to the rear of the cabin, hoping to get a look into the back window; isn't that what a good reporter would do, snoop? But before he could see anything a cop grabbed him from behind by his arm.

Simon again showed his ID; maybe this cop was a believer.

The cop's reply, "Yeah, and I'm Santa Claus, see my uniform?"

Simon was busted. Reporting was proving to be a tough profession. Simon was shown the way in with the spectators, but that was fine with him; he always got his news from them anyway. He started shoving his way where the lips were moving the most. Mason's Mill was at its best when tragedy rained down upon them. He spotted the moving lips. Naturally it had to be three woman, yak, yak, yak. One of the three waved him over.

"Did you hear? A stranger rented a cabin and was shot in the face, he was. One of the cabin dwellers saw another man run out the door no sooner than the blast was heard. You want my name for the *Happenings*?"

Simon should write an article about the person telling the story. She was older than Methuselah; she should be the one to be carted away. As he wrote what she had to say she peered over his writing pad, keeping a tight grip on her eyeglasses. She had to make sure he was writing what she told him. He seriously doubted she could even see, her glasses the thickness of a bar of soap.

"The first thing I need from you is for you to tell me who told you this story about the stranger. I can get your name later."

"Why, it was the other man in the cabin with him. I just don't know where he ran off to." Simon prayed it would get better.

He continued searching and spotted Nellie, a woman with a terrible temper when put upon. She was short and plump with a head full of matted white hair—frizzy it's called. She claimed to know more than Harriet the psychic. A thought then crossed Simon's mind; he had not seen Harriet in quite a while. It was no secret she took the loss of her friend badly, but it had been weeks; surely she wasn't still occupying a bed in the rest home. Was she the one that would put a star on his paper? He would make a note of it and check it out.

"Nellie, I was going out of my mind trying to find you. You are the only one I can trust to give me the scoop as to what is going on."

"Simon, you know I will, but you have to take my picture first and I want front page center."

Simon's camera hung on his neck like a noose, but a hanging would be too good for him.

"Where else would I put your lovely picture? You deserve the spotlight."

Nellie giggled; she wished Simon would ask her out, or better still, occupy her bed for a few nights. She hadn't had a man in her bed for well over thirty years and she was hungry—the younger the man the better. Her take on such an age difference was that it was acceptable, but only if it referred to her. She was sixty-seven and barely hanging on and she wanted to get it on with a man in his thirties; what fairy land is she living in?

"There are two women in there—sisters, I was told. They committed suicide. They both lost their husbands in a boating accident. And it was right here in our fishing lake."

Simon's mouth was hanging open, ready with a comment, when another woman overheard what was being said.

"No, no, Nellie, you got it all wrong. It was a man and a woman doing the nasty. When the woman's husband found out, he was quick with his rifle, he blew them to bits. The cops are in there now picking their parts off the walls. Now that is the truth."

The branches on the trees were falling on Simon's head. He needed to move out of harm's way. He knew his paper was mostly full of bull crap, but this was too far out even for him. But whatever the truth, no news would be good news.

Ben was present when Mr. Hewlett's penis was found. Who would have thought "Willie boy's" shoes, his most coveted possession, would contain the very thing that cost him his life? The highly shined brown shoes, still laced, had been neatly placed under the bed. Was Willie so anxious to get it on that he failed to untie his laces, or did someone take the time to retie them after his penis had been shoved inside?

Ben was making good use of the toilet. Things were wrapping up. Henry now had the stretcher before him. Willie's running days were over; his body would soon be put to rest. A body bag was brought in; there would be no possible way onlookers could sneak a peek. His belongings were tagged for evidence. The investigators were puzzled as to the absence of his wallet. If the person that committed this murder thought by removing his wallet it would look like a robbery, that person should be denied the right to vote.

Ben was informed of the missing item; it would be his job to see if it had been left at Mr. Hewlett's place of employment or at his home.

The caller's mementos were beginning to get crowded with the addition of Willie's wallet stuffed with pictures of his twelve kids; the caller would have to transfer the collectibles into a larger box.

No one could deny Mason's Mill had a murder on their hands. Ben would be given the full cooperation of his superiors to conduct a thorough investigation; he would be the head honcho.

It was a long time coming, but Ben was finally given the chance to find his rainbow.

CHAPTER SIXTEEN

Sunni pulled up stakes and moved out and on. Marc returned to school with his mother's insistence to take up residence in a dorm during the school week. She had much on her mind; she did not need to worry about Marc's daily commute to and from. He would visit on weekends only. And the sheriff of Mason's Mill still had a murder to solve.

Mr. Hewlett's body was taken away. The crowd began to disperse and Ben informed Norman the game was over. It did not take a genius to figure out who the body belonged to. When the bank's workday and the president was a no-show, assumptions took over.

Ben followed through with everything that was expected of him. He now had three deputies added to his sparse force. Two were to assist him in the investigation while the third handled the affairs at the station. He detested working with unknowns; he hated it more that Robert put himself out of commission. Ben would start with interviewing all the women "Willie boy" had escorted into the cabin. This in itself would end up putting more hours on the books than the police force had ever encountered.

When the presumed turned out to be true, Simon's paper was ready to put the printing press in motion. The darkened heading would certainly grab the townspeople's attention:

The horror of Mr. Hewlett's death ends with part of his anatomy missing

The *Happenings* was pressed into Ben's hand by one of the deputies assisting in the investigation. Outraged, Ben yelled out his thoughts, "This has to stop."

The paper consisting of several pages was crunched into Ben's big hand when he stomped into Simon's Antique Shop and so-called newspaper business.

Simon was swishing his hands back and forth as he watched the printing press in action. He would increase the cost of the paper from $2.00 to $2.50. If he noticed any slack in the sales, he could return to the original cost.

Ben slammed the paper down upon Simon's desk. The rambling sound of the press would not end soon.

"Is there something sick in your brain, or do you just not have one? I have no idea where you received the information that you are printing, but let me tell you, you have been misinformed."

"Oh, I don't think so, Sheriff. A good reporter goes directly to the source. I just happened to be at the medical examiner's when I overheard them talking about Mr. Hewlett."

Ben had to really restrain himself from punching that smug look on Simon's face. "Someday, someone will put an end to your disgusting paper."

"It certainly won't be you, Sheriff. I have the right to print what I want, when I want. It's called freedom of speech."

Ben's anger reached its boiling point and he reached for the closest thing, a telephone directory, and threw it at Simon. Simon did not duck fast enough, and it caught him in the eye; he would have a shiner for weeks. Simon was thinking, if he sued the sheriff, that would make fantastic headlines, one of his best works:

The sheriff of Mason's Mill, Ben Davidson, brutally attacks newsman, lawsuit to ensue

Simon kept staring at what he had written on a sheet of paper. The townspeople loved their sheriff and would without a doubt take their own action and probably blacken his other eye; his printing press would hum no more. His genius headline, now just bits of paper, was thrown into the scrap pile. Besides, he had another story to follow: Harriet Anderson.

Ben called on the medical examiner to advise him that a resident of Mason's Mill had acquired information that should have been kept confidential. It so happened the medical examiner was about to place a call to him.

"Ben, I'm aware of the leak. I have no idea how this could have happened; I guess informants are everywhere. Some things cannot be controlled no matter how hard you try."

Although provoked, Ben realized it was senseless to cry over a person like Simon, who at best was working with half a brain.

"Ben, I've completed the autopsy. The person responsible for this crime I believe enticed Mr. Hewlett into thinking he was in for a fun-filled night of sex. There is no doubt in my mind that Mr. Hewlett's murder was premeditated. If you have the time I would like to show you something."

Ben did not have to be asked twice; he was already on his way to the autopsy room. The medical examiner welcomed him and guided the sheriff to what he wanted him to see. Ben did a quick study upon entering; there it was, a door marked "bathroom." This time he would be prepared. Willie was lying on a slab. Ben avoided looking at what had eliminated him from life.

"Ben, if you'll notice, there are many abrasions on his wrists and ankles. No doubt, he thought he was in for a night of kinky sex. He was also gagged, most likely to prevent him from screaming out when his penis was removed. An instrument sharper than a razor had to have been used, more than likely a scalpel; it was a clean slice. I can think of nothing worse to end a man's life. I would determine that nylons were used for tying the victim; there are no rope burns. Has any evidence been uncovered that would back up my belief?"

"Not a fingerprint, fiber or weapon has been found, let alone nylons. It's as if an invisible force entered and left, leaving no trace that a crime had ever been committed. I have men working around the clock with no results. If someone does know something they are remaining silent. But I refuse to throw in the towel; it's over when it's over and not before. The person responsible will be caught, and when that happens I pray she receives the death penalty." Ben thanked the medical examiner for his expertise and said his good-bye.

The crime would remain on the books for a very long time.

Simon walked casually into the reception area, signed in, and then asked for the room number of Harriet Anderson.

Alayna, the receptionist, smiled cheerfully with a hearty reply.

"She is no longer a patient at this facility."

That announcement did not deter Simon.

"Has she returned to her place of residence?" Simon put on quite a show with his wide-gapped toothy smile.

"I'm sorry, sir; I cannot give out that information."

"Sure you can. I'm her brother. I just arrived from out of town, and she's expecting me."

"If she were expecting you, she herself would have given you the information you are requesting." Alayna still retained her smile.

Maybe if he showed his reporter's badge, she would comply. He continued to smile at her, she continued to smile back. He was getting nowhere. Maybe if he asked her out? He noticed a wedding ring; *Perfect. Married women always cheat on their husbands.*

"Since I'm new to your town, maybe you could show me the sights. Before I call on my sister. When can I pick you up?" You have to give Simon credit, he had more nerve than nerve gas.

Alayna, still smiling and in her sexiest voice, whispered sweetly, "Sir, I would rather go out with a hobo before I would even entertain the thought of being seen with you."

Simon was not only humiliated, but embarrassed. He had never had such a putdown. He leaned over; she could smell his funky breath.

"Well let me tell you a huge secret. Every woman I've been with said they've never seen a man so hung. But even if you changed your mind with that coveted knowledge I would deny giving you that enormous amount of pleasure."

He glanced at his watch, and then at the woman who refused him.

"Well, it's time for me to take my leave. Please have a miserable day while you think about what you just gave away."

Alayna continued to smile.

But Simon had an ego as large as his penis and his spirits lifted, as he knew they would. After all, he was a reporter with great credentials; any woman would love to have him. Nellie would.

Simon would have to run a new front page in the *Happenings*. The headline screamed out its words:

Are we missing someone from our little town?
Harriet Anderson, come out, come out, wherever
you are

Simon's paper at present was full; he would have to wait until tomorrow. He was wondering if the sheriff would blacken his other eye. If so, he could wear sunglasses. It was September, and the weather man predicted many sunny days. Simon refused to give in to the sheriff and his fist. A great reporter takes his chances.

The *Happenings* hit his newsstand bright and early the following morning. As expected the headline shouted at the residents. The newly priced papers were gobbled up. No more debates; Simon planned to enact an increase every six months.

Robert hobbled into the police station with the "fresh off the press" release.

"Ben, you're not going to like this."

Simon would wear sunglasses through October.

Ben needed to see Harriet. She was in her thirtieth week with no complications, and the babies were growing at a rapid rate,

Ben had heard women are most beautiful when pregnant, and that was definitely true of Harriet. She was catnapping when he entered. He touched her hand, and she smiled that one-dimpled smile he loved so well.

Ben leaned over, offering her the moisture of his lips before asking her how her day had gone. "Sweetheart, how are all of you doing? Dr. Rolan was smiling when he left, giving me a thumbs up."

"Ben, something has been on my mind for quite a while, and I can't keep shoving it to the side. I know you have been keeping something from me, and I know it's because of what I've been through. I also know it has to do with the Doc and his wife, because shortly after Dr. Rolan took over my care, I had a vision of the Doc and his wife fiercely arguing; it had to do with Sunni. Miriam was going to leave him, but tragedy struck shortly after her bags were packed. They lost their lives in a fire, didn't they?"

Ben was stunned but relieved. He would not be the bearer of bad news; it had already been delivered by means from the other side.

But Harriet was not finished with what she had to say.

"No matter how hard I try, I'm unable to see why Miriam was going to leave him. And don't try and tell me it was the Doc that took a match to his own gasoline supply."

Ben tried to keep his mind from working, failing badly. He hated it when his sweetheart worked her magic by picking up on his thought-waves.

"I know what you're thinking, Ben, and it's not so. The Doc loved Miriam; he would never have taken her life, no matter the reason. Ben, what I'm trying to tell you is, they were murdered. The evidence was lacking to support the investigators' findings that it was arson. But Ben, the worst of it is, I'm unable to see the face of the perpetrator."

Ben began to show excitement but Harriet quickly brought him back to reality.

"Ben, do not go there. Your superiors will never allow you to reopen the case because of what I saw in a vision, and you know this. I feel badly for you, but you need to put your efforts where they will do the most good. I'm struggling to do the same; I need to concentrate on the positive. I'm done grieving for my friends and loved ones. I've accepted God's will."

Ben felt squeamish each time Harriet read his thoughts, especially after they made love and she said, "You have doubts with all my moaning and groaning. Some women might fake it, but I am definitely not one of those women. My darling, you're more than enough man for me." Ben was thankful the lights were turned off; a man should not blush.

It was time to show her what she was unable to see. He laid the *Happenings* by her side.

"Simon is again up to no good, first with the paper on Willie, which I showed you, and now this."

Harriet unfolded the paper. She read the headlines and the brief story that followed. She started to giggle.

"Sweetheart, I thought you would be upset. This doesn't bother you?"

"Ben, the man's a nuisance and an attention grabber, but in reality has he does us harm? No."

"Well…he's going to be wearing shades for a while."

"Ben, you didn't?"

"Yeah, I did, and now he's got a twin to match from the article on Willie."

"Ben, you have to keep yourself under control. Swinging the fists doesn't solve a thing."

"Maybe not to you, but it sure felt good to me."

Harriet could not help herself, she started laughing. Ben joined in. What a family the triplets are going to have.

Ben needed to get everything off his chest. The case he was working on was wearing him down. He had to think about his up and coming family.

"Sweetheart, the investigation is going nowhere. My deputies and I have crisscrossed the roads so many times the pavements need to be resurfaced. It didn't take us long to run out of residents, so we started interviewing the children. How stupid is that? And to make matters worse, all the women we talked to denied being involved with Willie. I kind of expected denial from the married ones, but the singles? Some have even gone so far as to say they had no idea who I was talking about. These are the same women that not only wrestled with him in bed, but shared meals with him in town. Are these people for real? Plus, I just found out today that Willie was tied up…not tied up in the way you think, but for kinky sex. The person who did this is a psycho, and she is roaming around out there, and unless I stop her, she will do it again."

When he finished, he placed his elbows on the edge of the bed, cupping his head into his hands. He was tired of being a cop.

"Ben, look at me." He did as she asked. "What evidence do you have?"

"That's just it; there's no evidence, not even a hair."

"So, you've done everything you can possibly do. It's over, Ben; you're beating yourself up over something you have no control over. You need to call it a day and move on."

He knew she was right. He and his deputies had covered all bases with no results. They were spending more time at the police station than tracking down the non-leads. He would call off the investigation. He would not allow this murder to eat up his brain space. Harriet had to repeat his name several times before he became aware she was speaking.

"I'm sorry, sweetheart. I was just thinking of what you said. I'll notify the authorities tomorrow that the investigation is over, that we've come to a dead end, but I will request the file to remain open."

"That is a definite," was Harriet's reply.

Ben rushed on with what he really came to see her about.

"I think it's time we set our wedding date. How about tomorrow after I terminate two of my three deputies' services? I'll keep just one until Robert is back full time. "

"Well, it sure took you long enough to ask for my hand."

"The hell with the hand, I want your body." The kiss lasted long enough to arouse them both.

"Gosh, sweetheart, it seems like forever since I made love to you."

Harriet was quick with a response. "I quit counting after thirty days."

Ben got as close as he could without falling on top of her. Their embrace lasted but a minute before the babies kicked him away.

"It looks like they are already in charge." Their laughter could be heard in the hallway.

Ben returned to the station with a smile, he couldn't remember the last time he was truly this happy. He loved Harriet beyond reason. He was dialing before he claimed his chair behind his desk. Pastor Riley was amazed at Ben's request; he never thought Ben and Harriet would ever marry, although it was apparent they loved each other deeply. He wondered what precipitated this decision.

Pastor Riley was agreeable to the time of 4:30 p.m. tomorrow; he was just surprised it would be at St. Mary's Hospital instead of Pleasant View Nursing Home. Ben and Marc had agreed to keep Harriet's condition private, along with her new location, until after the babies' births. But with the wedding and Simon's nose trying to sniff Harriet out, they decided to let Pastor Riley announce the wedding and the upcoming births at Sunday's service.

Pastor Riley arrived at the hospital early, but the main principals were already in place. Marc was on one side of the bed, and Ben on the other, while Harriet stayed rooted in the middle, triplets directly below. The pastor now understood the rush to wed. *Is Miss Anderson ready to deliver?* he wondered. He was a man of God; he would not be their judge. He felt blessed that the wedding went smoothly, that the "I do's" would not be said while Harriet was bearing down in labor. A few pleasantries were exchanged after the congratulations.

The wedding party would have been idiots had they not noticed the pastor eyeballing Harriet's stomach. They did not have to tell him that he was staring at a woman whose belly contained three babies, but had they not, Simon would have a heyday at their babies' expense; they would not allow this to happen.

Ben was the one to make the announcement.

"Pastor Riley, it will be a while but eventually you will have three new parishioners."

Marc had a chair ready and the pastor fell onto it, but quickly rose, hand extended. He voiced his congratulations three times. He wished Ben could make the announcement; that guy had a gift with words. Ben could post a notice and the walls would stretch with his presence. Pastor Riley would pray hard for the right words. His prayer was answered, he posted his own notice:

My dear parishioners you are in for the surprise of your lives.
Find out at church services this Sunday. The announcement will be precisely at 10:30 a.m.

It worked, the townspeople were pushing and shoving; they all wanted front-row seating. Pastor Riley looked at the time on his watch—9:33 a.m. He needed a bigger church.

Simon believed in the church. Did he have religion in his heart? Probably not, but where there are people, there is news. Church services were held first, and the parishioners did not mind waiting for the surprise; God has priority. When the time arrived, everyone was anxious.

Pastor Riley was smiling, all eyes focused on him. It was a grand feeling.

"Yesterday, I married our sheriff and Harriet Anderson." Not a sound could be heard, nor a movement.

Finally a man seated near the back stood. He shouted, and no one could miss hearing his words. "Is this a joke?"

Pastor Riley quickly answered, "Now why would you think this is a joke,? They have loved one another for years. You all know this as well as I do."

The man again shouted, "After all these years the milk's been free, now he's buying the cow?" The old geezer thought it funny and started to laugh, assured the congregation would join in. The silence ended with gasps.

Pastor Riley was horrified at his comment.

"I don't believe I know the cow you're talking of. I pray it's not someone you love and hold in the highest esteem." A clap sounded and then another, until all those in attendance nearly broke the sound barrier.

Pastor Riley finally had everyone's attention.

"Will everyone bow their heads and say after me, 'Lord forgive me for thinking evil thoughts, wipe from my lips the words that hurt those around me, and guide me into the path of righteousness. Amen.'"

The townspeople began gathering their prayer books and a few personal belongings from the pew benches. They assumed their pastor had finished.

"Could I please have your attention for a few more minutes?"

Some of the parishioners had already exited, skipping around others in their quest to be the first out the door.

Pastor Riley shook his head, thoughts pounding his temples. *Why are they in such a hurry? Sin always waits? Satan will accomplish his evil sometime during the week; forgiveness will then be given in next Sunday's service.*

The remaining congregation turned their eyes towards the pulpit. Pastor Riley waited patiently for the rustling sounds to settle again into total silence.

"Thank you. Before the cow grabbed everyone's attention…" This time laughter was called for and everyone obliged.

If bets were taken, odds were Pastor Riley's message would have the townspeople scrabbling for more of the same. Ben's services may no longer be needed. For the first time in his young life, the pastor had managed to grab all the attention. He considered it a blessing.

Pastor Riley waited patiently for the laughter to subside. It was now curtain time.

"Ben and his wife Harriet are expecting, but not with just one baby but with three. She has totally recovered, and was transferred from the nursing home into the hospital to wait out the delivery of the triplets. Ben gave his permission to release this information. He asks for you to be patient and not visit until after the babies are born. We as good Christians should respect his wishes. When and if I get a further report I will pass it on. Have a pleasant day. God awaits you at next Sunday's service."

If the shock could have been felt, the church would have been in shambles. The women began rushing about, colliding with each other in their haste to add a bit of their own gossip; the fun of their day had just begun.

Simon's thoughts turned back to the receptionist. Damn her—if she had given him this information he would be standing with the best of the reporters, the increase of the paper justified.

The *Happenings* will not see better days; the cost will remain the same.

CHAPTER SEVENTEEN

Sunni had been in school for more days than she could count. Her money had not been transferred.

Mary, Mr. Hewlett's private secretary, picked up on the first ring.

Sunni screamed into the receiver. "This is Sunni Harrison. Where in the hell is my money?"

Mary nearly dropped the phone. "I'm sorry, I have no idea what you are talking about."

"Then give me to somebody who does." When she received no instant reply, Sunni screamed again. "Are you lame, or are you just slow with requests?"

"I'm sorry. I'm transferring you now, Miss Harrison." Sensitive Mary's day was ruined. At the least little incident, she would burst into tears.

"This is Rebecca Torri. May I help you?" Becca, as she liked to be called, was a stunning woman. She was a tall redhead with a spray of freckles across the bridge of her nose. Her eyes were green, her smile intriguing. She carried herself with pure confidence. She was twenty-seven years old and unmarried.

"This is Sunni Harrison. I'm sure you know who I am."

Becca noticed the sarcasm, but kept her own voice upbeat. "Yes, I know who you are. How may I help you?"

"Mr. Hewlett promised me he would transfer the money that I requested. A canoe to China would have been faster."

"I'm terribly sorry, but Mr. Hewlett is deceased. I've taken over most of his clients, but I don't think you are one of them."

If Sunni could have climbed into the phone, she would have strangled the person holding the receiver.

"If I have to come down there somebody will pay the piper. Now find out where the hell my money is."

"If you will please hold, I will find the person handling your account."

A running Becca would not calm this woman; she took her time. Think of paybacks.

Becca returned with a sweet reply. Sugar so thick it could turn into a cube.

"Miss Harrison, everything you requested has been taken care of and has been forwarded to the person you chose to be your personal banker. He should have the information you are seeking. Is there anything else I can help you with?"

Sunni slammed the phone down. Becca was prepared, holding the telephone away from her ear. Becca ended the conversation as if Sunni were still on the line. "May you also have a fabulous day."

Becca's thoughts when she had free time would ponder why Miss Harrison never asked the cause of Mr. Hewlett's death. "Strange" would be the best word to describe Miss Sunni Harrison. The human race comes in all shapes, sizes, and dispositions.

Sunni was happy, not because her finances were now taken care of, but because Mr. Hewlett would no longer flush someone's hopes and dreams down the toilet. He got what he deserved. She smiled, then tossed the thought of him away. She needed to call the sheriff.

Ben picked up after several rings.

"Why is it that no one answers the phone on the first or second ring?" Sunni's attitude had not changed from the last call.

"Pardon me?"

"No, I will not pardon you. Phones are to be answered. Why the delay?"

Ben recognized the voice. He ignored the stupidity of that question. "Well, hello to you too, Sunni."

That seemed to settle her down. She frequently professed her hatred for the sheriff, but this time she forced herself to be kind; he had the power to shelve the hunt for Sloan.

"I'm sorry, Sheriff Ben; this has not been a good day."

"Tell me about it. I'm receiving more and more of those myself. How are you doing? Long time not to hear from you."

"Sheriff Ben, I'm so miserable and unhappy."

He picked up on a choking sound. Was she crying? If so, it was about time.

"Sunni, I know what you're going through, I've been there. There's nothing worse than losing one's parents."

"Are you serious? Do you honestly think I'd take up brain space with thoughts of them? I look at them as being here one minute and gone the next, 'finite.' It's Sloan—I can't eat or sleep for thinking of her, and my studies are failing because of it. Surely you must have found out something by now?"

Ben held the phone away from his ear and looked at the receiver; did he just hear what he thought he heard? Sunni was a person he could easily learn to dislike.

He was somewhat brisk with her. "I haven't heard a word. If you leave me your phone number I will call you if I hear anything."

She would not recognize an attitude or a compliment. "Have you a pencil handy?"

Ben rolled his eyes. He was seriously thinking of not writing down her number but thought better; he refused to turn into someone like her. He jotted the number on a tablet and without further comments said good-bye. This would be one phone call he would be elated to make if Sloan were to turn up safely.

Sunni hung up the telephone. She felt betrayed by her best friend. Sloan had turned her back and walked. Walked where? Her pockets were empty, and where does a person go without money?

It will be years before she and Sloan come face-to-face.

CHAPTER EIGHTEEN

Harriet was now a Mrs. and very despondent. She could explain the melancholy if Ben were at her side; confessions are good for the soul. She was about to bring three babies into the world and place them into a cradle of lies. She had managed to keep the secrets buried, but the changes in her life were forcing her to dig them up. She needed to shed the coat she had been wearing and expose what lay beneath. Meanwhile, the babies were doing a boogie; she caressed them, soothing their fretfulness.

Dr. Rolan popped his head in the door with a joyous smile and a hearty hello.

"Want some company?"

Harriet enjoyed his open friendliness; she couldn't have selected a better doctor.

He kept chatting while checking the babies' monitors. "I don't think you are going to make it another three weeks. The babies are getting anxious. They're tired of sharing, they want their own space."

No matter her frame of mind, Harriet had to laugh. It was a small joke on the doctor's part, but he was extremely serious and a bit concerned.

"The babies' heartbeats are beginning to get a bit irregular. It could be because of the position they are lying in. I think it's time for the family to say hello."

"But you said thirty-three weeks was safe; I'm only thirty weeks."

"There are other forces at work, such as the babies; they decide when the time is right."

"I would never endanger the lives of my babies, but do you think a few more hours would make a difference? There is something I need to take care of."

"I think we can hold off for a while."

The doctor glanced at his watch. It read 8:40 a.m. "Would I be giving you enough time if I schedule the c-section for, say, 5:00 p.m.?"

"Let me check with Ben, and I need for Marc to return from school. We might be cutting it a little close."

"I'll tell you what; let's just go with tomorrow morning at 7:30. I'll alert the nurses to keep a close eye on the babies. If they cooperate, I'll see you the first thing in the morning. And now show me that beautiful smile."

She did as she hoped her babies would do, she cooperated.

Harriet thought about the order of things. She would call Marc to come home immediately. The story of how he came to be has a different beginning from the one he had been told. She knew she couldn't do a face-to-face. To see the trust fade away would have destroyed her. Years ago, she composed a letter to be given to him if she were to die. She no longer could hide under the cloak of death. The lies will end when he accepts her letter.

Marc was between classes; he would be in his dorm. Deep in thought, he answered on the first ring, the telephone occupying the same space as the books scattered across his desk.

"Marc here, what's up?" All the dorm guys answered the same; it was as if a code had been enacted. He was tapping his pencil on his work papers waiting on a response. He was just about to hang up; he had better things to do than to listen to someone breathing.

Of course, Harriet hesitated; she was thinking of changing her mind.

"Marc honey, it's me. Did I catch you at a bad time?"

"Oh my God, it's time isn't it?" He was ready to grab his truck keys and say good-bye to his dorm.

Harriet laughed; she loved this man, her son with a heart full of goodness.

"No, honey, I'm not in labor, but by this time tomorrow you will be a big brother."

"Oh my gosh, does Ben know? What a dummy I am, of course he knows."

"No, Marc, I have yet to tell him. I wanted you to be the first. Dr. Rolan just left. If everything goes according to his plan, at this time tomorrow you will get your wish: you will own the title big brother."

Marc wiped his tears. He was running with his thoughts. Twenty-two years to become a brother. But in less than two hours, his almost twenty-three-year-old world will come crashing down.

"Marc, I need to see you—it's important. Would you mind coming to the hospital now?"

"I'm on my way, Mom. I'll see you in a bit."

Harriet replaced the receiver with her right hand. Her left hand held the messenger, the damaging letter that could banish Marc from her life. She needed this time alone with her son. Ben would have to wait.

Marc was in a hurry; his mother needed him. With his keys in hand, identification in wallet, he slammed the door to his dorm room and ran down the stairs and out to his truck, which was parked nearby. He wrestled with his keys, feeling for the ignition, and soon he was speeding down the road. He was less than an hour away from the hospital and the untold truth.

Marc finally arrived; he was anxious and excited at the same time. He ran down the corridor straight for his mother's room. She was attempting to sit up, failing badly.

"Mom, let me see if I can help." As he wrapped his arms around his mother's back to pull her forward, she attempted to wrap her arms around her son, knowing this could well be her last time. He managed, somewhat, to get her in a reclined position.

Harriet refused to release him. She had something to say. She whispered in his ear, "I will always love you, Marc."

He tightened his embrace. "Hey, what is this, confession time? All right then, here goes."

"Mom, no one will ever love you as much as I."

Was Harriet sad? Of course—she was thinking about the consequences. She started to cry.

"Mom, what's with the tears? This is a happy time. Sometimes river beds dry up. Do you think we could also apply this to tears?"

Harriet gave a half-hearted smile. "Marc, I've struggled for years trying desperately to do the right thing, but I've failed badly. Doing the right thing is wrong when it starts with a lie…. Sounds confusing, doesn't it? But it is explained in detail in a letter that was written years ago.

Call me a coward, I will own up to it. The contents will be quite disturbing; you might think about reading it in the waiting room. All I ask is that you not say a word until the letter is finished. You can read it here or in another room."

Marc could read his mother's facial expressions. She was in agony. He had the letter in his hand, his name written on it with a noticeably shaky hand. His eyes tried to burrow into the mystery buried within. He reached over, taking his mother's hand into his.

"Mom, if you don't mind, I would prefer to read it in your presence." She nodded as her eyelids began to fill. The envelope had taken on a slight discoloration, the signs of aging. He gingerly tore the flap away. The unfolded letter was now secured in his hands.

My dear son Marc,

Where do I begin? How do I explain things that happened a lifetime ago? I beg you not to judge me too harshly. As you begin what I call a journey into your past, please keep my love for you in the forefront.

I fell hard for a man by the name of Phillip Chadsworth. Our love was mentally powerful, but quickly became physical when I found out I was expecting. Phillip assumed the baby was his, it was not. He wanted to get married immediately, and because I truly loved him, though harboring a lie, I wanted the same. His parents were shocked; I was considered a servant, though I carried the title of Governess. I was not worthy to carry the Chadsworth name. It's easy to lie, when knowing the truth would destroy a family. They permitted me to stay on, while tutoring and caring for their little girl. I was grateful, for I had nowhere to go. When my baby boy arrived the Chadsworths were elated. They welcomed what they thought to be their grandson with open arms. Their warm reception left no doubt Phillip and I would marry. At the tender age of six months my son and I no longer co-existed. I was forcibly removed from their home. My baby boy would grow up without the warmth of his mother's arms. Yes, Marc, you have an older half brother. His name is Joseph Clayton Chadsworth.

Marc took a breather, rubbing both his misted eyes with his middle finger and his thumb, head hung low. He did as told; he made no comment.

His reading continued.

Marc, your life also began with a lie. A lie perpetrated by your father. But let me start at the beginning. When the power of wealth stepped in and stole my baby, and took away my lover, I became severely depressed. I was stranded with very little money and no resources, except the power to see the future and look into the past. I forced myself forward, hiding my grief; I was determined to get my baby back. I opened a place called The Truth Beyond. Soon the money started rolling in, money I used for private investigators to find where the Chadsworths had hidden my little boy. It was apparent he no longer lived at the Chadsworth Mansion.

The years were gaining in numbers, when a friend named Marnie decided she had been party to enough of my misery. She wouldn't take no for an answer, we were going barhopping. Sleazy we were not, but I have to admit, I had the time of my life. It was that night I met the man that was destined to be your father. Without realizing, I must have been looking for someone to fill the void in my life. It was love at first glance.

As bad luck would have it, though I was unaware of it, your father had just been released from prison. He spent most of his life behind bars. It started with small-time robberies that kept the iron gates swinging in and out. Good behavior is a phrase our system uses as an excuse for early release. When this happens, "that system" carelessly removes the public's safety net. I am perhaps one of thousands who happen to be in the wrong place at the wrong time. He was not who he pretended to be and was already married when we said our "I do's." I was given many warning signs that continuously flashed, but I turned a blind eye to everything that was not to my liking. I think the worst thing was his drinking and drugs. These alone should have killed him, they did not. To put the blame totally on him would have been wrong, I had to assume partial responsibility for my stupidity. Using the phrase "I was desperate for companionship" is a lame excuse.

The three months we spent together ended quickly when he was arrested in yet another robbery, only this time the owner saw him and tried to stop him, resulting in your father beating him to death. He would have gotten a life sentence, had the man not already been told by his doctor that he had but three to four months to live. Your father told me he would kill me if I deserted him.

The months dragged on and while awaiting his trial you arrived. You deserved a good life, one without him in it. I prayed nightly for a life sentence. When the verdict was read, the thought of suicide came and then went. I could never leave you, you needed me as much as I needed you. Your father was sentenced to seven years, reduced to five and a half for time served while awaiting trial.

I ran for my life to save yours. I swore before God and country no one would ever take you. It was then I decided to change my name from Jennifer Carr to Harriet Anderson and yours to Marc Anderson. On the original birth certificate that I have stored in my safety deposit box, your given name is Adam Carr, father unknown; to attach your biological father's *name to that paper would have sickened me. I was determined he was never going to find us. To speak your father's name would leave a bitter taste in my mouth, so with pen to paper, I write his name, Trevor Hartman. Your father thankfully is no longer with us. Shortly after his release, he was killed in a barroom fight. A grave injustice has been done to you, and the words "I'm sorry" seem trivial. I'm left with nothing, if I lose your love and respect. Can you forgive me?*

Marc refolded the letter, his tear ducts cleansed. He rose from his seated position, never once taking his eyes off his mother, who had fear etched across her face. His hands reached for hers.

"Mom, do you not know me? You have nothing to be sorry for; sorry should be on the lips of the people that inflicted such agony. I will make you a promise: as long as I have a breath in my body, you will never again know sorrow or pain. I have but one thing to ask…never use 'forgive' in my presence."

Never underestimate the powerful love of a son for his mother. They would stay clutched together for several minutes, until like before, the babies pounded him away. To begin and end a day with laughter makes everything in between seem insignificant.

More words were not needed; questions and answers would wait for another day. A kiss was shared, good-byes until morning.

Marc would return home, but a good night's sleep would not be his; he allowed his brother to tap into his brain, where he would remain until they'd shaken hands and shared a hug.

Harriet was already dialing. Ben this time answered on the first ring. Sunni's impatient question about not answering the phone on the first or second ring was still hammering his ear.

"Ben, I need to see you. Can you get someone to fill in for you?"

"Sweetheart, you sound a little down. Should I be worried?" He was not the wait-and-see type. If there was a concern, pile it high, he was used to wading in it.

"We have to decide on the babies' names. Tomorrow morning we join the ranks of parenthood."

"Don't say any more. I'm on my way." The sheriff had been assigned another deputy until Robert returned on a full-time basis. Robert's temporary replacement was equipped to handle any emergency should the sheriff have to leave on his own emergency.

Ben recalled a comment Robert made yesterday. "Harriet's not the only one to see into the future. I predict we will be conducting police business in a pig's sty if I don't put my hands to work."

True to his word, every other day, broom in one hand, a rag in the other, Robert conquered the never-ending dust bunnies, his crutch holding him up. Whatever clung to the floors, walls and furniture he always managed to send Ben's way. He would attack the Kleenex box, one after another, until the dust forced his allergies to the surface, and he would then escape to the great outdoors. Robert's obsession was Ben's reward; never could he find a better deputy.

Ben parked his patrol car as an ordinary citizen. Maternity was on the fourth floor. Running was not his thing, until the elevator opened on his sweetheart's floor; then the speed at which he ran would qualify him to participate in a marathon. Harriet was semi-reclined. Ben never missed a running step, dragging a chair over to sit at Harriet's side. Their lips made contact immediately. He was now seated, their hands locked.

Harriet started the conversation.

"Dr. Rolan said the babies' heartbeats are becoming a little irregular and he thinks it's time to deliver. Don't look so frightened; if he was overly concerned, I'm sure he wouldn't have granted my request to wait until tomorrow morning."

Ben was taken aback; a funny look crossed his face with the thought, *Why would she choose to wait? That is totally unlike her.*

"Because I have something to tell you."

Is there an exercise available to hide what a person is thinking? If so, Ben would check it out. Reading people's thoughts was not Harriet's forte. This was a gift she would gladly have given back. She was grateful it only occurred when her body strength was at its weakest point.

"Ben, what I'm about to tell you is something I should have told you years ago. You may ask, why now, at this precise moment in time? It's because I need to start our lives together on a clean slate. You may think you know me, but you do not. My past called on me many weeks back; it was the day I found out 'we' were pregnant. When I finally found the courage to tell you, that chance was taken away, for that was the night I lost my Beth."

She continued on, repeating what she had told Marc. Ben's hands continued to stroke hers as she told her tale, never once removing them, until she finished. This big man with this tiny woman full of babies refused to move. His kids could kick away; he was there to stay.

Ben's lips covered her entire face, settling on her lips.

"When do I get to meet him, your other son?"

Was there anyone she could love more than Ben? With a handful of Kleenex, he collected Harriet's tears as they fell.

"Ben, there is more."

His massive hands covered the sides of her face, commanding her to look deep into his eyes. "Sweetheart, I really don't care about the more; we are living in the here and now."

She could not hold back.

"First, I need to tell you about Beth, for she was an intricate part in my beginning. I was raised in an orphanage after I lost my parents at the age of six. After a long ten years, the Chadsworths selected me as a governess for their little girl Alexandria. Ali, as she was called, lived a life full of distress until she couldn't stand it a minute longer. She thought her only option was to run away, and run she did, right into the arms of a college man. She was barely seventeen when she married, and that little girl moved to Mason's Mill; her name was Beth Parker. Now you can see why I loved her as I did; she was in my care from the tender age of three to the age of nine. It was then that I was thrown out. I met up with her again when I went into business for myself. She is the reason I moved to Mason's Mill. I miss her so much."

Harriet's tears continued to fall but the story went on.

"I fell helplessly in love with her older brother Phillip; he was sixteen to her three. But a dark cloud came and hung over me when Ali/Beth's father began raping me, night after night."

One box of Kleenex turned into two, Ben sharing. He entered a place he did not like to be. The monster responsible for this horrendous crime would be hunted down, and a pain like nothing he ever experienced would end his life.

"No, Ben, two wrongs do not make a right. I lived with hate for years but I learned to forgive, for out of that rape I was given the gift of life, my son Clay. I told no one, but I was in a dilemma. Who could have impregnated me if I didn't have sex with Phillip? My baby's life hung in the balance. I had no choice; I invited Phillip into my bed, and then I placed the blame on him. Lives are going to be shattered when the truth is told. The only good that will come out of this is my precious Beth will never hear the word 'rapist.' Ben, you are the only one I've told about the rape. I will in time tell Marc and all those involved, but you must allow me to decide when the time is right."

Ben sadly nodded. Of course it affected him, but it happened to her, so what else could he do?

"But you have told Marc about his brother, did you not?"

"Yes, I called him at school to come to the hospital; he left shortly before you arrived. I told him to bed down at the house. Oh Ben, telling him about his brother was the hardest thing I've ever had to do. We wept together. Our son has the heart of a giant and the sweetness of a newborn babe. Without him my life would have had no direction. Ben, I know I should have told you years ago when we became an us, but the fear of losing you won out. Please forgive me." His kisses said it all.

Baby names would have to be put off. Harriet's water bag burst, causing Ben to fall back looking at the mattress in bewilderment.

"You better ring for the nurse. I think our babies are about to demand our attention."

He yelled out when the nurse answered the call button. "My wife's water just broke. Call the doctor."

Harriet grabbed at her stomach, trying to bend over with the coming contraction. There would be no warm-up session; this one contraction was at its peak, lasting more than five minutes. Harriet screamed. The pain was like nothing she had ever experienced. Then from the deep recesses of her mind, the memory of childbirth rushed forth. She remembered this feeling, but this was much, much worse. She didn't like it; she refused to go through it, she wanted out, she continued to scream. Nurses came running, alerting Ben that Dr. Rolan had been called and was on his way.

Harriet caught a breath.

"Ben, you need to call Marc. Tell him to hurry, the babies are on their way." Another contraction grabbed her, refusing to let up; she screamed out that something was wrong.

Ben tried to comfort her. "Sweetheart, what can I do? Maybe I could rub your back, do you think that will help?"

"Rub my back, are you crazy? Get the hell out of my sight. I can't do this anymore; I need to get out of here. God, why doesn't someone help me?"

Harriet attempted to roll out of her bed. Her feet were almost to the floor, but the nurses were quick and managed to grab her before she made a run for it. It was like a battlefield, Harriet fighting for her freedom while the nurses fought to restrain her. They accomplished what Ben thought impossible. The bed rails were now secured, Harriet was going nowhere.

Ben was pacing, hands on hips, upset with Harriet's comeback. The nurse heard the conversation, if that is what you would call it. She approached Ben and placed her hand on his back.

"Sheriff, sometimes the pain causes the mother to say things she wouldn't normally say. When the doctor arrives, I'm sure he'll give her something for the pain."

Harriet was rolling back and forth. Her breaks in between contractions lasted just a tiny minute. The nurse performed her duties faithfully; she was constantly checking the mother's vitals and the babies' monitors. Other than the pain,

Harriet was doing okay; her blood pressure was a little on the high side, but nothing to become alarmed about.

The babies were showing no stress. It was a struggle, but the nurse managed to do an internal exam during a screaming protest. She found Harriet was already dilated five centimeters but the baby was in a breech position. The nurse knew Harriet was scheduled for a c-section in the morning. She wondered if the doctor could turn the baby, and if so, could Harriet deliver the triplets vaginally? But most importantly, would it be safe?

Dr. Rolan would have to make that decision.

CHAPTER NINETEEN
THE READING OF LYDIA'S WILL

Eight cooks, twenty-five maids, Art the butler, Max the chauffeur and Nurse Doleanna were called into Phillip's study. Phillip stood alongside the family's seated lawyer, Leo Cantrell, with an announcement.

"I've asked all of you to join me, because that was Lydia's wish. She has mentioned all of you in her will. As your name is called please step forward with acknowledgment, you may then retire for the remainder of the day with thanks for your continued support."

The gasps continued when each name and amount was revealed. The happy sounds rang out as members of the staff hugged one another, envelopes containing the checks gripped tightly in their hands as they scampered throughout the grand hall. Twenty-five thousand dollars could only be described as "WOW."

Max stuck his chest out. Did he think by doing this, by looking more confident, he would receive the same or more? Not likely, but it was a pleasing thought. He would most certainly retire to Mexico, where he'd heard a person can live on $500 a month with a maid. Now that's what he would call living. But Max would never desert Mr. Phillip, as he liked to be called, until he found a replacement.

Maxwell Turnbarry heard his name called and moved forward. Phillip tapped his lawyer on the shoulder, leaned over and whispered something into his ear.

Leo Cantrell was a short, very hairy-looking man, moving fast into his eighties. His brain usage afforded him an affluent lifestyle, but he shared his wealth with no one. A list of his assets would not have made him any more desirable. Leo turned the chair over to Phillip. He now stood beside his client.

"Max, you have been in our employ for more years than I can count. Your loyal service to our family could never be rewarded with money. Lydia, the wise woman she was, understood this…"

Maxwell's chest fell; he cannot retire.

Phillip continued. "But since money is all we have, Lydia wanted you to have enough to retire on. She said you mentioned Mexico; she thought one hundred fifty thousand dollars would help."

Max knew his place and had never crossed that line, until now. Clay was at his father's side when Max received his check. Max couldn't help it, he hugged them both, the warm embrace shared. There was no mistaking the wetness upon his face, the envelope now clutched within his hand. Phillip and Clay smiled for they knew their mother was doing the same. Max was told to pack his bags, his services were no longer required. Mexico would wait no longer.

Art patted Max on the back as he departed. Their work habits brought the two of them together quite often, and they could consider themselves friends.

Phillip the spokesperson continued.

"Art, never a day went by that you didn't bring sunshine into my mother's room while she lay dying. From day one, you always managed to put a twinkle in her eye and a smile upon her face. You were more than a butler, you were her friend. Clay and I are extremely grateful for that show of kindness. My frequent visits with her always ended with talks of you. She had but one wish, and that was for you to find someone to share your life. She apparently saw great potential and the makings of a great husband for some lucky woman. My mother was wise; it would be to your advantage to take her advice or at least keep your door open."

Art had to laugh while keeping his tears away from prying eyes; so many years and yet the love of his life refused to give up on him. He looked upward with a smile while thinking, *You win, Lydia, I will find someone to love; never someone like you, but someone, I promise.*

Phillip didn't hesitate.

"So it is with great honor and respect, according to her wishes, she bequeathed the sum of five hundred thousand dollars, to a man definitely deserving, in her eyes and ours."

Art stumbled backwards, his hand covering his mouth. Tears forever locked inside stayed there; had they burst forth they would not have been for the money but for the undeniable love he now knew Lydia had kept hidden from him. He walked towards the desk thanking Phillip while shaking his hand and accepting the check.

Clay returned to his distressed wife. They gave the appearance of one body sharing the same chair, his wife's head buried into his chest. Art nodded in his direction; never would he interrupt one's grieving process. Clay acknowledged him.

Art was about to exit the study when Phillip sounded out, "Art, from this day forward your life is your own. Make good use of it."

He would never again see Phillip or Clay…maybe Lydia, for he would die in a plane crash two months down the road; he had finally met someone.

When Art departed, words again spilled from Phillip's lips.

"Doleanna, what can we say about you? When our mother got sick we called on God's help. We pleaded with Him to send someone not only to care for her, but love her as well, for with love in the heart, passion is in the care. What a divine blessing you have been. But before you receive the rewards heaven has to offer, Lydia first wanted you to be showered with earth's blessings."

Doleanna, still in her nursing uniform and cap upon her head, was standing with her hands clasped in front of her when Phillip brought over a chair and told her to sit. She did as she was told. She was weary, worn out from the nightly tears; she loved Lydia as much as she loved her own mother, and that was saying a great deal. Phillip noticed her drawn look and fatigued appearance, but that was not the reason for the offered chair.

"Doleanna, I am honored to present you with a check for one million dollars."

Try and imagine someone giving you a check for that amount of money. Imagine away, but never will you know that feeling unless it happens to you.

Doleanna was beyond astounded; she could not come to grips with understanding that amount of money. She was a woman born into poverty but determined to do something with her life. She prayed nightly for guidance, months passed and finally her prayers were answered.

She spread the word. Jesus had come to her in the night; some believed, most did not.

"You are my disciple, you will tend to the sick and injured. This is what God the Father asks of you."

She graduated top in her class at the age of twenty-one, and from that day forward her cap was always in use. She was already looking ahead. She would now work in the poorest sectors of town providing her services, while helping those deserving pay their utility bills. This would continue until Lydia's generous gift was spent.

Phillip, Clay and Sloan embraced Lydia's Jewel. Doleanna gave Sloan more than the necessary shoulder to cry on; in their brief three months she gave lessons in the dynamics of love. Many will live out their lives never experiencing the power of that kind of love. They will weep together when she waves good-bye.

Phillip joined Clay and Sloan, allowing their lawyer to do what he was paid to do: finish with the reading of Lydia's will. After all the numerous charities, foundations and scholarships were named, Leo got to the gist of the will.

"Clay, your grandmother included a handwritten message. It is addressed to you, but her wish was that it be read aloud. With your permission I will continue." Clay nodded then glanced towards his father with his eyebrows raised. He gave his father a "What's up?" signal, but his father shook his head; he was never informed about a letter.

"My beloved Clay, if Leo is reading this, then I guess I've passed on. Oh well, that's life. I pray I will manage to go through the pearly gates and receive all the glorious things Heaven has to offer. But I take with me the most precious a memory, and that was when you presented yourself to my world. I had no idea how such a wee hand could carve such a huge place in my heart while scribbling your name on the walls that provided shelter. You made my house a home, giving life where none existed. That home now belongs to the little boy who gave it a soul. I will truly miss you."

Clay dropped his head, choking on his tears. It was now Sloan's turn to hold him close, trying to give comfort when none would come. Only God knows how much he will miss Lydia.

Leo did not wait for the tears to subside.

"Phillip, the remaining properties and assets she bequeathed to you. That about wraps it up. If you have any questions feel free to call me night or day."

Phillip, Clay and Sloan rose from their seats, as did Leo. They in turn offered their hands in thanks. Leo obliged with his handshake. He gave the appearance of someone in a hurry. He walked quickly out of the study hunched over his briefcase that seemingly was a strain to carry.

He waved his good-bye with his back turned. One thing you can say about Lydia's lawyer, when he's done with business, he hauls ass.

If you think Clay had qualms with the will, think again; the love for his father could never be measured in dollars and cents. It was as it should be, parents leaving their earthly possessions to their child or children. He was beyond grateful for Lydia's home, the memories of his youth stored in every nook and cranny. With her passing she took his heart.

They left the study, Phillip's arm draped over his son's shoulder, Clay's arm around his wife's waist.

A drastic change is the only thing that will return Sloan to her former self.

Days sped by, October shoved September aside. Sloan had a hard time coping. She had found a mother substitute, but they had had so little time together. Clay would find her in bed crying after a long day at work; nothing he could say or do would provide the comfort she needed. He never witnessed anyone behaving like his wife. He knew she loved his grandmother—that was without question—but this bordered on obsession. Of course, Sloan would not have behaved in such a manner had she been able to talk about a family Clay knew nothing of. Lydia knew, and was her only means to release the stress associated with that loss, and release it she did, on a daily basis, while Lydia struggled with her own life.

Sloan's tears were divided, some for Lydia, the majority for her mama and papa. She made herself believe she was happy, and she was to a certain extent, but she longed to feel the warmth of her papa's embrace and to be called "baby girl" again. She missed the private time spent with her mama. And when she thought about her sisters giggling over really stupid stuff, she would cry. She labored hard with tears for her baby brothers, missing their sloppy kisses. But the hardest thing to deal with was when Sloan's memory flashed a scene of her one-year-old brother DanDan. He was struggling with his first step, and then ending with a grand finale of fifteen. The family's applause was deafening and the solemn little guy's first toothless smile was caught on film, never to be shared with anyone. Had she not made a promise to Lydia about keeping the death of her parents a secret, Sloan would have confided in Clay. She knew he could have helped her understand the reasoning behind her family's death. But Destiny again stepped in, knowing this was not part of its plan, at least not at this time.

Clay was finding it depressing to return home night after night to find Sloan in the same fetal position he'd left her in, Kleenex a part of the floor's covering. He sat on a chair drawn close to her side, hunched over, hands clasped together, thinking. He scooted even closer, pulling her clutched arms away from her chest.

"Babe, I've been thinking. What we both need is a change. What do you think about moving in that grand old house of my grandmother's?"

For the first time in days he got a reaction. Sloan pulled herself up, legs tucked under, her nightie doing a poor job of covering her breasts. Clay couldn't help but notice she was minus her underwear. She leaned forward, her hands pressed firmly on the edge of the mattress.

"You would give up this beautiful apartment and move just to please me?"

Clay took her hands into his, and gently placed a kiss upon her lips. "I would buy all the wishing stars in the heavens, if it would put a smile upon your face."

She wrapped her arms around his neck, working her way onto his lap. Her hunger returned as her lips sought and held onto his. His arms swept her up. Hunger that hadn't been met in days exploded. He would ravish her body, longing to hear the moans and groans, her screaming for more and more. It didn't take long, he was thankful the servants had gone. Her screams of ecstasy continued to ring out, he stopped counting after five. The relief Clay felt was extreme; he worried his sex kitten was a figment of his imagination. The bed was given such a workout that the fitted sheet, top sheet and coverlet, along with the pillows, were nowhere near their mattress.

Clay was exhausted. He had performed at his highest capacity, and his bride was well taken care of. He smiled; he would give her an hour to recoup before he again approached her. Sloan was not only willing, but was more than ready. He never thought anyone could compete with his sex drive, but she outdid him. Her needs bordered on the extreme. He called that a bountiful blessing.

They would take nothing with them other than their personal belongings; all household items would remain behind. The apartment would stay in the family. While Clay was making arrangements to deliver all their personal items to his grandmother's home, Harriet was preparing for her own delivery.

Clay is about to be a brother to three additional siblings.

CHAPTER TWENTY

Marc came tearing down the hallway, noticing the nurses and doctors rushing in and out of his mother's room. He slid across the floor, stopping short, tennis shoes squeaking in protest. Harriet watched his approach. He was being cautious. He glanced about the room, where there was a buzz of activity he did not want to interrupt. Ben was by Harriet's side holding her hand. He acknowledged Marc with a nod; other than that Ben did not look well. Marc wondered if Ben would be able to withstand the delivery. Time will certainly tell.

Harriet took her son's hand.

"Marc, my sweet, thank God you make it. Dr. Rolan was just in and confirmed the babies were on their way. He flew out of here to make sure everything was ready in the delivery room. I thought I was going to die—the contractions were unimaginable. I behaved very badly. The anesthesiologist said multiples magnify the pain.

I know he just said that to make me feel better about my hysterical outbursts. All I know is after he gave me a spinal, I was free from pain. I wish he had been here when they started."

Harriet could laugh now, but Ben was showing no emotion. Marc made his mother aware of Ben's actions or lack thereof. She was so caught up in her own concerns she took no notice of Ben's. She waved her hand in front of her husband's face to get a reaction.

"Ben, are you okay?"

After several attempts he finally acknowledged the flapping of her hand. He calmly asked, "What is that you are doing with your hands?"

"I needed to get your attention; you didn't seem quite with it. Are you sure you're okay?"

"Yeah, I'm fine. How are you doing?" He was carrying on a normal conversation as if he were talking to an acquaintance.

Harriet struggled upward, taking his face into her hands. "Ben, honey, I know you are frightened of the unknown, so am I, but there isn't anything the two of us can't do, so long as we have each other. I love you and our babies will too."

Ben finally made eye connection. He returned in full gusto. "If you're ready, I'm ready. Let's go see who our kids look like."

The nurse took charge of Ben and Marc, guiding them into the room where they were to outfit themselves in surgical gear. They were then led into the delivery room. Harriet was draped and ready. Ben and Marc had never seen so many doctors and nurses gathered together in the same room. Dr. Rolan required the assistance of two other doctors to help in the delivery and to be on standby should an emergency arise. Each baby was to also have its own pediatrician and NIC nurse. Ben and Marc moved as close to Harriet as possible.

Dr. Rolan was ready.

"Harriet, I will tell you what I am going to do, so there are no surprises. Are you ready to say hello to the wee three?"

She was anxious but managed to say she was ready.

"I'm about to make an incision…you will feel some pressure."

Baby A announced her arrival with a hearty cry, and then settled down immediately.

You would have thought the baby was his—Dr. Rolan was that excited.

"It's a girl and is she a beauty. I've never seen such a mass of dark curls. There is no doubt, she is going to be a heartbreaker."

Harriet couldn't contain her joy. She wept openly. "I can't believe we have a baby girl." Ben wiped away her tears as they mingled with his. He then began kissing the side of her face.

Baby B quickly followed her sister; her cry lasted a little longer, probably because she wasn't going to be first in anything.

"You have another girl, and it appears they shared the same placenta. You have two of the same—what a blessing. I envy you, Ben; God is surely in your corner."

Harriet's and Ben's lips locked. She felt surrounded with God's presence.

Baby C's bag of water was still intact; immediately upon its rupture, he began protesting, letting out a howl that could be nothing other than a boy. Dr. Rolan cradled in his arms what every father desires.

"It's a boy. You have a son, Ben. I don't think you will have to worry about your girls' welfare; you were just given their protector."

That protector's cries would continue throughout his examination. Harriet, Ben and Marc could not contain their tears and laughter. Every member of the medical team shouted out their congratulations, their smiles hidden behind the masks. You could see heads nodding; everything seemed to be okay with the babies.

Dr. Rolan strolled over with a robust smile upon his face. "Well, you did it. Congratulations are in order, and trust me, you all will be hearing a lot of them. There are a few things I would like to go over with you. All three babies are strong and were breathing on their own following their births, but they were born ten weeks premature, and because of this, they will be put on a ventilator. This is only a precaution; sometimes babies forget to breathe, so the machine picks up the slack. And believe me when I say this, it's a struggle for the little ones; they tire quickly.

"The other thing is, they will have to be tube fed because their sucking ability has not yet developed. Now that's an easy fix. We encourage the mother to let them nuzzle against the breast, letting them feel and taste the nipple. At any given time their instincts could take over and latch on. We estimate their stay in the NICU will be to finish out what would have been the duration of your pregnancy. And finally, I would lay odds on your wanting to know their birth weights, right?"

Heads bobbed.

Dr. Rolan pulled out a folded sheet of paper with weights noted. Remembering a weight for one baby, no problem; two, a little iffy; three, impossible, at least for him.

"Baby A's weight, two pounds one ounce. Length, sixteen and a half inches. Baby B's weight, two pounds three ounces. Length, sixteen inches. Baby C's weight, two pounds fifteen ounces. Length seventeen and a half inches. You did a fantastic job Harriet, screams and all."

Embarrassed, Harriet dropped her chin to her chest. Dr. Rolan started laughing; he was playing with her.

"Harriet, Baby A was trying to present herself to the world butt first. There isn't a woman alive that would have reacted differently, so don't you dare hang your head in shame. Now that that is cleared up, let's talk about what's really important: your babies. Most people give no thought as to what a newborn endures during the birthing process, and in your case, the stress of a vaginal birth would have been extremely tiring due to their early arrival. I'm amazed at their body strength for their wee size. This is the first time I delivered triplets and I want to thank you for the privilege; they made my day. And now, I think it's time for the nurse to get you settled into your room. You're going to need all the rest you can get, and remember the doors to the NICU are never closed to the family. So take care. I'll see you in the morning." Dr. Rolan was smiling as exited the delivery room.

Ben and Marc waved Harriet off as the nurse and an aide guided her bed through the doors and down the hallway to the elevator. She would be on the sixth floor, same as her babies. Ben and Marc all but ran to the gift shop. Ribbons with rattles attached would grace Harriet's doorway, two pink and one blue. Ben with pen in hand filled out his son's, while Marc filled out his sisters'. The weights and lengths were now listed along with their birth date, October 6, 1985. The two men looked at each other, realizing they were missing the most important information: the babies' names.

Harriet was resting comfortably—it's called sleeping. Ben and Marc were also wiped out and they had done absolutely nothing to acquire that condition. They had their own thoughts playing around in their heads. Ben stared at his wife, amazed at how she had carried three babies within her when she herself was a mere sixty inches tall. Marc was worried; how will his mother care for three babies when Ben is away at work? Both men were lost in thought when Harriet began to stir.

She was weak and worn out when she spoke. "We did it, didn't we?"

Ben and Marc rose from their seated position to face her. Ben was given the honor to answer, as was his right. Marc moved away. This was Ben and his mother's moment; never would he intrude.

"There wasn't a day in my life that I didn't dream of having a wife and kids, lots of kids. But as the years gained in numbers, my wants were stomped on. I was dreaming about something that would never be. I surrendered. And then came you, a woman so beautiful and kind, and I was so undeserving, and yet you opened your door and allowed me to enter. I embraced your love, while accepting the fact I would never hold a child of my own, but you proved me wrong three times. Thank you."

Those words spoken from Ben's heart left Harriet breathless. She reached out and pulled him close, whispering in his ear, "Thank you for loving me and our son Marc." They pulled apart, gazing lovingly into each other's eyes.

Ben was the first to break the spell. "Sweetheart, our babies are lacking names. Have you given any thought as to what we shall call them?"

Harriet did not hesitate with an answer. "There is no other name that would be more appropriate than Hannah for our firstborn daughter, in honor of your mother, and I think her maiden name, Taylor, is perfect for our second daughter. What do you think?" Poor Taylor, she will not be first even in name calling.

Ben's response was a show of tears. His mother and father died tragically in a hit-and-run accident when he was thirteen; the guilty party never surrendered or was captured. His only remaining grandparents on his mother's side raised him until the age of nineteen. They died within one year of each other; their ages at the time of their deaths were sixty-eight and seventy-three. Ben's mother was tucked away, but never out of his thoughts. She will now be held in the highest honor by being remembered through his daughters. What a tribute!

But Harriet wasn't done with the selection of names. "And Ben, if it further pleases you, our son will bear your father's name, Nicholas."

Never again will there be a day that will measure up to this moment in time. Ben had the world in his hands, he could ask for no more.

CHAPTER TWENTY-ONE

Sloan was instructing the packing crew as to what would be taken to her new address. She was no longer showing signs of depression. She had buried her vow to Lydia deep within her. Never would she betray that trust. Clay was at work and would pick her up at day's end. They would make Lydia's home, their home.

Clay's servants and now also Sloan's were told of their upcoming new address. This would add many more minutes to their travel time. Sonja was hesitating; this would cut into her time with her husband and children. Clay could see this was going to be a problem; he would cut her hours, allowing her the same precious time with her family. Sonja's paycheck would remain the same. What he did for one, he would do for the others.

Everything was coming together. Clay had retained control of his life, his wife no longer a concern. He was seated in his brown leather swivel chair deep in thought; a pencil that should have been using its lead, was instead being twirled between his thumbs and index fingers. Sloan invaded his every thought, took control of his mind. He wanted to feel her body against his, take in her scent, run his fingers through her hair, and taste the sweetness of her lips. He was hungry for her; he didn't think he could finish out the day. But his lingering thoughts were shoved aside when he heard his father's voice.

"My boy, I hope I'm not interrupting, but if you've got a minute, I would like to have a word with you?"

"Come in, Father. There is no such thing as time when it comes to you; you're my favorite person."

Phillip smiled at his boy's comment. Clay always managed to find the right words to make his father feel special.

"I know you said I could use your apartment, and in the beginning I was excited, but then the 'what if's' took over. What if you and Sloan would like to stay in the city for a few days or weeks? I would feel like an intruder. It would be much more to my liking to have my own place, and I found just that place today. I can be like you used to be, join the ranks of the healthy, walking to and from work. I can think of no better pastime."

Clay could understand his reasoning, and could tell by the tone in his father's voice he was excited about his decision. He removed himself from his chair, threw the pencil onto his drafting table, and made his way to his father.

"If this is what you really want, then let's do it."

Father and son embraced. A few more words were spoken, finishing their conversation. Clay then retreated to his work station, his father the same. But before he forced himself to concentrate on the work before him, he tried again to call his mother; this would be his fourth try of the day. The never-ending unanswered calls were becoming more and more troublesome. There was no doubt something had happened, not only to his mother, but Ali as well. He needed to find out what that something was. As much as he dreaded leaving his wife to fend for herself, Clay's desire to see the other half of his family was greater. If something unthinkable had transpired, he could not live his life without knowing. He would have to make arrangements with Andrew, the sooner the better.

Sloan was hanging out on a stool fitted with casters facing the door of their soon-to-be evacuated apartment, hair twisted in all directions, two Chinese chopsticks keeping the disorderly hair in place. She was dressed in a pair of cinnamon-colored shorts and a sleeveless white t-shirt. She wore no bra. She found out early in their relationship that Clay loved to watch the sway of her breasts as she moved about. This caused an erection like no other. She was swirling back and forth, as were her breasts, her hands pressed firmly on the seat between her legs, using her bare feet for the adventure. She was impatient for her husband.

The help had been dismissed hours before. Sonja had a fabulous meal awaiting them: lasagna and a tossed salad served with garlic bread. This was Sloan's chosen meal. Sonja did as she was instructed. Sloan was tiring of the elaborate meals. *Don't the wealthy ever enjoy regular, down-to-earth meals?* she wondered As time passed, she decided she would take it upon herself to prepare many meals. She really enjoyed the art of cooking, if you would call hamburgers and fries an art, or better still, a hot dog with chili and onions. Now who wouldn't call that yummy?

Clay tried to dissuade her to no avail, although he had to admit some of Sloan's down-home cooking was becoming his favorite. Sloan did make him a promise though: only Sonja would prepare meals for guests. She never voiced her say, but wondered if the reasoning behind this was because Clay was embarrassed to serve what he would consider low-life food.

Some things were better left unsaid; after all, it was such a small thing, why bother?

Clay was having trouble opening the door. He needed to slow down; hurry never got anything done right. But damn, he was perspiring, his need could not be put on hold for much longer; he wanted to see, feel and taste her. Finally the door gave way, the two of them propelled themselves into each other's arms, the stool sailed across the room, becoming partners with a lounging chair.

He took her face into his hands, holding tightly as his kisses ran rampant. He sucked on her lips, tasting the sweetness. He had her trembling within seconds; she began to sway, his lips refusing to allow hers to leave his, but she did break away.

"Clay, I need for you to make love to me right now, right here—hurry, my love." Sloan slid from his arms, removing her scant clothing, making herself ready. His clothes also were no longer a factor. He removed the chopsticks from her hair, never once taking his eyes off hers, and gently gripped her hair, pulling her face to his. Their lips moved and sucked as he slowly began to make love to his bride. The rapturous moans and screams sounded out endlessly although they could not be heard by fellow residents through the well-insulated walls. He had never experienced the intense heights of orgasms that she evoked.

Clay gathered Sloan close into his arms once the last bit of energy had been snatched. Evil thoughts crept into his mind. There was no room for doubt; he would kill before he would allow anyone to take her from him. He shook his head, freeing the grisly deed from his mind. He laughed to himself; he knew he could never do such a thing. But he had to ask himself, *Then why does that thought keep working its way into my mind?*

Arrangements had been made. Gus would pick them up. Clay was to be a no-show at work; he would accompany his wife to their shared quarters, the Chadsworth Mansion.

Sloan was the first to awaken. She gazed lovingly at her husband. Why had this man remained single for so long? His qualities, if rated, would surpass all. Did all men perform like her husband? Papa must have; she remembered well the moans of her mama. Sloan had become addicted to sex; if it was withheld, she would suffer greatly. She reached over, caressing the hair on her husband's chest. She threw her leg over his, leaning over to search out his lips. His quick response did not surprise her. Morning sex, she was finding, was the best, the body fresh and alert.

Gus had been waiting for well over an hour from his appointed time of pickup; he had no alternative but to ring the buzzer announcing his arrival. He hoped he would not be interrupting an early morning sex call.

When the buzzer sounded, Clay and Sloan immediately tore away from each other. Time got away from them. They couldn't move fast enough. Clay grabbed his bathrobe, while Sloan made a dash for the shower. Clay's thought on running remained the same, but eventually his steps did take him to the speaker.

"Gus, we've overslept. Give us a half hour." Gus smiled a knowing smile. One thing he knew about his boss, he was an early riser.

Clay and Sloan took one last look at their apartment. They would hire a cleaning crew once a month to keep the apartment in pristine condition.

They all but ran to the limo voicing their apologies.

Sloan's face was flushed and that flush would reappear each time Gus caught her looking at him in the rearview mirror. She knew that he knew the reason behind their tardiness, and she was embarrassed. Gus grinned all the way to the Chadsworth Mansion.

Clay would again carry his bride over a threshold.

CHAPTER TWENTY-TWO

Ben left the hospital confident Harriet was in good hands. Marc would get a good night's sleep at his mother's and would return to school first thing in the morning. He would do as his mother requested, weekend visits only. Ben assured him if a problem arose, he would be notified.

Ben slept like the dead; for the first time the annoyance of the crickets chirping did not keep him awake. After a brisk morning shower, he slipped into his uniform. As he was combing his hair, he dialed the phone number to his sweetheart's room. On the first ring there was a pick-up (Sunni was wrong, he was amazed). Harriet's sugary voice sounded. Shortly this will be the first thing he hears in the morning and the last before he retires for the night. Nothing could be grander.

"Ben, is that you?"

"Pray tell, I have competition?" He could visualize her smiling that one-dimpled smile.

"Never, my darling, never. Besides, who would take on a woman with a stomach that moves like a bowl of jell-o and with three babies to boot?"

"True, true." Laughter was heard on both ends. Ben quickly took on a serious note. "How are you doing, sweetheart, hopefully no pain?"

"It hurts somewhat where Dr. Rolan made the incision. Other than that I feel great. I don't remember feeling like this when I had my other sons. Sons…to be able to say that, nothing could compare, the sins of my past no longer hidden. The world is really a beautiful place when the soul is cleansed. And the answer to your next question, the babies are doing what is expected of them: sleeping. Can you believe it? Our babies are having no problems. In a few minutes I'm going to cuddle with them. The nurse wants to see their reaction when they are introduced to my breast. I'm so excited; I wish you could be here."

Ben had to sit down. He was overjoyed; tears clouded his eyes. *My babies are sleeping.*

"Sweetheart, if I could, I would, but duty demands my attention. I'll see you this evening when my shift is over, and when you're cuddling our little ones, give them kisses from Daddy."

A pot of coffee had just finished brewing; Ben poured himself a tall cup and settled down to read the daily delivered paper. His mind read the words, but he didn't comprehend; his mind was on his bride and his babies. He had to get his act together, he had to work, his income was vital. He knew nothing of his bride's finances; when they are disclosed he will be stunned. He was still living in his trailer next to the station; his move to his bride's house would take place when she came home.

Robert was seated at Ben's desk. He was to have his cast removed today; his return to active duty would follow. Earlier in the week Ben had placed a call to his superior advising him the services of the stand-in deputy would no longer be required as of that day. The second the door to the station opened, Robert was on his way out. Ben had to do a little sidestepping to get out of his way. Robert couldn't get out fast enough; the itching from the cast could not be tolerated a minute longer. A quick hello was all Ben received.

Mail from yesterday was sitting on Ben's desk. He thumbed through it, throwing much into the trash. Yes, they also received junk mail; whatever building has a number on it, trash follows. A small manila envelope caught his attention; the contents were from Police Chief Roger Walker. Ben took off his hat and placed it onto the rack. He pulled out his chair, steadying himself as he lowered his body; he was trembling. The envelope lay on his desk facing him. He took a deep breath as the letter opener sliced through the flap. He shook out the contents; two unsealed envelopes fell onto the desk. Truth was waiting to be told. The first letter to be read was simply addressed "Mom and Dad." Cindy's confession screamed out at Ben. He crushed the letter in his hands. The other letter was addressed to him and was from Sarah Bingington, Cindy's mother.

Dear Ben,

To write this letter took every last ounce of my strength. Time stood still when we discovered the body of our beautiful daughter Cindy. What words does a person use to describe heartache and despair? There are none. I keep thinking it's all a bad dream, she will call in the morning like she always does, then morning comes and the phone is silent. She was our reason for living, our purpose in life. To go on without her is something Ken and I cannot do. Ben, you have no idea how lucky you are, you will never have to endure the excruciating pain due to the loss of a child. But before Ken and I say our final good-byes, I have one last request: you must never give up the search for the person that killed our Cindy and her little friend Timmy. When asked, we denied anything was missing from Cindy's apartment. We lied, Ben: Cindy's black-rimmed eyeglasses were nowhere to be found. We have no doubt this maniac also has something of Timmy's. This deranged killer is collecting souvenirs from his victims. Cindy's letter is a lie, prove it.

Thank you, Sarah and Ken.

Timmy's whistle was a part of his person. When his body was found, Ben assumed it had slipped from his neck into the depths of the water. Sarah was onto something. Now all he had to do was find the eyeglasses and the whistle. Then another thought swept over him. Willie's wallet was also missing. Was this too a part of the equation? What if the Parkers' and the Harrisons' deaths were intentional, and what about baby Zac and Silva? Could Mason's Mill have a serial killer living among them? But what good is this information if everything that belonged to the victims was destroyed by fire? Ben thought of baby Zac; was something of his taken? He couldn't help it; he damned the Doc for discouraging him from talking to the Parkers. If something of Zac's did go missing, did Beth just shrug it off, thinking it would eventually turn up?

In Silva's case, her entire estate was bequeathed to the church. Most of her personal belongings were sold at auction. Masses of file cabinets and stacks and stacks of ledgers recording her employees' working hours for as many years as she owned the property had yet to be sorted through. Ben never missed the monthly meeting; he was as much a part of the town as the townspeople. He could see Silva in his mind's eye as if it were yesterday, standing at the podium, that bright red folder flapping above her head on the night she died. How would he know if something were missing? It would have to be something he knew of, like the red folder.

Oh my God, that's it. The folder — that was like her diary, a coveted item listing all her good deeds. If we do have a serial killer living among us, the killer would know this.

But Ben knew the case would never be re-opened. Maybe someday, someone will see the holes in this case and re-investigate, but he knew it would not be him. His retirement age was fast approaching; he would not stay past that time. His babies would be walking and talking, and this would give him enough exercise to keep him on the move.

Ben reached into his pocket for a packet of Alka-Seltzer; his gut was killing him. He took the time to flush away his glass of Diet Coke, substituting a glass of water. He watched the tablet sizzle, praying it would put an end to his suffering.

Cindy's letter tore at his heart. He too didn't believe a word she had said; something was missing in the tell-all confession. Or was it only a mother's intuition that someone took her daughter's life? Ben took the crumpled letter and tried pressing out the wrinkles. He re-read her letter out loud, and then voiced a comment, "Damn, I wish the Doc were still alive. Maybe he could read between the lines, for he too was present throughout the interrogation." Ben stuffed Cindy's letter and her mother's letter back into the envelope, which he would place into his strong box, a place hidden within a wall in the trailer. He would study the words in Cindy's confession when time allowed.

The door slammed shut, forcing Ben to look up towards the intruder. Robert rushed through, swinging his arms in front of him like Al Jolson; he even had Jolson's stance. Maybe he would give a rendition of "Mame." But the only sound coming out of his mouth was, "I'm back."

Ben rolled his eyes. "Robert, I have some news. Are you ready?"

"Depends. If it's good I'll make the time to hear it, if it's bad save it for later, I have to put in a slight effort to clean."

Ben's eyes starting rolling again, but he would have his say. "Robert, we will soon be welcoming new residents. I've already made arrangements for you to meet them tonight."

Robert was already busy mopping the floor but stopped to acknowledge him, the dirty water from the mop forming a puddle on the floor. "You know me, I'm always ready to meet new people, especially new neighbors. Are there any single women?"

Ben felt sorry for his deputy; his propensity to clean should spark the interest of any woman. Maybe a notice in Simon's paper would help. The headline could read:

Man will marry any woman who hates to clean.

Ben's thoughts ended, bringing him back to the present; Robert wanted to know if there were any single women.

"By golly, there are two, and there is no doubt in my mind that over time they will clamber for your attention." Ben turned away to grin. Had Robert seen, this would have given him a clue something was amiss.

Robert was ecstatic. His comeback was appropriate. "Are they pretty?"

Ben put aside his grin and acted on his serious side. "Pretty would not apply to them. Gorgeous is by far the only word to describe them. It's about a half-hour drive from here. Do you think you can put your cleaning on hold?"

"This isn't cleaning, Ben, this is called a lick and a promise. Cleaning is getting down on your hands and knees. Now just where is it that I'm to meet them?"

"St. Mary's Hospital is their home for the time being." Ben started laughing at the dumb look on Robert's face. He still didn't comprehend.

"Robert…Harriet just gave birth to our babies. The girls I want you to meet are Hannah and Taylor. Harriet chose those names in memory of my mother. And to complete the package, we have a son. He will be called Nicholas after my father. Is this not a grand day?"

Robert dropped the mop and jumped on him. For a split second Ben thought his lights were going to be put out; Robert definitely had the right to be pissed for making him believe a woman was in his future. Robert's arms engulfed Ben, dancing him around in circles.

"Oh my God, Ben, you're a daddy! Just how wonderful is that?"

The dancing continued until Ben got dizzy. Robert continued without his partner; you would have thought he was the daddy. He really needed a woman to give him a child. Ben for the first time saw Robert in a new light. He would make the greatest father. Ben decided he would make a serious effort to find him a woman.

He would take on the role of matchmaker.

CHAPTER TWENTY-THREE

Sunni was sick of sharing a room. Why should she tolerate the noise and constant disruptions associated with living in a dormitory? She wanted her own place. Why should she wait till graduation to move? Money was definitely not the problem. Manhattan awaited her. This was the weekend she would stop by a realtor's place of business. She would buy today.

She was wearing a pair of washed-out denim jeans, a loose-fitting blue jersey top and white tennis shoes with no socks. She rummaged through her closet for a long-handled purse. Thrown onto the floor was the canvas handbag she had with her when she was informed she was a millionaire. She had not used that bag in weeks; it was far too bulky to lug around with all the books she had to carry.

Her keys were sitting on top of her study desk along with her wallet. Sunni shoved her work material to the side, making space to place her large handbag. She flipped the flap, exposing the zipper part of the bag, and struggled trying to get it open. Something was caught. Sunni managed to get her finger into the slight opening and discovered paper was the culprit. After many tries the jammed piece of paper tore free. By this time Sunni was furious and wondering why she wasted so much time on something she hardly ever used. She yanked the handbag open as if the jam were the handbag's fault. The letter from her mother had caused the problem, the letter given to her by the evildoer Mr. Hewlett. Sunni looked at the envelope's face, where her own name was written in her mother's perfected hand. She hesitated; what her mother had to say was of no interest to her. She had her hands on the center of the envelope ready to tear it in half, then there was a pause. Her name, so perfect, seemed to scream out the word "OPEN." Sunni was a trifle bit curious. *What the hell, I may as well read what the bitch had to say.*

My dear sweet Sunni,

I informed the bank if anything were to happen to me, I wanted you to have a letter I wrote not too long ago, the need to express my feelings huge.

The day you were placed into my arms was the day happiness gave way to new meaning. The sun was brighter, the stars more brilliant, the darkness of the night more beautiful, all because of you. After several years of trying unsuccessfully to have a child, your father and I decided to adopt. An associate of your father gave us the name of a lawyer that guaranteed we would have a baby within weeks. He definitely lived up to his promise. The day he called, I will never forget. He had a baby girl, a newborn, did we want her? Did we want you? The splendor of that moment will live with me all the days of my life. Thank you for giving us an endless supply of joy and laughter. But most of all for bringing a love like no other, thus making our house a home.

Your mother's name is CeCe Thorman. She was an unmarried woman at the time of your birth, and for reasons she refused to disclose, she chose not to keep you. I do know this much, she must have suffered greatly for she held onto you for several weeks before relinquishing her rights. Please do not hate me for not telling you the circumstances surrounding your birth. The years of waiting for a baby were unbearable. I lived in constant fear you would leave us once you found out. I was selfish to keep this from you, please forgive me. Seek her out, honey; this is your right as well as hers.

Good-bye, precious daughter.

Rage exploded. Sunni twisted and crumpled the letter before throwing it onto the floor and stomping on it in a final show of anger. Her mother was not her mother. How could she not tell her? What lawyer had they hired to find them a baby? She snatched the letter from the floor, eyes scanning the written note. She looked on the backside and found nothing. Her mother had failed to mention the place of her birth. *Must I live my life under a cloud of darkness, not knowing who I am?* Hate will now control her life.

Sunni took her keys and wallet and tossed them into the bag that had contained the information that in time she would seek. But for now, she had to shelve her hate. She would bring it up when she had time; today she had to find an apartment.

She had forgotten her anger associated with the Jaguar and purchased another. She climbed in and gunned the engine. Sunni was in a hurry.

Driving in New York City was a nightmare, one that Sunni would welcome after her schooling. She acquainted herself with the streets of New York the day she dropped her bags at the dorm. She would have no trouble finding a real estate office; the address was in her purse. Sunni drove into a nearby parking garage, took the assigned ticket and parked.

A door chime sounded, alerting an agent that a potential client had just entered. A young man a slight bit older than Sunni stepped forward. He was of a medium build and height but not as tall as she. His blond hair was his asset; his blue, blue eyes also were to his benefit. He knew how to impress, his suit an Armani. He not only looked the part, he owned it. The commission alone from the sale of an apartment in the heart of Manhattan would pay for her Jaguar and more.

"If you are looking for an apartment you need not look further. I have the perfect place."

Was Sunni dealing with yet another psychic? One was enough in her lifetime. She hesitated; she had no patience to deal with pushy salespeople.

"I am looking for an apartment, but I don't need to be conned into something you've been trying to dump on an unsuspecting customer."

"Miss, my reputation is my calling card. I can give you many references if you so desire." The young man held out his hand. In spite of herself, Sunni gave hers in return. His offered name was Todd Sheppard; the name suited him. She replied with her own.

"The apartment I would like to show you just came on the market. It's in the heart of Manhattan, prime property for select few. And if I do sound pushy, it's because I am; this property will not last. We are within walking distance, a block at the most; do you think you would be interested in looking at it?"

Sunni could have turned and walked away; she did not. That little guy sitting on her shoulder was shouting, "It doesn't cost to take a look." She gave Todd the answer he was seeking. She did not mind walking. If she did elect to buy, she could get acquainted with the surrounding shops and businesses.

The walk was just what Sunni needed; she calmed down considerably, and was agreeable to conversation. She found herself opening up, something she never allowed herself to do with anyone other than Sloan. She confided in Todd the reason she chose Manhattan as her home. He was a slow walker; he was giving her sound advice as to what he considered would be the best location to start up her business.

Todd stopped walking and pointed to a brick building. A few steps up would take them into the apartment complex. He asked if Sunni found it to her liking. She not only found it to her liking, she signed two contracts, one for the purchase of the apartment and the other authorizing Todd to find her a suitable place to start her business, money no object. It was not a concern; she had another three years for completion of her studies. She decided money was meant to be spent and spend it she will. The day she steps down from receiving her diploma, she will step up the ladder of success, placing her signature "Ni's House of Design" high on the face of her company.

Clay and Sloan's evacuated apartment will be one floor above Sunni's.

CHAPTER TWENTY-FOUR

When Harriet was told she would be released in a week Ben was overexcited. The week seemed to drag, but as days do come and go, the week did end. Ben was thankful it was a Saturday. He would spend every second, minute and hour with his bride; there would be no interruptions. Marc offered to stay away and resume his regular visiting the following weekend.

Ben stopped at the florist located inside the hospital and left with two dozen red roses with long stems, thorns removed, clutched in his hand. And yes, he realized they would be joining the many flowers that now overcrowded Harriet's room; the flowers will soon take over their living quarters. The townspeople had kept their word and stayed away, although reluctantly. The desire to see all those babies was overpowering, but instead they would have to wait until Harriet and Ben gave the go-ahead; until then, they heaped on the flowers.

As he walked towards Harriet's room, Ben was attempting to whistle a tune; he would have done better with a harmonica.

Harriet was dressed, packed, and more than ready to start her new life. She was sitting on the bed; in her hands were the roses from Ben's visit last night. The fragrance was delightful, her face pressed deep within the petals. Ben stuck his head around the door. Youth had nothing on her. If everyone had her beauty, mirrors would be obsolete.

"Hi, sweetheart. It's been a while, but have no fear, Ben is here."

Harriet threw the roses onto the sheet, making a beeline for her now husband. Their kiss lasted longer than either one of them expected; they could not get enough. Ben was roused to the point of pursuing the hospital bed.

"It seems like forever since I held you this close. I can't wait to get you home."

"Ben, I don't think Dr. Rolan would agree to this, do you?"

"I don't know. Should we ask him?"

"If you do, you better be prepared for his answer."

"Do you think he'll say no way hoza?"

She started to laugh and then held back. "Ben, please don't make me laugh, it hurts too much.

If you're serious, go for it, I certainly wouldn't put up a fight. My need is just as great as yours."

Ben rang the buzzer, and the nurse quickly answered.

"Is Dr. Rolan in the hospital?" Ben asked.

The signal at the nurses' station identified the room and its occupant; Ben was a regular visitor, his voice recognizable. "Yes, he is, Ben; he just finished signing your lovely wife out. Would you like to see him?"

"Yes I would. Tell him it's an emergency."

Harriet shook her head, reaching out with her hand trying to hush his mouth. "Ben, why did you say it's an emergency? He's going to rush in here thinking something is wrong with me."

"Well, something is wrong with you; you need a man, and not just any man—it's Ben to the rescue."

Harriet grabbed onto her stomach. Her laughter could be heard up and down the hallways and past the nurses' station. To the nurse sitting at the desk going over some of the doctor's notes, it sounded like a distress call. She came running and found Harriet bent over clutching her stomach; she appeared to be convulsing. The nurse tried to get her back into bed, but Harriet couldn't get herself under control. Ben finally stepped in and informed the nurse what was wrong with her. Of course the nurse was relieved, but this was so uncalled for—she got the be-jangles scared out of her. She left quietly, shaking her head, although she did follow through with a statement.

"Dr. Rolan was notified of the emergency; he should be here in a heartbeat. What the tears of laughter were about I don't think I want to know. You can tell Dr. Rolan if you wish."

As the nurse left the room, Ben winked at her. Harriet apologized. But by the time she got to the nurses' station she was smiling. Happiness shares the same space as sadness; both are contagious.

Dr. Rolan rushed in; he was, as the nurse said, a heartbeat away.

"The nurse informed me what just transpired; laughter I can partake of, so deal me in."

Harriet and Ben were so into this doctor. Should they confess? If the need arises, by all means, confession is good. Ben started the conversation. Harriet hung her head, modesty still her virtue.

"Well, it's like this; we haven't been together in so long, we both feel that if we don't get back in the saddle soon, the horse will leave without us. Do you get my drift?"

Harriet shook her head, and then tried to hide her face; the collection of words that sprung from her husband's mouth would stagger anyone's imagination.

It was the doctor's turn to belly over. "I never heard it put quite that way, but who am I to tell you 'no' when the body screams for attention?" Laughter soon subsided.

Dr. Rolan moved on to talk about the babies. Harriet and Ben each took a chair, placing them side by side. Hand-holding seemed to pacify them for now.

"I would like to visit with the babies and see how they react to the breast. Would that be agreeable?"

Harriet was quick with a response. "By all means, please do. The NIC nurses think the babies are doing their best due to their prematurity. They seem eager, although they still haven't latched on. Do you think there is a reason for concern?"

"No concern at all. Besides, I miss them. They may not have latched onto the breast, but they have no trouble latching onto a person's heart." A mere mention of their babies would never fail to bring smiles.

Dr. Rolan exited Harriet's room to fetch a wheelchair; he claimed the honor of wheeling his special patient into the NICU. Ben held her hand as the wheels spun towards the nursery.

Hannah, Taylor and Nicholas were in separate incubators grouped together; the three nurses in charge of their care were comparing notes when the parents and doctor approached. There was no need to remind the visitors about the safety issues; they had already scrubbed, and each placed a hand into a porthole. Gently caressing the tiny fingers and a gentle touch to Hannah's leg brought a stretch and a yawn. Harriet's free hand covered her mouth as a tear rolled down her cheek. Ben leaned over to get a closer look at God's tiny miracle; his lips pressed tightly together, the urge to tear up was held back.

After several minutes Taylor, still in second place, finally got her rubdown, receiving the same treatment as her older sister, although she opened her eyes to take a gander at her parents. Apparently satisfied with God's choice, the sleep fairy called her back.

Nicholas protested the touch, letting them know who was boss. His crying would not stop. Harriet began to get upset; she touched his nurse's arm, asking if she could hold and comfort him in the rocker that was placed in front of his incubator. The nurse smiled and compiled. While the nurse disconnected various wires, Nicholas continued to scream his annoyance. Harriet felt as if the nurse wasn't moving fast enough. She wished she could shove her aside and take care of him herself; a mother does best.

Nicholas was now wrapped tightly and placed into his mother's arms. The blades of the rocker started moving. A song of love Harriet had written while awaiting the babies' delivery began to ring out. Ben was awestruck; he had never heard Harriet sing. Her voice echoed throughout the intensive care unit. Nurses stopped what they were doing and turned towards the sound. Babies that had been crying stopped. Nicholas was now at peace. When the melody ended, the nurses quietly applauded. The nursery was now quiet and calm.

Dr. Rolan took Harriet's hands into his. "You have the gift of song that needs to be heard. We would be grateful if you would make a tape of the song you sang. Do you think that is possible?"

"I would be honored."

"Now, how about seeing if we can get those babies of yours to nurse?"

Baby Nicholas did not fuss as Harriet was made ready to receive her son to her breast. Ben stood alongside her intrigued, the mother of his son giving all of herself. Nicholas instantly started searching, his tiny lips moving back and forth, the nipple Harriet held in place ready for his acceptance. Her little man was really trying. He started to fuss. The nurse and the doctor agreed it was best not to get him too upset; they would put it off for another day. Harriet was again discouraged. Refusing to accept another day of trying, she drew Nicholas closer and leaned over, the nipple at the tip of his mouth, then he opened as wide as his tiny mouth allowed and grabbed hold.

This little man of Harriet's and Ben's was determined he would get his nourishment directly from the person making the delivery. Cheers sounded from the three nurses in charge of the Davidsons' triplets. Dr. Rolan was all smiles, astounded. Ben fell to his knees at the foot of the rocker, arms encircling part of his family. Harriet was not alone in her tears of joy. Their little guy quickly tired. The tug on the nipple released, the drool of milk wiped away, he was at peace in his tiny incubator world. Harriet had more than enough milk; she had been pumping since delivery. The tube feeding contained only the best, milk from mother's breast.

She asked for Hannah. There it happened again; Taylor is last. The same steps were taken in removing Nick's sister. She did not fuss, nor did she wake up. She from the first day had been the most complacent. Harriet again began to sing, her wee baby girl attempting to open her eyes. Harriet was ready. She pushed the tip of her nipple across Hannah's lips, expelling the milk within. Hannah gave it her all, but failed miserably.

Several minutes passed; Hannah just couldn't get the hang of it. Harriet was weepy and extremely disappointed. Dr. Rolan could see why Harriet was upset; if Nicholas could do it, why not Hannah? She was offered Kleenex as Hannah was removed from her arms. Ben kept rubbing her back, trying to give her some measure of comfort. She, like her baby girl, failed.

Dr. Rolan knelt in front of her. "Harriet, did you not notice how Hannah did not appear as interested as Nicholas? In my opinion, she's not hungry. I would lay odds, she would start her search eagerly if she had to wait another hour. Feel like staying around for a retry?"

All Harriet could do was nod, her show of tears unending. Hannah was returned to her safe haven.

Dr. Rolan retrieved Taylor himself, cuddling her close. Her eyes were open. He stared down into her wee face and it was love at first sight. She grimaced, betraying a dimple. Dr. Rolan wished she were his; being gay never meant he couldn't raise a child. He would look into a surrogate, although time was not on his partner's side. Henry White, his soul mate, was his concealed partner.

"Shall we see if Taylor is more enthusiastic?" Reluctantly Dr. Rolan relinquished her into her mother's arms. Her eyes remained opened, the breast lay before her. Leave it to Taylor, she would show her older sis how it's done.

Bravo, Taylor. You can now claim first place in the chow-down department in reference to your sister Hannah. Harriet glanced up at Ben smiling; he was beaming with pride. Dr. Rolan somehow knew she had a lot of spunk.

Harriet would give Hannah another try. Hannah was beginning to fuss, a good sign she was either hungry or dirty. Her primary care nurse changed her diaper first, and then disconnected all the attached wires, wrapping her tightly. Hannah seemed to be searching, her head bobbing in all directions. Harriet gently took her to her breast, praying like she had never prayed before. If Hannah wasn't hungry, something was wrong with her. Hannah was strong; Harriet had a hard time directing her to her nipple.

"There, there, baby girl, please calm down. Mommy's going to feed you, okay?"

The struggling continued until Hannah's energy level was spent. She fell asleep. Harriet refused to give her back to the nurse; she would stay until Hannah nursed, even if it meant spending the night. Ben understood; he too would spend the night. On the fifth try, mission was accomplished. Harriet would lay testimony to the fact Hannah had more suction than Nicholas and Taylor combined; she also clung to the nipple longer. Harriet and Ben could now go home. Although they were both exhausted, their spirits could not have been higher.

Harriet would divide her time; daylight belonged to the babies, evenings belonged to Ben. The babies were introduced to the bottle as an alternate feeding. When able, Harriet would breast-feed. She would deprive no one of her time. She also refused to allow Ben visiting hours Monday through Friday; the stress of driving to and from the hospital was wearing him down. Arguments from him were to no avail. He would do as Harriet ordered.

Ben and Marc took one weekend away from visiting the babies to move Ben's personal belongings from his mobile home to Harriet's home, where they would be stacked against a wall in the living room. When time permitted, they would go through his things, deciding what to keep and what to dispose of. His household contents would remain with the trailer.

Harriet had suggested giving the place to Norman, for when the day came and he was no longer able to work, he would have a place to truly call home. Ben heartily agreed.

Marc would continue to visit weekends with his sisters and brother. He would stay in the three-bedroom home until the babies arrived and shoved him outdoors. At that time he would rent a room in a boarding house owned by one of the farmers, his decision.

The babies were gaining weight and becoming more alert. They were now six weeks of age. Everyone settled into a happy and content routine.

It was time to call Phillip.

CHAPTER TWENTY-FIVE

Clay carried his bride over a new threshold.

The servants were lined up, and Clay was to make the introductions. Sloan was embarrassed; she had come farther in life than she ever thought possible. When each of the servants' names were called they did a curtsy, showing respect for the new mistress of the house. Clay received the attention he was entitled to when he spoke.

"There will be no changes. You will continue as if my grandmother were still present. If over time my wife prefers to arrange things differently she will so advise. I have nothing more to say, unless my wife wishes to say something?" Sloan shook her hung head; Clay noticed. He quickly dismissed his staff of employees. They scattered to different areas, duties calling.

He was a little upset with his wife and let her know it. "Sloan, you embarrassed not only yourself but me as well. Never drop your head in the presence of servants, it's very belittling. You must be kind, but show authority."

She had a quick comeback. "What would you have me do? Walk up and down in front of them, hands tucked behind my back like I was a drill sergeant giving them an inspection?"

Clay had been too hard on her too soon; Sloan would find her way eventually, time definitely on her side.

He was just as quick with an apology. "Babe, I'm sorry. It's been a trying day, and I'm showing a bad side. Please forgive me?" Her reply was a lengthy kiss that gave a guarantee of more to come.

Sloan quickly settled into her new home. Nothing was discarded, rearranged or changed; she loved Lydia's touch, for the older woman paid close attention to detail. Clay was pleased the home he grew up in would remain as it had always been, though he would never have stood in his wife's way if she decided otherwise. Together they roamed the hallways. The servants' quarters in a separate wing of the mansion Sloan would not enter; this belonged to them, this was their private sanctuary. Life would be restored to this grand old house, she would see to it. She could envision children running up and down the staircases, possibly sailing down the handrails, sliding across the marble floors, skating allowed if they so desired.

Yes, this will be a home where everyone from every walk of life will be welcomed.

Clay guided her down the Grand Hall as it was called. It was on the main level of the estate, its walls decorated with a gallery of pictures of ancestors dating back to the 1700s. The frames looked as old as, if not older than the portraits themselves. Sloan covered her mouth, giggling at the hairstyles and clothing worn not only by the men but the women as well. Clay had her by the hand leading the way when he caught her laughter. He turned.

"I agree…pitiful, isn't it? Can you imagine getting dressed each morning in such adornments? The time involved in caring for the beards and mustaches had to have been tiring."

They both started laughing until Sloan came to the picture of a beautiful woman from their time.

"Clay, who is this woman? She doesn't belong on this wall; she should have a place of her own."

Sloan turned towards him. She had caught him off guard; he had forgotten about the fraudulent photograph. Clay did not know what to say. How could he explain a part of his life that he himself had just learned of? He still had not talked to his mother to allow everything to be revealed. Until such time he would continue with a cover-up.

"Let me put it this way, I really don't know this woman. She has been on this wall for as long as I have lived here." Clay was somewhat telling the truth.

"Your father must know. Did you ever ask him?"

"Babe, my father in his youth had a difficult time. If he does know anything, I think it would toss bad memories into his face. I for one would hate to dredge up a part of his past that has long been buried. If you want to take it upon yourself to question him, be my guest; but please don't ask me to be a willing participant."

"Oh Clay, I wouldn't do anything to upset your father; he's my favorite father-in-law." Sloan smiled that smile he loved so well. He reached out and she welcomed his embrace, situation now under control.

Six weeks in her new home and still counting as Sloan scratched the days off the calendar. She was hoping she would miss her period, but she did not. She never approached Clay on the subject of children, sure that he would bring it up in time.

Clay was at work when he approached his father's office. He knocked; never would he invade his father's right to privacy. His father sounded out, "Come in."

He was at his drafting table deep in thought, never taking his eyes off the project before him.

Without looking up, he spoke. "What's up?" When no comment came forth, he looked up. Immediately he was on his feet walking over to give his boy a hug. "My boy, why do you insist upon knocking? My office is your office."

"Because your office is your office, Father, and I will always respect that."

They stood face-to-face. Phillip's hands were now on his boy's shoulders when he spoke. "Come on in. How about a drink? It's late enough in the day."

Clay glanced at his watch, not because he doubted his father, but to estimate how much more time would be spent away from his wife. Another hour and he would head home.

He never knew where he would find his wife upon his arrival; she could be lying naked on a comforter in the entrance foyer, hugging the bear rug in his study, occupying the sofa or simply waiting in bed. Sloan never failed to surprise him with different means of entertainment. She could write a book on the techniques she applied in their lovemaking. This woman was no longer a pussy cat; she was a full-blown lioness.

Clay turned his attention back to his father; he was getting aroused. "I'll have a scotch, no ice please." He quickly took a chair to hide the evidence, while his father fixed two identical drinks. Phillip handed his boy the drink and took a chair alongside the table that divided them, his own drink secured in his hand.

"So what's on your mind besides the desire to see me?"

Clay joined his father in a smile and slight laugh. "Father, I think it time to introduce Sloan to our circle of friends and many associates. She's met my closest friends, only because they persisted in tearing down my door with their knocking."

"I agree. I would feel privileged if you let me take charge." Clay was in agreement.

Phillip glanced at the calendar on his desk. "Let's plan on November thirtieth, that's on a Saturday. My secretary can take care of the invitations; she has all the names and addresses in my rolodex. I think Mother would have been honored to have the black-tie affair in her home. Do you agree?"

Clay could not have thought of a more appropriate place. in his mind's eye he could see Lydia rushing about, making sure the finishing touch had her hand in it. He smiled thinking that thought.

Phillip continued. "When I get finished, this will end up being the social event of the year and your wife will make everyone sit up and take notice. What a glorious day that will be. Leave all the details to me. Your job will be to focus your attention on your wife. Now get out of here and go home; this shop is closed to you."

As he headed out the door Clay turned and thanked his father. In his eyes, God elected Phillip as one of his leaders, and Clay felt blessed to be a part of that life.

Gus was waiting; he now chauffeured Clay to and from his workplace Monday through Friday. Today was the last day of the work week, and Clay's wife could expect him home early.

No matter how many times Clay was picked up and delivered, he always acknowledged Gus with some sort of pleasantry, although today his thoughts were on his mother and Ali. He will be out of New York and on his way to Chicago the day after his wife is welcomed into the folds of High Society. This time he will not procrastinate.

CHAPTER TWENTY-SIX

Harriet dialed the operator. It was early in the morning, and she would be leaving shortly for the hospital. But first she needed the phone number of Chadsworth & Chadsworth Architectural Firm. Phillip had been on her mind for several days. She would no longer put off talking with him. A woman's voice sounded at the other end of the telephone line. Harriet's heart began to flutter wildly; the feeling was beginning to make her sick.

"Chadsworth & Chadsworth. May I help you?"

"Yes, please, I would like to speak with Phillip Chadsworth."

"May I ask who is calling?"

"If you don't mind I would like to keep that confidential. If you would just tell him it's a person from the happiest time in his life, I'm sure he will accept my call."

"One moment please."

When the receptionist relayed the message, Phillip immediately picked up the receiver. "Jena…?"

"Yes, Phillip, it is I."

He couldn't believe it. There was no way he could count the number of times he had dreamt of this moment. The sound of her voice brought back memories of the nights they spent together, discussing their future, stars in their eyes, clouds under their feet. Did this phone call just happen or were there other forces at work? After all these years, was she seeking him out? Did she want to resume what they were forced to end?

"Jena, you made my heart race when my receptionist relayed your message. Just yesterday Clay and I were talking about you and Ali. We were concerned when you didn't answer your telephone. If he had kept a record of the calls it would fill a book. And what happened to Ali's promised visit? She never even gave him the courtesy of a call. I'm sorry, Jena, I'm going on and on…it's just that we were extremely concerned for you as well as Ali. We envisioned everything bad that could have happened. Thank God everything is okay. I assume you've already spoken to Clay; he must be relieved."

"No, Phillip, I have not spoken to Clay. There are reasons that I prefer you did not mention this call at this time. I need to see you; it's extremely important. Do you think you can come to Mason's Mill without his knowledge?"

"I guess I can. But Jena, I need to know what's going on. Should I be worried?"

"I can't discuss anything on the telephone. If I could I would, but what I have to say is strictly person to person."

"By the tone in your voice, I get the feeling it's not something I want to hear." He could detect a hint of sadness in her voice. Phillip would have a hard time dealing with the unknown on a day-to-day basis if he did not make arrangements immediately.

"I need the directions to your home, and if it's agreeable I could be there by tomorrow."

Jena gave him the necessary information with an additional request. "Phillip, if it's at all possible I would like it to be a morning visit."

"I will try, weather and road conditions permitting. Until then, I think I will start praying." Was what he heard, a tearful good-bye? He would do what he said, he would pray.

Jena (alias Harriet) hung up the phone and started to weep. Just hearing Phillip's voice brought forth the vision of him. He was once her life; she had loved him and still felt the pangs of that love, and now she was about to put such an unimaginable hurt on him. She prayed he would be strong enough to endure. Was she enacting revenge? Never. If that were so, she would have gotten her evens years ago. Her way of thinking changed with the appearance of her son Clayton. He had the right to know his real father, be it good or bad. And the finale, Phillip had to be told of the tragic death of his sister.

So much on her plate, Harriet prayed she could hold up.

She rushed out of the house, late to visit her babies who were waiting to be cuddled and fed. Dr. Rolan had already confirmed the babies would be home in time for Christmas.

Six more weeks and the fun begins.

.

CHAPTER TWENTY-SEVEN

What just happened? Jena called me instead of her son; something is dreadfully wrong. Phillip did not have time to spare; he immediately got on the phone, his pilot always on standby. Rick Matters picked up on the third ring. He was forty-two years of age and had been Phillip's personal pilot for several years. He was divorced with four girls, all teenagers ranging in age from sixteen to nineteen with not a year missing. He was tall and slender, fair of skin and blue-eyed, his wavy blond hair the exact color of his eyebrows and mustache. He had many women friends.

"Rick, I need for you to fly me out of Kennedy Airport no later than five tomorrow morning. Please make the necessary arrangements with the airport authority; my destination will be Chicago O'Hare Airport. I will also need a car to drive. Check with the trental agency I use, see if they have a Bentley or Rolls Royce available. If a

"

problem arises you can call me at the office or my home. Until then, take care."

There was no dillydallying around; Phillip was in a hurry.

He had to come up with something to tell Clay, but what? Business trips were planned in advance. He was deep in thought when his boy knocked on his glass door. He rose from his seated position and walked to the door. The instant the door opened he had his arms around his boy, hug intense.

"Hey, what's up? Is something wrong?"

Phillip brushed a tear from his eye. "I just had the urge…call me sentimental."

"Okay, but I just received a chill. Are you sure there is nothing wrong?" Had Clay known he possessed the powers of his mother and exercised that ability, he would have picked up on the plight facing his father.

"Absolutely. Come on in. What's on your mind?" Phillip could not look him directly in the eye; he just lied to his boy, something he thought was a thing of the past.

"I just dropped by to confirm lunch. Is it still on?"

"I was just about to head out to your office; you saved me a trip. I'm sorry, my boy, lunch is out. I have a list of things that need to be taken care of, and the way it's looking I may not make it in tomorrow." His excuse was acceptable; many times they had to check how things were going on the job site. He and Clay finished what they had to say and reported back to the work at hand.

Phillip for the first time in his life was glad a project was not in the works. His concentration was on Jena. In a matter of hours he would come face-to-face with the woman his life of dreams was based on.

Darkness was still in force when Phillip's feet touched the floor. He had not slept, prayers repeating themselves. He rushed into the shower. Coffee was already in the make, timer set the night before. He pulled out a chair to sit upon, towel damp from the shower clinging to his lower half. *Jena, Jena,* was the thought of the day. The black coffee slowly made its way down his throat, its wake-up call unnecessary. The wall clock read 4:10 a.m. He had to get a move on. The suitcase was waiting for the grip of its owner's hand, parked by the front door of his newly acquired multimillion-dollar apartment. He had packed a few things to tide him over if for any reason he was left stranded.

The called cabbie was waiting. Phillip's tan Armani jacket provided not only warmth but comfort. His choice of clothing was a navy blue Dolce & Gabbana pull-over shirt with Bikkemberg jeans, his loafers by Gucci. He looked the part; wealth and good looks a perfect combination. He hoped Jena would notice his well-toned body. When she left unwillingly he was a boy; today she would see a man.

The plane was ready for takeoff. Phillip greeted Rick, and then tossed in a comment. "Weather looks good. Let's hope it stays that way."

"From what I've been told today and tomorrow will be sunny. And I did as you instructed; a Bentley will be parked inside your hangar at the airport."

Phillip climbed aboard. The *Wall Street Journal*, his choice of reading material, was lying on the opposite seat. He really tried to read, but Jena kept interfering.

He moved his seat to a reclined position and closed his eyes. Sleep claimed what it was denied last night; Jena was forced to leave. Rick repeated himself three times before he got a reaction that they had landed. Phillip felt much better; the little amount of sleep revived his attention span. He could handle anything; at least that was his intention.

The Bentley was secured and waiting as promised. Rick was given further instructions in regards to Phillip's return. He would wait out the day, and it would be a very long day.

The suitcase took up little space inside the trunk. Phillip put the car in gear and headed towards Mason's Mill, directions to the farming community lying on the passenger seat. It would be a two-hour drive. He drove faster than the law allowed, tickets his least concern. It seems like an eternity when you are anxious for the unknown.

The bridge slowed his approach. He had one thought: *So this is the place where my heart has been hiding.* The shopping district was huge for such a small town. A sign noted 1,387 total residents. It was severely weather-beaten and the total was quite faded. Phillip doubted the count was correct. He passed a multitude of cars thinking, *This is one happening shopping center.* He passed the police station just as Ben walked out the door. Ben missed the Bentley by seconds, and Phillip lost the chance to see his competitor. He continued to follow the map with its twists and turns. There it was, just as she said, "You will see a red mailbox with the name Anderson." Phillip pulled onto her steep driveway. He looked down at his hands grasping the wheel. Had they not been attached to the wheel he would not have been able to control the trembling. He could not move; his heart was racing to a tempo that could only be described as nearly fatal.

Harriet had just finished pumping. The weight of her breasts had been heavy, and relief followed. She was one of the lucky ones, with the gene to reclaim her slim body. The visible stretch marks she acquired were from her firstborn; few were added from the additional births.

She told Ben she was going to put an end to her past that day. She asked him not to call or stop by, and he promised he wouldn't.

The night before she had informed her babies' nurses that for the first time she would be unavailable for their daily feedings. She would continue her routine the following day.

The front door opened. She stepped onto the porch and held her breath. The love of her youth stared back at her. For several seconds they were back in the privacy of her bedroom, the longing for each other evident. Her feelings exploded. This was not just a fire burning, this was a volcanic eruption. She never expected this; she loved Ben, but her body was screaming for Phillip's. He couldn't get out of the car fast enough. She turned back into her house, Phillip behind her. He kicked the door closed. Their lips searched for the days lost.

He whispered into her ear, "I've never stopped loving you."

She held nothing back; she took him by his hand guiding him towards her and Ben's bedroom. She was still in love with Phillip. She took her time, undressing him, savoring his body, her lips continuously searching for his, her hunger for him much stronger than that for her husband. It was his turn to undress her, her eyes closed as his kisses traced the outline of her now naked form. He gently picked up her feather-light body and tenderly placed her onto the bed. Their lovemaking held no bounds; they explored each other as if it were their first time. He drew back when he noticed the visible pink line betraying her c-section.

"Jena, what is this?" His fingers began tracing the incision.

"Phillip, my darling, I will explain everything, but for now please make love to me. I desperately need to feel you."

He was gentle with her; if something were wrong, he did not want to hurt her. If she wanted and needed him, he would see to her needs, he loved her that much. The morning was spent making love; thankfully it refused to race into the afternoon. They lay entwined, hands still at work exploring the wonders of the human body, while their lips reveled in the splendors that a kiss brought forth. Jena was the first to break the spell.

"Oh Phillip, what have you done to my heart? I thought I had put you out of my mind. But that saying, out of sight out of mind, only holds true if that person doesn't reappear. What we are doing is wrong, terribly wrong.

"I am married to a wonderful man and now I have betrayed him. To confess would put an end to our marriage, something I can't and won't do.

The scar I have is from a c-section. I recently gave birth to triplets."

Phillip pulled back, shocked. The woman he loved his entire life freely gave him her love and body, and now claimed to be married with children. Was this a slap in his face? He removed himself from her bed, the bed she shared with her husband.

He quickly dressed with a comment. "I hurt you badly years ago, and now you decide to pay me back. That's it, isn't it?"

"No, Phillip, you have it all wrong. You mustn't be angry with me. I did not mean for this to happen. The moment I saw you, a force like nothing I ever experienced came over me; I desperately wanted you. To deny that love would be hypocritical. But what we feel for each other now cannot go forward. In the beginning I thought we had a chance, but your father took that away. I made a new life and I am happy. Forgive me for giving you the impression we would be together again."

Phillip's back was facing her.

"Phillip, I did call you for a reason. I need to focus on my family, and to do that I have to release the past and all the horror that came with it. But first, I need to shower and dress. Would you mind waiting in the living room?"

Phillip could have run, shouting an obscenity as he left, and for her to "Go to Hell." But what would that accomplish? It would not make his love go away.

"I will do as you ask."

The scent of his body clung to hers; she would have to scrub it away. She cried the words, "Phillip, my darling, I will never forget you. Forgive me." Tears mingled with the flow of water from the shower head. She was forced to admit she loved Phillip far more than Ben.

The fragrance of Oscar, Jena's favorite perfume, flowed through the living room. When she found what she liked, she never wavered in her choice, except for now: Phillip was out, Ben was in. Phillip chose a chair facing the sofa. Jena, now dressed in shorts and a t-shirt, sat barefooted across from her lover, his green eyes embedded in her brain.

They stared at each other as if memorizing their images. Jena leaned forward, her hands clasped together.

"Phillip, what I'm about to tell you is going to hurt you worse than you can ever imagine. I committed a grave injustice. God in his goodness may forgive me, but I seriously doubt you will. Phillip…Clay is not your son; he is the son of your father, he is your half-brother."

Phillip jumped from his chair screaming the worst kind of filth that no one should ever hear.

"What in the hell are you talking about? Is this some kind of sick joke? There is no way my father impregnated you. Is your hate for him so strong that you will lower yourself to tell such a falsehood? Jena, please don't do this. If you want me to get on my knees to apologize for the wrong my father did, I will, just don't tell me Clay is not my son."

Tears worked their way to the surface, not only in Phillip's eyes but Jena's as well.

"Phillip, your father was evil; he raped me from the beginning of my employment. When it started, it was innocent enough. He would come into my room using many excuses—was I satisfied with my living quarters, was my bed comfortable, did I need more blankets?—on and on, until one night he drew me to him, telling me he loved me, that I reminded him of your mother when she was young and always eager to make love. He said he had a desperate need for nightly sex, and your mother no longer was a willing partner. Night after night he pleaded, many times on his knees. I kept refusing, pushing his hands off my body. I really thought he would tire of the notion of having me. It never happened.

"I began to hide, which was foolish. He always found me. I existed on less than four hours of sleep each night. I wasn't giving it my all in the care of your sister. I finally had enough. I told him if he continued to bother me, I would report him to the proper authorities for trying to entice a minor. He flew into a rage; he grabbed me by my hair and threw me onto the bed. He ripped away at my night clothes; he then fell on top of me. The weight of his body was suffocating. I tried to scream, but the force of his hand shoved over my mouth prevented this. Phillip, he brutalized me. I was a virgin and he tore into me. I bled for many days. The pain was so intense, I begged God to end my life, but He had forsaken me."

Jena dropped her head, ashamed. She was emotionally drained. Tears at rest returned in full force. Phillip held his; his anger was way too powerful. His father had raped the woman he loved; he did not doubt her.

He needed to take revenge on someone, but whom? His father was dead. Had he not been, Phillip in all likelihood would have killed him. He would continue to damn him for months; hate would forever rule the remainder of his life. He refused to visualize the horror his father had inflicted upon his sweet Jena.

Jena was sobbing nonstop. Phillip went to her side and drew her to him. Words could not ease the pain she had revisited. Several minutes passed before at last she regained control.

"Phillip, I am so very sorry. I never wanted to hurt you; you must believe that, if nothing else."

"Jena, I know you are sorry, and I am also sorry. You have endured far more tragedy than I." He was now seated on the sofa, his arm draped over Jena's shoulder. He was thinking there would never be another day to compare. He was about to know more.

"No, I do not think so. Phillip, your sister Ali is no longer with us. She and her family perished in a horrible house fire."

Phillip was thrust into a nightmare. He was having a hard time dealing with the rape and now he no longer had a baby sister. How much cruelty can be inflicted on one's life in a single day? He dropped his head onto Jena's shoulder. There was no shame in weeping for the little sister who was set to return home after being away eighteen years. If tears were counted, Phillip's by far would have outnumbered Jena's.

"Jena, how am I to tell Clay I am not his father and that Ali has died?"

"Phillip, I believe he needs to hear this from my lips. After all, I was the deceiver; you were not a party to the sham."

"I don't know...I've been with him for twenty-eight years and not to hear it from me could be devastating. I need time to think this over. To make a decision at this time is too overwhelming. You will have to bear with me. Will you do that, Jena?"

"Whatever you decide I will abide by your wishes."

She continued, her heart now on her sleeve. "Phillip, when Clay found me, I had no time to prepare for questions and answers, let alone tell him about my then pregnancy. It was that night that I lost Ali and her family. I went into shock and was placed in a nursing home until my subsequent recovery, which was the reason for the unanswered calls. But there is more. I never got the chance to tell him he has a brother, Marc, that is six years younger, and now he has an additional three siblings: Hannah, Taylor and Nicholas. I can only pray he will be pleased."

Phillip could not grasp all that was being told to him. Surely he did not think she would wait for him. He turned his back and she moved on. He had no one to blame but himself.

He responded to her comment. "I have no doubt that after the shock wears off, he will board his plane immediately. Will you allow me the pleasure of telling him?"

"What you are asking is for me to let you shoulder all the responsibility…but if that is your desire, I will honor that decision."

But she was not finished, she had more shocking news.

"Phillip, I have more to tell you in regards to your sister. Her eldest child, Sloan, was not in the house at the time of the fire. She is alive, but has gone missing. We've distributed and hung posters everywhere; so far there is no news of her whereabouts. We take solace in knowing a part of Ali lives on through her beautiful daughter. All that is left is prayer for her safe return."

An alarm blasted in Phillip's head. There was no way his Sloan could be the one Jena was speaking of. If that were so, she would be his daughter-in-law/sister-in-law/niece.

"Jena, I think I heard you wrong in regards to her name."

"I know what you are thinking: Sloan is for a man, not a woman, but her father chose that name out of tradition; the firstborn child, girl or boy, is named after the grandfather. If you knew her as well as I, you too would think the name a perfect fit."

The look on his face caused her concern. "Phillip, is something wrong? My God, you look as if you heard the worst news possible."

He prayed he would just die and get it over with. How does he tell his son/brother that his wife is his niece? A sin of such magnitude has no manual of instructions on what to do. He dropped his head into his hands and cried for what could not go forward.

His boy/brother would have to end his marriage or see bars. Jena was now on her knees trying to comfort him, for what she had no idea.

"Jena, I have a request. Would you give me enough time to sort through all you have told me before I make any announcements?"

Her forehead furrowed. "Is there something I should be concerned with?"

"No, no, you just caught me by surprise." Pandora's Box has just been opened, letting all the ills escape. Woe to the receiver.

"Jena, Clay is sure to call you; he never misses a day. He must know nothing of what we discussed until I think the time appropriate. I need to break the news gently, if there is such a thing."

She did not hesitate with an answer. "When he calls and asks where I have been, I will tell him I had to go away for a while, that being the truth. I'll throw in the comment, 'Why, did you miss me?' That should throw him off guard to question me further. I placed a tremendous burden on you; I pray everything will go easily."

It was time to call it a day; Phillip had never been so weary and lost. Jena arose from her seated position; she knew it was time to say good-bye, this time forever. And then, as if on cue, their lips touched and clung, this moment to last their lifetime. She began biting her lip and shaking her head, the tears blinding her vision when he released her hand and walked out the door. She had one consolation; she will forever remember the splendor of his kiss.

She closed the door; she did not watch him drive off.

CHAPTER TWENTY-EIGHT

Phillip was not driving a straight line, his tears falling like rain in a rain forest. He would recall no memory of leaving the shopping center or crossing over the bridge. He drove until the gas reached a dangerous low, then he pulled over to the side of the highway. His head fell onto his hands while he gripped the steering wheel. He wailed like a baby that had had no food for days.

His fulfillment in life was taken away when Jena announced his boy carried his father's genes. Of course Phillip had doubt, until she outlined the date of conception; he himself had not shared her bed until thirty days later. The memory of your first time stays with you. Of course Jena was deeply apologetic and saddened for deceiving him, but he would not be the man he is, if he did not understand. She was carrying a child, she had no money, where would she go? She had to think of her baby.

If no one had yet qualified in the *Guinness Book of World Records* for crying the most tears, Phillip would be the first. He seriously tried to stop, but it was useless.

A tap on the window forced him to join the living. He quickly swiped his hand across his face, trying to erase the agony. A police officer began shaking his finger signaling for him to lower the window. The days were turning cold; November had a couple weeks remaining. Phillip did as instructed.

"I was parked a ways down the road and you've been here for well over fifteen minutes. Do you have a problem?"

"No, sir. I'll get on my way immediately."

The officer leaned down and noticed the puffiness of Phillip's eyes and the blotches covering his face. "Sir, I need to see your driver's license. You appear to have been drinking."

"No, sir, I just had a really bad day." Phillip provided his driver's license. The officer then told him to get out of his car. He was made to walk a straight line; no problem there.

The officer was extremely kind and thoughtful.

"Apparently there is something troubling you. Why don't you go home and try and work out your problem. Tomorrow will be much better, trust me."

Phillip thanked him and was about to offer his own comment, "If only that were true," then decided against it. For all of his wealth, this would not make his problem disappear. He was in a situation he could not run from; he had to face it head-on.

Phillip put the car in gear, waved at the officer and pulled onto the highway. At the first sign he saw for gas he would pull over and fill up. He would then put in a call to his pilot, Rick. Phillip was approximately an hour out of Chicago. He would be home before nightfall.

His worst nightmare was about to begin.

Rick made no comment when he noticed the condition of his boss. Neither said hello. Something or someone had taken the wind out of his boss's sails. Their air time was spent in silence. Rick knew there was nothing that would wash away the sadness etched on his boss's face; this man was suffering badly.

Back on the ground, Rick took the lone suitcase and placed it into the trunk of the waiting limo, but he could not let Phillip leave without saying something.

"When you feel all is lost and there is nowhere to turn, call on Jesus."

Phillip turned towards Rick just as he was about to enter the car. "Thank you, Rick. That's the best thing I've heard all day. I think I'll take your advice." Phillip gave a half-hearted smile.

Phillip's phone was ringing when he stepped into his apartment. He thought it best to ignore it; to carry on a conversation would be nearly impossible. But the persistent ringing could no longer be held off.

"Hello." He was always polite when he answered the phone.

"Father, you were gone longer than I thought you would be. I pray it wasn't a bad day."

His boy's voice gave him reason to choke back his tears. "No, it was an okay day, I'm just beat. Do you think we can talk tomorrow?"

Clay could detect that all was not well with his father. "Okay, let's hear it. What's up? I can tell by the tone in your voice all is not as it should be."

"Clay, please, I'm exhausted, I need sleep. We'll talk tomorrow."

The sound of a hang-up caught Clay off guard. He stared at the receiver still clutched in his hand. He could not remember the last time his father called him Clay; not once in this brief exchange did he say "my boy."

Sloan only heard one side of the conversation and Clay appeared concerned. She walked over to him and began stroking his neck.

"Honey, I couldn't help overhearing...Is something wrong with your father?"

He turned towards her, welcoming her presence. He pulled her to himself and gave her a deep, loving kiss. "Something is definitely wrong. I guess I'll have to wait until tomorrow to find out."

Sloan loved her father-in-law; waiting was the wrong choice. "I think you should drive over to his apartment immediately. I could go with you and keep you company. How about it?"

"No, babe. He said he was really tired, that all he wanted was sleep. Besides, maybe I'm reading more into it than it really is. Come on, let's take a walk on the beach; before long snow instead of sand will be our carpet."

He noticed the expression on Sloan's face; he had not convinced her they were doing the right thing by waiting. She grabbed a shawl resembling a coat to ward off the chill of the fast-approaching night winds. They headed out towards the ocean, each with an arm wrapped around the other's waist; they were lost in their own thoughts.

Morning would not come fast enough.

CHAPTER TWENTY-NINE

Phillip never hung up on his boy without saying good-bye. What was he thinking? Clay would have realized something was wrong. What he had done was stupid, but how do you call back words and actions once they've been released? He was struggling with the after-effects. The hurt was like none he ever experienced. How does a man who thought he was a father tell his boy, who he thought was his son, that he was not? Phillip was bone weary and brain tired. He needed to relax and figure out his next step.

He began to undress, tossing his clothing about, something he had never done. He had a place for everything; the floor was not one of them. The pulsating water from the shower head brought a measure of relief, while the seat within the shower stall felt the weight of his body for well over thirty minutes. No one could differentiate between the water and the tears.

Phillip toweled dry, then wrapped the same towel around his waist. He faltered in his steps towards the kitchen, thinking and thinking. He removed the stainless steel kettle from the stove and filled it with tap water. A cup of tea could supply some sort of comfort. The cup was resting in his hand, Phillip waiting for its comfort, when he suddenly sent it sailing across the room. His eyes focused upward, beseeching the heavens to open and hear his distress call.

"Why, God, why? Why did You desert me? Why did You allow this to happen? What have I done to You that's deserving of such punishment? I have always loved You and believed in Your wisdom and You turned Your back. How am I to trust You after this?"

Anger and hate began to do a number on him. Rick did not mean it quite that way when he said to call on Jesus.

Sleep eluded Phillip throughout the night. He came to a conclusion: there was no solution to the immense problem before him. He would just have to blurt it out and watch his boy crumble before him.

He was now dressed in a brown striped short-sleeved Gucci shirt and tan Burberry slacks; a pair of camel-colored Gucci slip-ons completed the look. When he stepped out of his apartment looking as he did, he would catch many a woman's eye until they saw the haggard look upon his face. He gave the appearance of someone fast approaching his seventies, while in truth fifty was staring him in the face.

He glanced at his watch. The hour was one minute away from 6:00 a.m. The office staff's workday would not begin for another two hours.

Phillip knew his boy was up and ready to go, although in the last couple months Clay's arrival was often delayed. Clay had a huge distraction in his wife/niece. Who could blame him? Sloan possessed all the qualities of a temptress. Any man would be foolish not to linger in bed with such a woman.

Phillip recalled the memory from the day before. Jena herself had turned into a woman that left him wanting for more and more. She tore into him like an animal that had had no nourishment for days. He dated when it was a necessity, and never did he have to ask to see his companion's art; she gladly showed him her works. And now he had a comparison; his needs from this day forward would suffer greatly. He had Jena's love, her husband had the benefits. He also knew she would come to know the enormity of the letdown when her desires went unfulfilled. He worked hard at satisfying those desires, wanting to make sure no one could do for her what he had accomplished. He knew he performed brilliantly when her screams of ecstasy rang out time after time. Phillip made a vow: he could not and would not give Jena up. He would somehow, somewhere, meet with her, if only to satisfy the sexual cravings of their bodies.

There was no way to keep skirting around the issue at hand. It was time to be the bearer of bad news.

The ring of the phone caused Clay and Sloan to hesitate with their lovemaking, their second performance in the make. She just started with the moaning and Clay hated to leave her in that condition, but he worried it could be his father.

"Sorry, babe, it could be my father."

Sloan wasn't greedy…well, maybe a little, but her father-in-law came first.

The sound of his boy's voice grabbed at Phillip's heart. "My boy, before you say a word, just answer with a yes or a no. Is Sloan able to hear your conversation? If it's a yes, you must move out of her hearing range, okay?"

"Yes, that's affirmative."

Sloan wrinkled her brows, holding up her hands palms up, questioning who was on the phone. Clay shook his head, giving her the impression it was not her father-in-law. He began moving out of the room, phone attached firmly to his ear, applying only such words as *yes* or *no*.

Sloan drew up, claiming the position of a yoga instructor while thinking how someone had the nerve to call on her husband so early in the morning. She tiptoed to another telephone located in her dressing room. She gingerly picked up the receiver, and then held it to her ear. A conversation was in place.

"My boy, I am really sorry for the way I spoke to you, I was rather rude. I guess I left you wondering why I acted the way I did. There is an explanation but I can't talk about it on the telephone. I need to see you in person. If your calendar at work is free for the day, I would like for you to come to my apartment."

Clay kept a lookout for the appearance of his wife. He spoke barely above a whisper. "I have one appointment, but it's an easy reschedule. Father, you sound really down; is this something to do with your health?"

"It very well could be, if a certain situation doesn't go my way. How about coming over for breakfast? We can talk about it then, and, my boy, Sloan must know nothing of this call. I'm sure you can think of something to tell her. In the meantime, I will call the office and leave a message on my secretary's recorder alerting her not to expect us. My boy, be prepared for a long day."

This time Phillip said good-bye.

Sloan heard every word. What was it that her father-in-law did not want her to know? What situation could cause his health to be in jeopardy? Only one thing came to mind: he had somehow found out the truth about her folks.

But what if he had? That was no reason to cause a health problem. If she had not made a promise to Lydia, she would have already told her husband.

While her brain was deciphering different scenarios, Sloan slipped on lounge wear and returned the phone to its rightful place. The door to her dressing room opened slowly; it was Clay.

"I was about to send out for a search and rescue team when I couldn't find you." His smile was genuine.

Let the lies begin.

"Who had the audacity to call you this early in the morning?"

Was Sloan acting pissed to throw off suspicion of her listening in on their conversation? Or was it to see if Clay got upset with the comment made in reference to the phone call? His expression did not change.

"It was a client; he's on the warpath, something to do with my blueprints. I have to get a move on; he's expecting to meet up by eight. I'm sorry, babe, but this could turn out to be a long day. Hopefully I'll be home for dinner." Clay had no running ability, but he showed a mean attempt as he ran into the shower. He would keep his father waiting no longer than necessary.

Sloan was seated near the door; she would send him off with her best smile and a warm embrace, always mindful to give him something to look forward to at the end of his day.

Clay held no briefcase in his hand; he was leaving his home empty-handed. Did he not know that omission would look suspicious? Sloan did not say a word. He pulled her up from her seated position and drew her close, her scent taking him places he loved to be. He began to kiss her earlobes, continuing onto her neck, working his way to her lips. She was swaying in his arms, her weight supported by his.

His words caused her to quiver. "Be prepared for a makeup session. I plan on having you climb the walls."

She was quick with her comeback. "If you keep talking like that, you'll have to tell the guy who called that your wife's body is craving attention. I think he will understand."

Gus was waiting to chauffeur his boss to work. He was greeted with an okay hello; what was lacking was spirit. Maybe a joke would help. He slid down the window behind him.

"How many lawyers does it take to get a man off death row?" When he received no response, Gus returned the window to its original position. He had but one thought: *It was a stupid joke anyhow.* He did not take well to silence. He liked noise, even if it was coming from his mouth. He was about to start talking to himself when a voice sounded from the back.

"Gus, I need for you to take me to my father's apartment. You've only been there once, do you need directions?"

"No, sir, I remember it well."

"I more than likely will be spending the day, so if you have anything you need to take care of, by all means do so. I will call when I need your services." Clay was pleasant enough when Gus pulled over in front of the Manhattan apartment.

"I'll be waiting for your call, Mr. Clay. Have a pleasant day."

Clay, lost in thought, gave no response.

Gus followed his boss's figure as he rang the buzzer allowing his entrance into the apartment complex. He prayed that when he picked him up, there would be a marked improvement in his frame of mind. He cared deeply for this man and his family; what happened to him would also affect Gus, and he was not talking about his employment.

Phillip's timing was perfect. His specialty, eggs Benedict, along with bagels, was being kept warm on a hot plate. He had no help; he was a do-it-himself kind of guy. Coffee was brewing, fresh juice chilled and ready to serve. The buzzer sounded, he walked to the speaker, heard his boy's voice and then released the door lock. His boy was here, there was no turning back.

Phillip held the door open. In mere minutes his boy would be told an awful truth. Clay stood in front of his father. Neither moved forward for several seconds, and then a feeling of love rushed over them and they embraced, holding on tightly. Philip brushed away a tear as he drew his boy into the apartment.

"I have your favorite breakfast. Come join me in the kitchen."

Each pulled out a chair. Phillip poured the coffee and placed the pitcher of orange juice on the table. The table had been set an hour prior. Phillip had the honor of serving his boy, while Clay stayed focused on his father's face. He got a glimpse of what was hiding beneath the surface; he was going to be told "all is not what it appears to be." He wondered where that thought came from. They would consume the food, while Phillip's mouth remained shut to the words that would destroy both their lives. Time was waiting.

Phillip scooted out his chair and went over to his boy, placing his hand on his shoulder. "Come, I need to talk to you."

Clay followed his father into the great room. Phillip pointed him towards a chair that would allow them to have eye-to-eye contact.

"You know I would rather die than hurt you, but all is not what it appears to be."

Clay was stunned as the exact words he had thought came rolling off the lips of his father.

"Clay, your mother called me a couple of days ago and asked to see me. I was so elated just to know she was okay, I would have agreed to anything."

Clay was overwhelmed with the news. He too could not have been happier. A relief like nothing he expected settled in.

"Anyway, that was the reason for my absence at work yesterday. I'm sorry I lied to you, but Jena pleaded with me not to tell you of her call until after we spoke. I could tell by the tone in her voice something was wrong. I thought since you hadn't heard from her in so long, she might have been gravely ill and she didn't have the heart to tell you. I would be the go-between if that were so. As it turned out, it was much worse than I thought, but not in that way. Clay, your grandmother apparently did not have all the facts. Thank God she did not, for had she known the truth behind your birth, I know for a fact she would not have lived as long as she did. What I'm about to tell you is something I too was unaware of."

The length of hesitation on his father's part was almost unbearable. His father hung his head, and the weeping began.

Clay felt a tugging on his heart; he had never seen his father behave in such a manner. He knelt down, placing his head next to his father's, his arms stretched across his father's back, praying he could give some measure of comfort.

"Father, it can't be all bad if she's okay, right? And whatever is causing you this much pain, you need to get it out in the open."

Phillip brought his head up. The puffiness had returned. He strained to look deep into his boy's eyes, his concern evident, his love undeniable. Clay was still kneeling when his father finally spoke the words no son should hear.

"My boy, you are not my son. You are my brother."

How does a person react to such news? Clay pushed away from his father. This was totally unexpected. His father was not his father but his brother… How could this be? He could speak no words; he was lost within himself. *Was my mother also not my mother?* Clay was about to enter a never-ending nightmare. He refused to believe what he was told. But wherever this tale was going to take him, he had to go.

"Father, you need to tell me what my mother said."

Phillip heard the blessed word *Father*. Soon it would come to an end. Habits can be broken.

"My boy, I don't know what I expected, it certainly wasn't that. She was in agony, reliving the horror of what she was forced to endure for years." His eyes again began to fill, tears ready to fall.

"My boy, I am sorry to say your grandfather is your biological father. My father forced himself upon your mother, resulting in pregnancy; you were the child of that rape. I will carry forever the sins of my father. I am so ashamed…please forgive my weakness in not securing a home for you and your mother."

A force of rage took over; Clay shook from the storm of tears. He would have given his life for his grandfather, he loved him that much. His angered feelings poured forth.

"How could he have done something so vile and perverted? And to think he had the gall to throw her out and keep her baby… What kind of man did I love? May God forgive him, for I cannot."

"My boy, I truly believed I was your father. Your mother and I gradually grew to love each other, but that love extended to only handholding and a few captured kisses until she realized she was pregnant. She went into a panic. She was provided all the necessities of life but no pay. She could not support herself, let alone a baby, if she were discharged. But her worst fear was the effect the rape would have on her beloved friend Lydia. She would rather lie than destroy that coveted friendship. She had no choice: I would finally share her bed, I would be the father of her baby. I struggled with accepting what she had done, trying to understand the why. And then like a bolt of lightning it struck me: your mother's motive was pure and simple; she did it out of her love for your grandmother.

There was no greater gift she could have given her."

Clay wept for the horror his mother was forced to live with, and the loss of a father he thought he had.

Phillip cried for what was to come. He prayed for the right words, knowing the tremendous impact it would have on his boy's heart.

"My boy, what I'm about to say is going to do damage to your heart. I wish there was an easy way of saying it, but there isn't. Ali is no longer with us; she is in the company of angels. I am so sorry." Phillip covered his face, sobbing for all the years he and his sister had lost; there will never be a family reunion.

Clay lost what little composure he had. His screams of agony bounced around the room. He tore at his clothes, slamming his fists against the wall. He then crumbled to the floor.

His weeping tore at Phillip's core, but Phillip would make no attempt to console him; Clay had to work through this tragedy on his own. When and if his boy reached for him, Phillip would be there. He was forced to put his own grief aside; he had to think of his boy, his own tears would only add to his misery. He kept shaking his head at the wailing sounds of his boy, wondering when he would stop. There was no doubt in his mind Clay was his boy, he did not care about his genetic makeup, and he would be damned if anyone would try to take away that honor. They would continue like before; no one need know about what his father had done. The Chadsworths' name would remain in good standing.

Clay's distress was easing, although he stayed slumped over. Phillip went to him, offering support. He put his arm around his boy's shoulder; they now sat, side by side.

"I can't believe Ali, who I loved my entire life, is not my aunt but is, or was, my sister. I should have flown out there after several calls went unanswered. I should have insisted on meeting with Ali. I knew she was nearby; I should have made more of an effort. Father, I assume you know the cause of her death."

Phillip hesitated, and Clay noticed his delay. "Please, Father, I need to know."

How could Phillip talk of her death without mentioning Sloan?

"My boy, you assumed she was living close by and you did what your mother asked of you; you could have done no more. Had your mother known that was to be Ali's last day, she would have taken you by your hand and led you to her." He caught his boy's surprised look. "Yes, my boy, the day you spoke to Ali was her last."

Clay's tears hung on his eyelids; until he blinked they would remain.

"My boy, her death involves others, and you need to understand the worst is yet to come.

Let's give it more time, so you can absorb all you've been told."

"Prolonging the inevitable will not change a thing. Ali is gone. How much worse can it be?"

Phillip was giving it his all to evade the issue at hand; his tiptoeing days were over. "Ali and her family perished from a fire in their home, leaving behind one child. That child has gone missing. She is eighteen and her name is Sloan. My dear boy, I am so sorry."

Clay jumped from his chair and began shouting at his father. "Where did you hear such nonsense? Surely you don't believe this is our Sloan?"

Phillip rose to face his boy, placing his arms upon Clay's shoulders to try to calm him down. "My dear boy, what do you know about your wife? Has she said anything in regards to her family?"

Clay began pacing, trying to remember what she had said. "There is no way my wife is the woman you are speaking of. I remember distinctly what she said when I made a reference to meeting her parents. She told me her father would never allow her to leave. She feared if she did not run away, she could never be with me. That would have been two weeks after Ali's death. Don't you see, she isn't who you think she is?"

Phillip could see how his boy could rationalize the discrepancies. But he had his own ideas.

"My boy, is it possible she lied to you? Think of it this way: her family is gone, she has no one, she is left stranded with only the clothes on her back, and there you are willing to take her away. Maybe she wasn't over the grieving, and to talk of it would force her to relive the horror all over again. Let's face it, she is really just a child living in a woman's body, enduring the worst kind of pain imaginable. Maybe she just shut it out of her mind and invented another family. There are so many variables, and I can understand where you're coming from. It's the two-week span that allows doubt, but this is her hometown, her loss is the town's loss, someone would have taken her in. You have to see it for what it is: we have two young girls with the same age, same name, living in the same town. There is no way this is a coincidence."

Clay looked down. He was crushed.

"My dear boy, look at me. You know deep in your heart she is one and the same."

"Father, I can't give her up. I love her. What am I to do?"

Phillip had thought long and hard with what he was about to say.

"Come sit by me. I have a plan."

CHAPTER THIRTY

Harriet felt empty when she heard Phillip's car drive away. She wished she had not washed away his scent; she longed to feel his touch, his lips upon her mouth. She locked herself within her bedroom and stretched out on the bed. She could hear the bed linens swishing inside the washing machine. She was angry at herself for washing them so quickly, for surely his scent would have lingered. She closed her eyes, trying to recapture their time together.

She traveled back to their beginning remembering their sexual playtime. They confided in each other they were virgins. She refused to think of herself as otherwise; the nightly abuse of rape did not enter into the picture. Neither knew what to do to please the other. He would fumble around in the dark, never quite giving Jena what she needed. She knew she was on the brink of something wonderful, then it would flutter away. This would happen time and again. She knew he managed to secure those wonderful feelings for himself for he would quickly collapse and fall asleep. She could not say he did not give it his all, but he was a greenhorn. She thought she found it with Trevor until Ben came along and now Phillip…there was no comparison. This fumbler had turned into a master of foreplay. Practice made perfect. A tinge of jealously showed itself. She envied every woman he took to his bed.

She could not turn him loose. If committing adultery is a sin, then why did God have to make it such an earth-shattering experience to which nothing could compare? Phillip gave to her what no other man was capable of achieving, the ultimate pleasure. He forced her body to demand sexual fulfillment no matter the cost. Her needs were greater than the thought of spending eternity in hell. As Ben so artfully put it, live for the here and now. She would worry about the hereafter when her body faded away to nothing.

She had to formulate a plan. She would think of one way, and then toss it aside. So many ideas, yet nothing seemed feasible. She finally settled on what she deemed to be the most acceptable.

She would tell Ben she needed time away from the babies to unwind. He would understand; there wasn't anything he wouldn't do for her. She would tell him she would use this time to possibly visit with her son, maybe spend the weekend. To cover her tracks, she would call Ben several times during the day. In her mind that was a perfect fix. No one would be the wiser.

She had to admit, there was a slight problem with her plan. Ben had to work. Even if she chose the weekends, he could be called to duty at any given time. Besides, she did not know if Ben could take care of three babies on his own. She wished she could have a trial run. There was no way she would ever give the responsibility to Marc; if something were to happen it would crush him.

She was seated in Ben's recliner lost in thought when she took to her feet shouting out loud, "Oh my God, I am so dumb. I can hire in a nanny, possibly two, maybe three." She started laughing.

"Well, I finally got the last laugh, you didn't beat me after all, Mr. Rapist. Your dirty payoff money will allow me to spend weekends with your son, the man you swore would never be a part of my life. But most importantly, your money will provide great care for my babies."

She could not wait to present her plan to Ben.

CHAPTER THIRTY-ONE

Clay was willing to listen to anything his father/brother had to say when it came to keeping his wife.

"This is what I propose. We will continue on with our lives as if nothing happened. Your mother need not know that Sloan is with us. As far as we know she has gone missing and will stay that way."

Clay was struck dumb with his father's words. "I can't believe what you are saying. You want me to live a life of deceit. I thought we were done with lies."

"My boy, do you want a divorce? Do you want to disclaim me as your father? There is much at stake here. There will be charges of incest brought against you if this is found out. You said you couldn't give her up; well tell me, what choice do you have?"

Clay started pacing the floor and then stopping as he rubbed his forehead. He was sorting through ways to find a solution to this gigantic problem. He decided it was better to sit and think.

If he accepts his father's proposal, he will commit himself to a life of incest.

A tangled web was in the process of being woven.

"What if my mother decides to visit with me, or I with her, what do I do with Sloan?"

"I don't think she will visit anytime soon; she now has three babies to care for."

Clay stood with that announcement. Was he ready to salute his mother for a job well done? "What…?"

"You are no more surprised than I. Can you imagine giving birth to three babies at our age? Wonders will never cease to amaze me."

Clay felt as if he were on a roller coaster. "Will this never-ending tale ever end, or do you have more in store for me?"

Phillip could not help himself, he had to laugh. He quickly apologized. "My boy, I'm so sorry. I know this is no laughing matter, but I'm sick to death of crying. Sometimes it's better to loosen up than to wallow in self-pity."

Clay had to agree. He was heartsick over the entire mess; he needed release, and laughter was the best cure. But before he could let himself go, he knew his father had more to say.

"Okay, spit it out. What do you have to tell me in regards to my newly acquired siblings, other than their names?"

"If I didn't know better, I would think you are reading my mind." Unbeknownst to him, his boy was honing in on his abilities. Phillip blurted out the remainder.

"My boy, besides the two baby girls Hannah and Taylor and baby brother Nicholas, you have another brother six years younger than you and his name is Marc. And that, my boy, is all I have to say."

Clay's mind began to race. In a matter of seconds he had acquired two sisters and two brothers. A strong desire to meet them could not be denied, but there again, he had Sloan. What would he say to her? He could travel only so much on business. He would always have to watch his back, waiting to be found out. Could he do this? If he wanted to keep his wife, he would have to. While he was lost in thought his father prepared lunch.

Phillip did what every father would do: protect his boy, to hell with the consequences.

Lunch was anything but quiet. Talk of business would finish the day. Prior discussions were put to rest, Phillip and Clay would follow through with the only life they knew; there would be no exceptions to the rule.

The end of the day did not delay; Gus was on his way. Sloan was waiting for her husband to return and Clay felt the bile rise each time he thought of her. His wife was his niece, he was her uncle.

While Clay was praying to God to forgive him for not giving up his life of incest, Sloan was making preparations for sack time.

CHAPTER THIRTY-TWO

Harriet remade her and Ben's bed, evidence washed away. She was preparing dinner when Ben stepped through the door. He removed his work shoes and slipped on a pair of waiting slippers while calling out his sweetheart's name. The woman by the name of Jena had returned to her past and stayed there; her replacement, "Harriet," was tending to her present-day duties.

Harriet was facing the stove, adjusting the heat control on sizzling pieces of chicken. Roasted potatoes, salad and French bread would be added alongside the evening's entrée. A slightly chilled bottle of white Chardonnay would complement the meal. Harriet had done a quick study in wines, knowing the finest and the least expensive. Chardonnay was of course the least expensive, but cost was not the issue; she enjoyed its taste, especially with chicken. Preference was the key.

Ben stood silent at the door leading into the kitchen admiring his beautiful wife. He could not believe his luck; a woman such as she did not deserve a brute such as he. She was refined, he was just a backwoods hick, but become a pair they did. Theirs was an unlikely match, but who was he to question destiny?

He quietly approached his sweetheart, gently placing his arms around her waist. She did not flinch; this was a ritual he performed each evening. Her hair was twisted in a French roll secured with hair pins. He kissed her neck while enjoying the scent of Oscar.

Harriet wiped her left hand on a draped towel and reached up to caress Ben's face. Yes, she loved him. He was a wonderful man and she would deny him nothing. She thought she had experienced all there was to lovemaking until Phillip took her hand and lifted her to heights she never knew existed. She had shared Ben's bed for years, long before they married; if he had more to give he would have done so. Phillip had moves that forced her to leave fingernail scrapes up and down his backside. She branded him; he belonged to her. She will put her plan in motion; she will be taken care of on a monthly basis, no ifs, ands or buts.

She swung around, her lips seeking his. Ben was gentle with his kiss. She tried to pretend it was Phillip's lips against hers but failed. Phillip would have crushed his lips to hers, seeking the contents within. Harriet's thoughts took her away: *Soon, my love, soon.*

Dinner now over, the used utensils, dishes and pans would not see hands at work, the dishwasher willing. Ben retreated to the living room to relax in his favorite recliner. The attached footrest welcomed his socked feet, the newspaper waiting for his eyes to scan.

Harriet now joined him. He put the paper aside.

"Well, did you have any problems with Phillip accepting everything you told him?"

"He was shocked and saddened. I really hurt him. I'm glad it's over. I just need to put this behind me and move on, okay?"

"I'm sorry you had to relive your past, I know it weighed heavily on your mind. Your past is now forgotten. I'm thankful it's over for your benefit."

Harriet nodded in agreement. But Ben had something that was much more important.

"Sweetheart, I've had something on my mind that I can't put off any longer. I need to know whether or not we are going to have more children."

"Ben, you have got to be kidding. Why would you even think that?"

"I just wanted to know your feelings, because I was thinking of getting a vasectomy."

Harriet started laughing. "Can you imagine the look on Dr. Rolan's face when you ask for sterilization at your age?" She could not contain her laughter.

Embarrassed, Ben turned a bright red. "I never thought of it as a laughing matter."

She had hurt his feelings. That was not her intention. This big guy of hers was sensitive.

"Honey, I am so sorry, it just struck me as funny. I mean look at us, we're old fogies still dropping kids, and now we're going to take care of the equipment that causes it?"

She could tell she was not reaching him with her sense of humor. She knelt down in front of him. "Forgive me?" When she still received no response, she stood, leaned over and whispered into his ear, "Let me show you just how sorry I am."

Did he pull back? What do you think?

While Harriet performed, she was thinking of her plan to escape into a world of sin.

CHAPTER THIRTY-THREE

Gus was thankful that his boss seemed to be his old self. He rattled on and on as was his custom. A chuckle every now and then escaped his employer's lips. The long drive ended but not before Clay had a request.

"Gus, I need to ask a favor of you."

Gus had a brief reply. "Ask away."

"I wish to keep the visit with my father private. If Mrs. Chadsworth were to ask about this day, it was a workday as usual. This must be kept between us."

"My lips are sealed, Mr. Clay." Gus with a zipper on his mouth, that would be a first.

Clay was comfortable that Gus would never speak a word of their conversation. "Thank you, Gus. Tomorrow we will continue with my work schedule as before. Until then, please take care."

Gus deposited his boss outside the mansion and drove off. He would return at 6:45 tomorrow morning.

Clay was home at his usual time. He stood rooted in front of the door to his mansion. It felt as if lead were in his shoes. Minutes passed. He began to sweat, although the cold air of November brushed against him. He did not have to hesitate much longer, for the door flew open and Sloan bounced into his arms. Her arms wrapped around his shoulders with a welcome kiss that spoke of a promise. Clay really tried, but his lips locked. He again tasted the bile.

It did not take a dummy to sense something was not right.

"Honey, what's wrong? Did something happen at work? Is there something I should be concerned with?"

Shall we start counting the lies?

"I lost a big contract for our company."

"Oh, is that all? You had me worried; I thought it was something really awful."

"Are you lame? That contract was worth fifteen million dollars."

She was taken aback. Clay had never spoken to her so sharply, and she was offended.

"Well forgive me. If you so inclined, dinner is ready to be served." She rushed indoors, tears brushed aside. She wished she had enough nerve to throw the dinner at him.

This did not go as he expected. How would he atone? He was thinking of the proper words to say. He loosened his tie as he made his way to the dinner table.

Sloan had taken a seat. She held her head down, hands folded in her lap. She had conferred with Sonja early in the day. She wanted to surprise her husband with his favorite meal, roasted duck with all the trimmings, which will now be lacking in taste.

Instead of taking a seat, Clay went to his wife and apologized on bended knee. "Please forgive me. There is no excuse for my behavior. The only way to rid my mouth of offensive words is to wash them out with soap."

How could she stay mad after such an outlandish remark? "If I had a bar of soap handy, I would do so."

While still on his knees and with Sloan facing him, their lips met. This time Clay gave it his best shot. Apparently, she was none the wiser. His mind could not turn off to the fact he was kissing his niece. He was thankful they were interrupted. Sonja was ready to serve.

Night entered before he had time to prepare. Sloan eagerly waited for Clay's nightly performance; when he failed to come to bed because of business, she always slept fitfully. He knew he could not perform to her satisfaction this night; he refused to try and then fail. He needed a few days to get used to the idea he was bedding down with his niece. Until he conquered this affliction, she would have to do without.

Sloan also put on a good performance. His kiss was flat. Oh sure, he had all the right moves, but the hunger was not there. Never question a woman's instincts, she always knows. She also knew there would be no lovemaking. Something more was going on than losing a lousy contract.

Tomorrow she will question Gus after his return from dropping her husband at work. Consideration was Clay's finest quality; if Sloan needed the services of his chauffeur, Gus was at her disposal.

As expected, Clay informed Sloan he would be late coming to bed. He had contracts to go over; he would see her in the morning. Breakfast was eaten in silence. She walked him to the door as was the custom, only this time she knew not to cling like a vine. Their kiss was long, but the hunger did not return. She waved to Gus, knowing within a couple of hours she would have the whole story; he never knew when to keep his mouth shut.

Sloan took a shower and quickly dressed. She would go for a long drive, sightseeing if necessary. In a few days the well-planned party of introducing her to society will take place. She was looking forward to meeting all the people who moved in Clay's circle. She had already met and approved of his best friends.

Nico and Sofie Adamo were by far the most charming and agreeable. Nico and Clay were head to head in height. He was a hunk of a man with broad shoulders and a small waist, his dark hair peppered with grey, and to turn your head a bit further, his green eyes could turn wax to liquid. He had a slight twist to a fabulous smile. He was all man. His wife Sofie was his perfect mate. She too was tall and very slim, having the figure of a runway model. She wore her waist-length silvery blond hair straight. Thick black lashes added more emphasis to her already large brown eyes. Lips that always appeared moist were natural; she chose not to wear lipstick. She owned the smile that everyone coveted, but it was her personality that drew many towards her.

Then there were Garth and Krista Casine. Garth was also gifted with height and a physique that many men envied. He did not own up to the fact he worked out continuously. His dark brown hair was kept short, laying claim to extremely curly hair. He would comment frequently to all those who would listen that if he did not keep it that way, he would be sporting ringlets. He thought of himself as the last of the great men.

He also could not keep his hands off Sloan when they were forced to be alone. Many times she would skip from room to room in her haste to get away. So long as she kept moving, she was okay, and yes, it was very tiring. Had she told Clay, they would in all probability lose their friendship. Garth to Clay was like a brother. Brothers stay together.

But it was more than that, for his wife Krista became Sloan's best friend, and their friendship grew into a kinship like that of sisters. Sunni will never reclaim first place. How does someone describe to others the most perfect person to see, meet and remember? That would fit Krista to a T. She had a figure that required no attention and would be considered short, five-feet-four inches in comparison to Sloan's five-feet-nine inches. She wore her medium brown hair with natural blond highlights cut shoulder length into a bob. She had beautiful hazel green eyes and full lips that never left home without the stroke of lipstick. She had the capacity to put a sparkle in your eyes and a smile on your lips after experiencing your worst day ever. She was in her element when it came to helping those in need. Krista was the best of the best.

Sloan chose a cushioned ornate bench on which to sit. She preferred the step, which was reminiscent of her days on the farm, but the cold weather prevented that. She kept twirling a two-carat diamond post earring. Her hair stylist had shown her how wearing her hair parted in the middle made her widow's peak much more flattering. She had chosen a Roberto Cavalli black wool jumpsuit with full-length tapered sleeves. It was collarless with a single roll of black onyx buttons starting at the neckline and ending a little past the waist. The chill of the early day forced her to wear a waist-length red fox fur. The long-strapped Gucci handbag lay across her lap. November was about finished; December was waiting to show its face of snow and ice.

Gus was later than usual. Sloan began tapping her black Gucci stilettos on the stone step, while watching the hands on her Audemar watch that never seemed to move. She was impatient for her mind to be put to rest in regards to her father-in-law.

In the far-off distance the limo was finally making an appearance. Sloan came running as if she were wearing flat-heeded shoes instead of five-inch spikes. She never failed to take Gus's breath away. He could not recall the last time he was given the chance to open the car door; Sloan was always in and out before he could do his duty, plus he lost the opportunity to take in her scent of fragrance for the day.

They greeted each other as if they were the best of friends. He was ready to put the car in gear. It was quite a distance before they would actually leave the estate, so he had plenty of time to find out her destination. But Sloan spoke hurriedly.

"Gus, I was just wondering where it was that you took my husband yesterday?" She almost caught him off guard.

"I took him to his workplace, Mrs. Sloan."

"Did you not take him to his father's first?"

"No, I took him straight to work."

She received an answer she did not want to hear. Clay had gotten to him first; Gus had been told to lie.

"Gus, I changed my mind, I'd rather stay home. If you have something to do, just go and do it." She was brash with him.

"Did I say something wrong, Mrs. Sloan?"

"I don't know, did you?"

Before she received a reply she was out and running towards the front door. Gus knew that she knew he had lied. He also knew she would not tell Mr. Clay about what had just transpired.

Apparently lies are okay if they fall from Sloan's lips, even better if they come from Lydia, but God forbid Sloan should be lied to.

She will find a way to expose the truth.

The conclusion of *Rest in Peace* will exceed expectations in *Book Three: Starting Over*.

Author / Evelyn Sciarratta

Mrs. Sciarratta resides in St. Charles, Missouri. She is a widow with five children, 17 grandchildren and eight great-grandchildren.

Rest In Peace is her first full-length novel.

The *Rest In Peace* trilogy is as follows:

> *Rest In Peace Book One: The Beginning*
> *Rest In Peace Book Two: Changes*
> *Rest In Peace Book Three: Starting Over*

The novel initially appeared as a synopsized serial newspaper feature in 1988. She's excited with the prospect that the new novels will bring as much enjoyment to readers as they brought to her as she was penning them.